I0818623

Becoming Super*n*atural

By J. Miller Wilson

ISBN 978-0-578-00429-7

To Ann, Ann Miller, Little Mamma, Lucy
(an ideal reader), Bandit (asleep on
the couch) and human spirit
that cannot be explained
or contained

Becoming Supernatural

www.houseknect.net/BecomingSupernatural.aspx

I soar to a better place,
Floating above the floor.
The world turns below me
Gulls fly on empty shores.

How can this be real?
I can't make you love me
Can this be how God feels?
He could be lonely.

'Cause I'm becoming supernatural.
I'm becoming supernatural.

Not content to be asleep,
I let my eye fly free.
Into realms of impossible.
I know you'd fear me.

Not feeling so super now
I can't make you love me.
Now I know how God feels.
I bet he's lonely.

'Cause I'm becoming supernatural.
I'm becoming supernatural.

How can this be real?
I can't make you love me
Can this be how God feels?
I know he's lonely.

'Cause I'm becoming supernatural.
I'm becoming supernatural.

Chapter 1 – Summer 1972

Mark Justin and his band of merry tripsters were cruising south on Texas 124, out of Houston heading to the coast, not Galveston, too many lights there to get the full sense of the event. They were headed for a remote beach up the coast. No one in the '64 Volkswagen van had seen it yet but it had arrived that night on the Texas coastline and every FM station from Victoria to Port Sulfur was raving.

"Listen compadres, I'm not telling you to do anything illegal but if your head ain't right and you're still dressed and dry, let's just say you'd better find a way to the coast in the next few hours. It's 2 A.M. Southeast Texas and the Rover wants to hear from all over what my friends are seeing and doing in the water tonight. There's magic in the Gulf and I'm taking your calls until dawn," announced The Midnight Rover, on Galveston's Power 98.

Mark drove the party van and sipped a cup of his favorite brew, a mixture of coffee and beer he called Maxwiser. Nasty but effective, it left no residual fuzz of a hangover even on the longest road trips. In his early 20's and still buff from running high school track, Mark was taller than most and handsome in a jut-jawed way with killer blue eyes and long blond hair.

With the summer rotation of UT students Mark's usual friends were long gone and the 'drive board' was where he found these paying customers for this little excursion. Forty eight hours ago he had tacked his card on the bulletin board in the commons under The Tower and advertised, "Experience the Gulf: one special night-$10 round trip." Now he had five companions, three girls and two guys, and more than enough cash to cover it.

Their destination was High Island, a small beach town northeast of Galveston across the bay, isolated from the lights and traffic. Mark had surfed Cosby's Beach for years and knew the cut through the dunes that opened to the wide long beach that should be deserted despite all the radio buzz. The idea was to party on the beach and skinny dip for a few hours in the most fantastic migration of phosphorescent plankton to hit the Texas shoreline in fifty years.

When the van rolled through the dunes, the coast was literally clear—not another vehicle in sight. And the water glowed. Mark drove slowly down the beach, taking some time to adjust to the dark and the amazing lights in the naturally phosphorescent surf.

Like an inverse shadow, the plankton reflected the energy from everything in the water. That night, a gallon of the Gulf contained hundreds of thousands of the bioluminescent dinoflagellates each secreting a mixture of protein and enzyme intended to light up and frighten away predators. It was this extreme concentration of the plankton that generated the rare light show in front of him.

The sea foam was electric white as it rolled up the beach and then dissolved into twinkling stars seeping into the sand. Breaking waves glimmered white-green at their crests, fish were streaks of lime flashing through the troughs and hermit crabs left sparkling trails as they scooted across the back wash. Even straight it was dazzling.

The tripsters went bananas. Before Mark stopped the van they stripped and piled on to the beach jumping up and down, dancing and singing, celebrating their sensory overload. After a beer-toast to new friends and psychedelic plankton, six naked screaming hippies sprinted into the water to see it up close.

At belly button depth they stopped moving and started laughing as another surprise surrounded each one of them. From every body a perfect ring of reflective light beamed life energy in all directions.

An aura revealed is an awesome sight. In this water it shown first as intense white-green (like a glow stick) close to the body, fading to lighter green within a foot, then trailing off to a deep green that disappeared into the night water about three feet away.

Mark and April stayed back apart from the others. They had hit it off since she called about the ride but now it was love at first sight, a common problem for him. She was so cute and relaxed he could not help himself. They were tall, slender and blond, a fine match for the gene pool.

But Mark had sworn off relationships; too many expectations with too much consequence and unpredictable results-not worth the effort, until now.

"Hell of a light show," he said to break the ice.

"You should see it from here. God, it's everywhere. Come on, slow poke," she laughed and pulled him deeper until the water was chest high.

Now their full body energy was reflected and lit up the water around them. They were close enough so that their auras were indistinguishable and she playfully pushed him away.

"You're all aglow Miss April. Lots of energy in that lovely body of yours."

But as he moved away she stopped laughing and just stared at him, at the water around him. Transfixed and amazed, mouth agape, she panicked.

"Stop a second. Damn it! I can't believe I'm seeing this. Tell me real fast Mark Justin and don't lie about it. Why the hell is your light not like mine?"

He couldn't answer the question. Instead of a white-green glow like all the others, his aura was an rainbow of red, green and yellow light, blending then separating and fusing again; ebbing and flowing to some unknown biorhythm. It swirled around him like a watery kaleidoscope pulsing color in all directions. To April it was inexplicable, powerful and frightening.

"Wow, that's a relief," he finally replied. "I thought you were looking below the surface." She didn't laugh.

"Okay, okay, there are lots of pretty colors. It's just the Maxwiser. You know it does that to everybody if you drink enough, so take it easy. But it's pretty cool, huh?"

"That's pure-dee bullshit, but it's so far-out I don't care. That is *the* most beautiful thing I have ever seen. All those colors, dancing around you like some kind of Tim Leary psychedelic ballet. It's fan-damn-tastic."

He just smiled and hunched his shoulders not knowing how to respond or explain the light show emanating from his body.

"I swear, Mark Justin. You are so trippy and you don't even know it. Come back over here right now. I gotta take your pulse from inside that thing," she said with open arms and a smile.

But spoiling their perfect moment, Mark noticed new lights flash across the beach. A pickup truck had cut through the dunes and was slowly heading down the beach toward his van.

At that moment his dream date ended and the freak show began.

In the bed of the pickup, standing together against the cab, a tall naked longhaired hippie wearing only a flapping black trash bag for a cape was flanked by two totally nude blondes each holding a kerosene torch high above the truck cab. They looked like a bargain-basement entry in an East Texas porn parade.

Mark quickly warned April and began swimming toward shore as fast as he could. Realizing how vulnerable they were, he felt more threatened with every stroke.

In seconds he reached shallow waters and jogged up the beach. From the dark side he grabbed his jeans out of the van and then walked into the torchlight. Hoping for the best he waved in Captain Trashbag, the bouncy blonds and the rest of the crew.

"Ahoy matie," shouted the captain shining his flashlight on Mark. "How's it hanging?" The blonds giggled on cue.

"Just a little party in the water. Looks like you're dressed for it so come on in and join us. It's unbelievable out there." Mark smiled, admiring the porn stars.

The captain and his naked beauties leaped out of the truck onto the beach, ready to party, but trouble was behind the windshield. Three fully dressed 20-something, stubble-faced, baseball-capped rednecks unloaded from the cab and stepped in front of the blonds. Two approached Mark.

"Got any dope?" one of them asked.

"Well, you know, not on me." Mark replied and extended a hand in friendship knowing it was the moment of truth with these guys.

Instead of returning the greeting the closest one slammed a meaty right fist into the side of his face, instantly knocking him down. The punch was strong but it was the skull-and-bones silver ring that gashed his left temple and chipped the cheekbone next to his eye.

The bone was nearly exposed and a bloody stream poured into his eye. In an instant he was half blind and on his knees, fighting off total darkness as the pain ripped through his head.

At that moment, his companions, Jason and Keith, stumbled up the beach into the flickering torchlight. Laughing and expecting to party with the newcomers, they had no clue about the danger in front of them.

But it was the third and the largest of the rednecks that clarified things when he pulled a Louisville Slugger from behind the seat and ceremoniously slammed it three times on the truck's weathered hood. The blows sounded like muffled gunshots across the windy beach.

"Alright you stoned out hippie maggots. I am not fucking around. You are trespassing on my beach. That means you shits are going to have to pay the freight."

"Hey man, don't be so harsh. Let's just take their dope and bail," said Captain Trashbag.

"Shut up, bag boy. I'm gonna have a little fun. Hey Bubba, you and Cuz empty out the van. Gotta be some good stuff in there. The speed is mine. You can have the rest."

April and the other girls had just enough time to circle around out of the water, slip into the van and put on their underwear before Bubba slid open the door. Their screams shook Mark to the bone as he tried to find his bearings and use the van's bumper to get back on his feet.

"Hot damn! Buddy, they got women too. We'll herd 'em over your ways," Bubba yelled as the girls ran around the front of the van and stopped.

“Hello ladies. You with these creeps?” asked Buddy whose 6’3” frame towered over them as he tapped the bat in his hands. His glazed eyes and wicked grin scared them beyond words.

“Well, the correct answer is, ‘Not for long,’” he said and took a few steps toward Jason.

“Dude, don’t you want to party?” Jason asked.

Buddy answered by smashing the barrel of the Louisville Slugger into his gut; a brutal crunching blow that dropped Jason to his hands and knees.

Breaking out in a toothy smile, Buddy added a quick two-step kick in the ribs that flipped Jason over and out on the beach.

Then he turned back to the other tripsters trembling in the torchlight. “Now, are we all paying attention? That’s good because I have a little announcement. I’ve decided to take some more batting practice and then I’ll be impounding your van back to my garage. Hey Cuz, you find the keys to that heap?” he yelled across the beach.

“Oh yeah. Some dope and money too.” Cuz said holding up the booty.

“Damn hippies. Don’t you know that possession of narcotics is *still* a felony in these parts,” Buddy said waking over toward Keith.

“So, here’s the deal, boys. I’m gonna finish off these maggots then we’ll get what we can for the van after we party with their chicks. Any questions?”

Mark was helpless. A thundering headache, bloody eye, and the nausea of a concussion overwhelmed him. He knew the whacked out speed freak meant to kill them all but he could only watch. So he focused on the bat.

“Alright scumbag. Your turn to meet The Eliminator,” Buddy said to Keith as he started to swing for a deadly headshot.

But in mid-stroke, two feet from Keith’s forehead, the bat stopped.

“Hey, gotdamnit. Let go of it! Now *that* is your death warrant. You hear me?” Buddy threatened as he yanked on the bat.

But it didn’t budge and suddenly he looked more like a crazed mime struggling to pull a bat out of thin air than a meth-crazed psychopath.

And then his voice changed too.

“Gotdamnit, now my hands won’t move either. Sumbitch is stuck to me!” He screamed at a stunned audience.

Finally the bat moved, *in reverse*. It arched back over Buddy’s head, swooped down in front, and then behind him again in an arching tetherball motion.

And Buddy rotated with it.

Suddenly he was the target; terror just inflicted reflected back by an unseen force.

“What the hell? My legs are stuck too. Bubba, help me gotdamnit! I can’t move. Stop it. You’re breaking my legs!” he yelled in sheer panic.

Bubba and Cuz dropped the girls and ran toward him but they froze in their tracks, invisibly hog-tied. The rednecks and the tripsters all watched as Buddy, now crying for mercy, slowly twisted in the sand like a human drill bit.

Then, as if picked up by a hurricane gust, Cuz and Bubba launched off the sand and flew over the cab of the pickup, crashing into its open bed. They cried and groaned for help but Captain Trashbag and the blonds had disappeared, taking cover under the dashboard inside the truck.

Mark’s stringy hair hid part of his bloody face but his eyes cut through the night and remained fixed on the passed out psychopath. Both of Buddy’s legs cracked then splintered as he continued torking deeper into the beach

April could see and *feel* Mark’s fury.

“Stop it, he can’t hurt us any more!” she yelled and grabbed his arm. “Stop it now! You are killing him!” she pleaded.

"What?" Mark broke his focus to look at her, "I got nothing to do with it. I'm not touching him."

But Buddy did stop his slow spin in sand.

Mark wiped his bloody eye and tried to smile at her.

"Well, you have to admit, his luck did take a turn for the worst," he said feebly trying to win her back.

But April loathed him. With his face grotesquely bloodied and swollen and wielding some kind of uncomprehendable power, he had morphed from adorable to terrorable in less time than it takes to smoke a cigarette.

"How could you…How can you do that?" she stammered and raised her voice to ask, "What on earth are you, Mark Justin?"

He couldn't answer; he didn't know either.

Suddenly, more afraid of him than she had been of Buddy, April ran to join her girlfriends gathered around Jason, still face down in the sand. Feeling Mark looking through her, she didn't look back.

"Hey, you in the truck, get dressed!" Mark turned his attention to Captain Trashbag and the blonds. "It's time for you to collect this garbage and get off my beach."

They struggled to dig Buddy out of the sand but with Mark's help they untwisted his legs and laid him next to his friends in the back of the pickup. Peeling out and swerving down the beach, the truck disappeared back through the cut in the dunes.

The glowing waves still broke in bright white shifts and the sea foam still dissolved into a million stars on the beach but the tripsters didn't care.

They were down.

Jason was bruised and coughing from a broken rib, Mark could barely see out of a swollen left eye and the girls continued crying as they finished dressing and got back in the van. Mark washed his wound in silence, doing his best to stop the blood and tears.

On the drive back to Jason's house in Houston, April never looked at him-no thanks or forgiveness there. She just hugged the door handle and sobbed.

He was not a mind reader but knew what she was thinking,

Get away from this monster as fast as you can before he does something like that to you.

They pulled up to Jason's house at daybreak and the boys quietly helped him into his room and bed. Keith decided to crash there too. He'd rather face Jason's Dad in a few hours than spend another minute with Mark.

"Dude, I saw what you did to those guys," he whispered to Mark. "Are you like some kind of extraterrestrial or from a parallel universe? You can tell me. I'm cool, you know, unless you'd have to kill me." His eyes went huge.

"Oh shit, wait. I didn't mean it." And he reflexed the two-finger hippy salute that makes everything right, "Peace, brother. No more violence."

"Me?" Mark whispered back. "You can't be serious. It was you, man. I saw it with my good eye. Don't bullshit me. You put a spell on the bat and another one on those three maniacs. You're a wizard aren't you? Wait," he held up a stop-sign hand, "don't erase my memory. I won't say a word."

And he folded three fingers to return the peace sign as he backed out of the room, bowing like an infidel and closed the door.

He was feeling better, even smiling, as he returned to his van. But the girls were gone. He retraced the route out of the subdivision but they were nowhere to be found. He was alone and suddenly deeply depressed knowing they had run away from him.

"Don't blame yourself, Markus. No one knows what really happened on the beach. Lives were saved-nothing else matters. Questions without answers will suck you dry. S-U-C-K, man. So drive. Just drive," demanded his inner dialog.

"Good advice, boys, but I can spell."

He took a deep breath and a long pull of Maxwiser then slipped a favorite 8-track into the player, found 'Good Vibrations', and the Beach Boys were live as he started the long drive back to Austin. He needed a few stitches but that would have to wait. He could make it.

But ten miles down the road, hands shaking, exhausted, and convinced his left eye was going to explode, he pulled into a 7-11. The pain, depression and anger opened an abyss and it swallowed him.

Nothing made sense and everything pissed him off. He would never have April or any girl that mattered and he had wanted to kill those guys. Kill them all. And he *would* kill someone before long.

"Who the hell am I?" He yelled at a passing semi.

"Hey mystery boy, we sent that one to Research. Take a number. Someone will be here soon to suck you dry," answered the voice in his head.

He was going mad and the only thing that made sense at the moment was to end this torture. Instantly he knew the 50-foot overpass just ahead was high enough to do the job.

And he was about to put the van in gear when the passenger door swung open.

"Hi. You headed to Austin?" asked a slim, short haired, smiling brunette.

"No, not going to make it that far. You don't want to be in here." He waved her off not looking.

"Yeah, thought so. You'd better let me drive," she said throwing a backpack on the floor and climbed into the passenger seat.

"Come on, rainbow. That's no way to think. It's time someone did something for you," she said reaching over, pressing her hand on his swollen face for a moment and then gently pulled him toward her.

"You *are* going to crash, sweetie, but in the back seat," she said and helped him curl up on the bench seat where he immediately passed out.

* * * * *

Perched on the lowest limb of the giant elm tree a mockingbird sang in the warm afternoon breeze as Mark awoke in his van parked in the shade about 20 feet from his Austin apartment. Abruptly sitting up on the backseat bench, he was looking in the rear view mirror at a face that was exactly as it had before the road trip.

"April, the naked blonds, the psycho speed freak that tattooed me and…"

He looked back in the rearview mirror and rubbed his perfectly smooth face and forehead.

"Did it happen? That could not have been a dream so, yes, it happened. Right?"

He listened but his internal dialog was off the air.

Looking around the van for evidence of the beach trip, he didn't see anything different from the usual dirt, trash and stains always there.

"It would help if the maid came in occasionally," he said as he got out and walked toward his apartment.

"Hey, Justin. How many times I got to say it? You pay single rent," said Jack Dearborn, owner and irritating slumlord of this six-unit off-campus complex. "Start shacking up and I'll need another fifty bills per month. Now tell old Jack the truth. That brunette has her own key, right?"

"No sir. There's nobody living here but us chickens. Just take a look at this disaster area," Mark said unlocking the front door. "Could anyone live in this mess but me?"

The door opened to a spotlessly clean den and kitchen area. From floor to ceiling it was immaculate. Beyond clean it was a disinfectant miracle. Even the Maxwiser rug stains were gone. He knew that Jack knew only a woman would live in a place this tidy.

"So Jack, tell me about that brunette. Was she perky and cute?"

"Yeah, sure, melted my heart. Hellofa job in here, though. I might have something for her if she'll do that to all my units. But it's still fifty bucks from you."

"You are so right, Jack. Fifty bucks it was."

He pulled out his wallet and stared at the money the five tripsters had paid for the beach trip.

"I'll be damned. It was real," he mumbled and took off his shoes to enter.

"Sorry Jack. She's not coming back. No maid or girlfriend I ever knew could do this."

He closed the door in Jack's face and slowly walked around, marveling at the sanitized kitchen with its bowl of fresh fruit, sparkling linoleum, and light petulie oil fragrance. The bedroom was equally impeccable; clothes hung, sheets changed, all Downy fresh. He knew from Philosophy 101 that Aristotle would call this the heavenly reflection of a cheap earthly apartment.

"She did this to be sure I get it. A Clorox epiphany for the prodigal son, coming-of-age, accepting his gift. There's just one problem, lady. I don't want it," he said aloud entering the spotless bathroom.

"Do you hear me?" he screamed at the perfect face in the mirror.

"I DO NOT WANT IT!"

Chapter 2 – 5 Years Later-Spring 1977

He hated it more than a bowl of steamed cauliflower; worse than a sloppy kiss on the lips from Grammy; even more than a sun burn. But like Grammy's loving wet one, this was unavoidable. Between ice-pick stabs the abscessed molar throbbed in heart rhythm as he sat in the waiting room of his friend and dentist, Dr. Peter Trent.

Mark's teeth were rotten since he could remember-the product of an early addiction to bubble gum, candy cigarettes, and atomic fireballs. Even twenty years after they first drilled his baby teeth (*what was the point in that?*) and dozens of tortured visits, he entertained the option of leaping out the second story window to his immediate left.

"Wouldn't be fatal," he concluded and the agony kept him seated, waiting for Dr. Painless.

A particularly harsh spike rolled his eyes and he realized he'd been waiting long enough to find half of the hidden animals in the back page of the latest Highlights Magazine.

"Pete's *never* late so it means only one thing-he's dead. He's lying back there upside down in a long vinyl chair, smiling, ODed on nitrous. Oh Pete, we hardly knew ye," he thought as his macabre vision rotated above and around Pete's body.

Details of the crime scene (*this was murder, not suicide*) were becoming clear when someone in the office called his name. It wasn't Pete's voice-it couldn't be-but instead it came from a striking redhead in doctor's whites standing in the doorway.

Mark felt a different pain, sharp and lower. Love at first sight, again, but this girl was older and in uniform.

"Doctor Ohmygod", he thought. "Hope she does molars."

"Hello Mr. Justin. I'm Dr. Nolan. Pete had a family emergency and I'm taking his patients this afternoon. I believe you're in need of a root canal and I've seen the film. Is that abscess any better?"

“What abscess?”

“Then it’s a piece ‘o cake for me. You’ll never know I’m in there.” she smiled showing perfectly white teeth and continued, “I promise you’ll be ready for rehearsal in 90 minutes. Guaranteed.”

Then she leaned forward and whispered, “Pete told me your little secret. You are *the* Tuck Nucker. He knows how much I love your show so don’t be mad at him.” And she leaned back, offered a petite right hand for Mark to shake and winked so cute he could eat her. He took her hand instead.

“Nice to meet you too, doc, and please call me Mark. Mr. Justin is my dad and Tuck ain’t working at the moment,” he returned her wink along with his best radio personality smile.

The show she loved, *Tuck & Others*, was an overnight sensation in Austin and his first career move since finishing the UT undergrad Media Communications program a year earlier. Every weekday morning he played the hippy-dizzy straight man, Tuck Nucker, for the best undiscovered voice impressionists in the country. In ninety days the show had leaped into the #2 spot in Austin’s morning drive slot and #1 was sweating.

He was a fake news anchor in a call-in, interview and fake news morning show. Every morning a different cast of politicos and celebrities dropped by to chat with Tuck Nucker and his listeners. His partner, who worshiped Jonathon Winters, could dead-on anyone in the public eye and the format was straight out of their UT student radio show. With the 20-something Austin demographic, it was a hit for *The Vibe, FM102.*

But very few recognized either Tuck or The Others yet and they wanted to keep it that way. Obviously Pete kept no such secrets from the beautiful Dr. Nolan.

“So, doc, have you done as many of these canal jobs as Pete?” he asked changing the subject.

“Probably a boat load more but not on any local ce-lebs. Honestly, you guys kill me. That morning when Elvis was trying on a condom? I almost wrecked the car. That’s classic. How does your partner do all those voices?”

“I have no idea. The station manager just wheels him in at seven and he takes off. My job is to keep us on the air.” He shrugged his shoulders but in truth, it was all scripted to be spontaneous.

“Yeah, we all have our trade secrets don’t we. Just follow me, Mark, and we’ll get you out of here lickedy-split.”

“Seriously, doc, I’m kind of a unique patient with special sensitivities. You know, my sensitivity with anesthesia is important to understand,” he warned as they walked toward the chamber of horrors with its electric chair and torture tools.

She stopped at the door, turning to confront Mark and his irritating fears.

“Hey, check these hands. Best in the office, maybe the state,” she said and held them out for inspection. “Small, agile, and oh so gentle. You’ll be fine.” She winked again and he melted.

“That’s a hellofa line, Dr. Nolan.”

“Call me Charlotte and take a seat, any seat.”

He slid into the long brown vinyl chair (*they had already moved Pete’s dead body*) and quickly took stock of all of the dental-obilia on the shelves around the torture chamber.

A blue 6-foot toothbrush that read *Use me or Else* on the handle lay across the top of three shelves. Two sets of oversized, smiling plastic chatter teeth guarded a foot-tall J&J floss box on the middle shelf and four colorful giant toothpaste tubes occupied the bottom shelf.

Un-amused, he closed his eyes and visioned Dr. Charlotte’s perfect teeth and what might be under the whites of that uniform. But nothing blocked the sound of her slender hands unwrapping, laying-out and prepping various instruments of destruction he didn’t want to ponder at all.

“And besides,” she said from behind, “You’ll never feel a thing. Just breathe deep and we’ll be on our way,” she said strapping the small gas delivery mask over his nose.

His eyelids flew open but he had already taken one breath and trying to talk he took another.

"But. You don't…"

Another. He moved his arm in protest but it looked more like a wave to 'bring it on'.

"Nitrous is very cool stuff and I know you're not allergic. You'll not float away, I promise. Just a tingly sensation, light and airy is all you'll feel. No worries. I'll take very good care of you," she whispered from somewhere nearby.

He relaxed, smiled and disappeared into the music playing over the suddenly high quality stereo system surrounding him. The pain dissolved into it along with his fears about past and future dental disasters. The light blurred as she bent over him to begin work.

"Just open for me and I'll add some Novocain to be sure we are ready. Open a bit mo…

She stopped in mid sentence. Stunned, confused, paralyzed, unable to move her right hand and deliver the needle to Mark's gum.

"Oh shit! I'm having stroke," she thought and tried again.

No luck. Suspended-she couldn't budge it.

"Mr. Justin, ah, Mark? We're having a slight problem here," she said struggling to move the needle. His eyes were open, staring into hers.

"Are, are you doing this?" she asked wondering if he had somehow hypnotized her. "Mark, can you hear me?"

He had to laugh out loud because she sounded and looked just like Ann Margaret. That was funny but not nearly as cool as the giant toothbrush floating off the top shelf and hovering above it, awaiting further instructions.

"A superb idea, Mr. Bristles," he mumbled and abruptly raised his forearms the way a conductor does to quiet an orchestra.

Then, on queue, the song on the stereo changed to a top-40 classic and his concert began.

Na nana na naaaa, nana na naaa, nana naaaa, nana naaaa. Na naah na naaaa, began the familiar tune.

Mark snapped his wrists and instantly the toothbrush picked up the beat, spiraling slowly downward, dancing on air as Mark directed.

Still paralyzed but too amazed to be afraid, Charlotte giggled as the syringe floated out of her hand to join the toothbrush doing the Wah Tootsie in front of them.

He smiled and the gas mask lifted off of his nose and boogied over in front of Charlotte. Nitrous oxide can be fatal if concentrated but mixed with the room air it was well below toxic levels. She was helpless.

"This is no stroke. It's a trip," she mused and then heard a new noise.

The clatter on her left sent a rip of laughter from her mouth as she saw the tray of prodding, cleaning and blunt-nose scaling instruments standing on end, swaying to the music like a tiny stainless steel chorus line.

Then the water-pic beside the spit bowl joined in, squirting little streams of water to the rhythm of the *Na Na* song. The air hose next to it snaked up the arm of the overhead light and didn't miss a beat as it hissed with the music.

Mark pointed an invisible baton at the middle shelf and the J&J floss box began a do-se-do with the plastic chattering teeth as they picked up the *na na* beat, floating down and then around the dancing tooth brush-syringe duet.

When the toothpaste tubes lifted off the bottom shelf and circled them like tubular angles, everything in the room that wasn't nailed down was in motion with the music. Even the silver-filling mixer cut in-and-out in throaty harmony, burping the in-between *duh daaas*.

He knew it was all a dream conjured by the gas. The lovely Dr. Nolan had actually been removing the nerve sheath and deep quick of his molar or packing the empty canals with antibacterial goo. That was the real root canal drill. This was too cool to be dental.

"Mark, can you put me down now?" Charlotte whispered to him as she, like everything else in the room, hovered just above the floor. He didn't hear here yet.

"I get it, I get it. Your sensitivities are duly noted. Damnation. Pete should have warned me buuuuuuut… he's not in on this secret, is he?"

She reached out and touched his cheek. "Thanks for the ride, Mark. Now let's work on the landing," she said as her shoes tapped the floor.

Weightlessness was exhilarating and the dance of the dental instruments was bewildering but she had enough sense to cut off the Nitrous as soon as she could move her arms. Now everything was returning to its place in perfect reversal as the song faded.

"A little nitrous and you spin up this? A freaking cartoon? How'd you do that?"

But she saw his eyes clear and knew he wouldn't answer the question. It was over. Even the syringe nestled back into her hand in just a few seconds.

"Mark, listen to me. I loved your dream or whatever it was and I don't care how you did it. Your secret is safe with me but I've got to finish that molar right now don't you think?"

"You bet. And just between us, I don't think the Tuck Nucker thing is much of a secret any more." He saw her green eyes crinkle and hoped that incredible smile was flashing behind the mask.

"You were right, Miss Charlotte." he added. "I didn't feel a thing but you could have mentioned the hallucinations with that stuff. They were so real. Like that Disney cartoon, *Sorcerer's Apprentice,* but with your tool set and dental gear all dancing around instead of the water buckets."

Now he was babbling and that awkward pause along with a where-am-I-what-the-hell-just-happened moment was a deep hole dug quickly. He was about to blow it if he hadn't already scared her away.

"Sorry, didn't mean to space out. It was just a childhood memory, I guess. Right? Anyway, do you mind if we finish up with only the Novocain. I'm a bit queasy."

"Yeah, that's a good idea. Let's do try it your way this time," she said and administered the shot.

Charlotte had rules about dating patients. Drilling and filling a man's mouth usually killed any romance potential. But after this experience she ached to keep this very funny guy and his magic in her life.

"Just relax, Mark. I said I'd take good care of you and I am a woman of my word."

Chapter 3 - 20 Years Later-Summer 1997

"Does this mean we're going to be more than just friends?"

"Only if you move my hand two feet lower. Now *that* would redefine palm reading as we know it," Madame Surgio said to his best friend, Mark Justin.

Madame Surgio was the mystic alter ego of Dr. Louis 'Shots' Shotley. In med school Louis had created the Madame to meet women and mooch drinks. Now twenty-five years later he was a successful cardiovascular surgeon living in Richmond's West End. But after a few drinks he still morphed into the Madame.

On this warm Saturday night the four couples that rotated hosting a monthly cocktail party were enjoying the night air on the Shotley's back yard patio. A few minutes earlier Louis had folded and wrapped a beach towel into a headdress and solicited his company for volunteers. Mark was the Madame's only taker.

"Hey, we'd better cut the Madame off before she starts reading the wrong wrinkles," Mark said and motioned to Charlotte and Sarah to join them for the read.

"Well, there he goes," Sarah said looking across the patio at the two men holding hands. She smiled and asked Charlotte, "You think Louis has a secret desire to be a woman?"

"Doesn't look like a secret from here." Charlotte glanced over and added, "Besides, all men do. They just won't admit it. Those guys over there, they love each other like women but compete like men. Good combination don't you think?"

"Yeah. Depth without penetration."

They both laughed out loud but stopped and cleared their throats in unison before strolling arm in arm over to watch the reading.

"You come to Madame Surgio because you vant to know the future. Madame sees zee past and knows zee future too. It is all right here," Madame said in a comic German accent.

Madame traced the three key lines in every human palm and studied them for a moment. The first impression startled Louis and he leaned down to get a better look at his friend's remarkable palm.

"*Unmistakable*," he thought and then began.

"We'll start with zee Life Line. It's this one near and above your thumb curving to the wrist. It's not your average Life Line. Well, it's perfectly average until zis break right there about two thirds of zee way down," Madam said pointing to a small gap in the line.

"After that it actually becomes two lines, both are deep and long but choppy. You've heard of zee proverbial fork in zee road? Well, you are about to take it. It is sharp, fast, and permanent but also it is life threatening. Could be a leetil illness or injury but definitely like zee son-of-a-bitch to split your Life Line like zat." He stopped and waited for a response from Mark.

"Damn son, I'm amazed. The danger and suspense, the lame accent. I could even be kidnapped by your evil twin, Madame Bullshit," Mark said with a wink to Charlotte.

"Come on Shots, you don't know that stuff's going to happen any more than a menstruating intern at the Psychic Friends Hot Line. And she'd never try to con me with an accent straight out of 'Hogan's Heroes. Can you believe that, Miss Charlotte? This is drivel. Let's go freshen our toddies and powder our noses." But Charlotte put a hand on his shoulder and applied enough pressure to keep him sitting.

"I don't know about that, Mark. You've got a lot of lines on that hand and I'd hate to leave with only the bad news to remember, right Madame?" she said glaring at Louis.

"Cutting zee crap as you vish." Louis understood and looked back at Mark. "Menstruating interns. Very clever Justin, but I just call 'em like I see 'em," he said and began tracing another line in Mark's palm.

"Your Head Line is next and begins its journey joined with your Lifeline above your thumb but take a closer look, my friends. It travels completely across your palm, down the edge of your hand and doesn't stop until joining your wrist." Louis couldn't stay in character any longer.

"Man, that's some header you got there and get this. It's broken at the same place as your Life Line. See it? About two thirds of the way down there. It confirms the upcoming life change," he said and looked up with another revelation.

"Congratulations Markus. That's the longest Head Line I've ever read and it tells me you've got enough juice in your noggin to power a small gymnasium," he said still marveling over the 5-inch Head Line.

"Now what the hell does that mean? Is this some kind of joke?" Mark was alarmed that Louis was getting so close to the truth.

"If you'd taken a little physiology you'd know that the average brain generates about ¼-volt of electricity. It propels the heart, lungs, mind, wiener, that kind of stuff. Your whole being is powered by the synaptic radiance generated by your brain and that Head Line is its blueprint. And you, little buddy, possess the Godzilla of Head Lines."

"Okay Madame, time's up. Does even a fraction of that mean anything?" Charlotte asked.

"Damn straight. It *all* means something," he said more seriously than intended but the signs in Mark's palm were frightening.

"Now, right now, I have to ask you this, Marko. Have you ever moved an object with your mind? It is possible."

" Mark answered nervously. "What the hell are you driving at, Ace?"

"It's just one of those things I follow. Some of the literature details how guys like Kreskin, Johnny Single and The Great Glenninson all have off-the-scale readings on a type of electro-encephalograph that measures cranium-generated energy. They do some incredible physical stuff like bending metal objects, moving small cars, levitating, and so forth. And they all have extremely long Head Lines. But probably *not* as long as this one," he said retracing the line and shaking his head.

"So I'm intrigued. I don't think you've ever used psychokinetic manipulation on a corn chip but perhaps it could happen if you weren't so anal. Constipation of the mind, so to speak."

"Mixing metaphors are we? Amped or blocked, Madame. Which is it?" Mark was laughing and pulling his hand away but Louis held on, not convinced it was a dead end.

"Okay, okay. One more little read and I'm done. See that deep vertical line that cuts through both Head and Heart lines?"

"Sure. What's it mean? Am I going to get pregnant?"

"Well Chuckles you'll be lucky if that's all that happens," Louis warned. "It says there'll be some fame with the upcoming life changing event. Not the good kind like in your old radio and TV days. This is more negative and destructive."

"Charlotte, can I borrow your lovely right paw for a quick second? Let's check your compatibility. I'm sure it's off the charts," he said taking her hand without looking up.

"And there it is, dear friends-our smoking gun. You have the very same break in your Life Line. More proof that something big is about to happen and that you're going through it together. It's engraved right there."

"Come on Lou, you gotta do better than that," Mark interrupted. "But on the other hand, so to speak, I really don't think you can." He decided to explain why, after watching for so many years, he had volunteered for a reading.

"You're such a con. Just admit that you don't have a freakin' clue about the future or any of that telegenetic crap you just laid on us," Mark said, pulling his hand back to fold his arms.

"It's telekinetic crap, you moron, and I'm real sorry if it scares you but remember? Y*ou* asked for it." And he leaned over to emphasize his last warning.

"Whether you hear it from me or just let it run over your ass, there's not a hellofa lot you can do about your fate. Got it?"

Mark retaliated by sweeping his left hand across the top of Louis's head and swatting the makeshift headdress into the boxwood shrub ten feet away.

"Hot damn!" He yelled and pumped his fist in the air.

Louis stood up glaring at Mark ready to knock his head off but Sarah stepped in between them.

"That's enough, boys. This is a friendly little town and we don't want your macho shoot out here. So stuff a cork in it," she insisted and put her arm around her husband. "Louis, honey, you need to sit down. You're scaring all the tourists."

"Sarah's right," Charlotte said grabbing Mark's hand. "Let's just call it a night, dear. Obviously you're late taking whatever it is that keeps you from becoming a complete jerk." She began pulling him in the direction of the back yard gate.

"Yeah, you really got the drop on me Marko, but no worries, son. Come on inside and let me buy you and your girlfriend a beer," Louis said taking Sarah's hand and they headed toward the house.

Mark swung Charlotte around and they caught up with their friends.

"So Lou, I'm curious about the telekinesis thing. You think it could ever be real?"

"Well Marko, it's like this. Since you're shooting blanks now, it's highly unlikely you'll become supernatural in your declining years. It was just a wild hair up Madame's derriere. That's all. But your Life Line doesn't lie, little buddy," he said opening the back door and then added, "Unfortunately I can't be specific so there's no sense dwelling on it. I say we grab another brewski and toast your celebrity," he said closing the door behind them and heading toward the refrigerator.

"Thanks a lot, my transvestite friend, but after that little show it's clear you need professional help. How about I pray long and hard in church tomorrow for Madame to grow a couple of crystal balls?"

Louis had had enough and pointed a beer at Mark, "Don't mock the Madame, little man. There could be hell to pay."

Mark thought about slapping him again but instead walked back out to the patio, beerless and frustrated. He decided to lie on the brick and stare at the moon until it lured his anger away.

The party broke up an hour later and the Justin's walked the half block to their house. Charlotte was exhausted and immediately headed upstairs to pass out in their soft bed.

Mark took to the den couch to watch TV until he fell asleep. Most nights he used the TV to muffle the inner voices that wanted to argue all things Justin all night long.

Over the years they had grown in number and volume and now he referred to them as The Debating Society, each voice some derivative of his own (*he hoped*), serving as an editorial board; liberal, conservative, theological, cynical, and more.

And they practically never stopped.

"Alright girls," he thought settling on the couch and picking up the remote. "Let's not overrate Lou's tomfoolery. I know you want to reminisce but you're not digging up our past at this point in our programming day. I'm putting you down before you get started. And there's no debating it."

But he glanced down at his palm, at the gaps in the Life Line. No debating them either.

So, with the TV front and center, spewing commercials and redundant weather information, the Debating Society was stifled, whispers behind the telechatter, and he quickly feel asleep.

The Sunday sun rose and the TV continued overlaying the voices in his head. But nothing could stop the fate about to run his ass over.

Chapter 4 - The Hall of Dead Preachers

Less than ½ mile from the Shotley's party there was another confrontation between more intense rivals. The preacher should have been long gone but this last task was worth the wait. He'd face them down then walk out and deliver the future for his church. After turning out the office lights, only the emergency fluorescents lit the hall of dead preachers.

There they were; always looking, judging, never changing-the silent history of Commonwealth Church. In ¾ profile, the twelve pastors were framed in gesso and gilt, 30 by 44 inches, with six on either side nailed to the mahogany paneling above the chair rail. They stared through the life of that church, as much a part of Richmond's history as the slave trade warehouses, the state capitol and The Confederate Museum.

Beginning in 1792, each took a turn shepherding tens of thousands from cradle to grave while hundreds of millions of dollars from the wealthiest Richmond families filled the church coffers. Gone but not entirely forgotten, their twelve legacies were compressed and distilled into abstract salutes for sparsely attended services during the annual Founders Week ritual.

Senior Minister Matthew Victor 'Vick' Springwell was number thirteen and they were twelve reminders of his unfulfilled legacy. They peered through the walls, pushed him and, in recent years, frightened him every day. Even after his epiphany of a new network that would catapult their church, *his* church, back to prominence, he would still be the odd man out. They would never accept him.

So tonight, facts certain, he was ready to face them.

His skin crawled as their twenty-four cold dead eyes followed him down the hall and they breathed their history down the back of his neck. He wanted to run through the sanctuary and out the Grant Street doors but instead turned and stared.

The twelve stared back, a posthumous board of directors he knew he couldn't impress. But the deal was sealed and they would listen to his sermon. Number thirteen about to launch their church in a magnificent new direction and they were going along for the ride, like it or not.

"Gentleman, I envy you up there all dead and done. Heroic lives buttoned down by kind history. I've tried to be guided by it but your ministry from the grave weighs on me and now holds all of us back. For twenty years I've tried to stay on your path, tending the local flock, not straying off the path but, gentlemen, I am not satisfied. Today we are breaking free of your quaint vision. We begin a new era that none of you could imagine and, by God, I will be worthy." His voice echoed down the hall.

He stopped to confront the first of them. Painted in 1804, Charles Nathaniel Townsend rode with Washington, had ministered at Yorktown and prayed for dying Americans as Cornwallis negotiated the terms of surrender.

"Doctor, they died in your arms, sons of America, and you brought so many back here to rest. Now, she's a wasteland; strayed too far from righteousness, Doctor, but I can bring her back to you. A spiritual revolution is on the brink and it is dedicated to your legacy." Vick said to the most decorated minister in Virginia history.

He stepped next to stare down the portrait of Thomas Robert Lee, the hell-fire-and-brimstone preacher of the Lee family and Commonwealth minister through the dark days of destruction, surrender and Reconstruction after the War of Northern Aggression. In the battles for Richmond, the sanctuary and grounds were spared Yankee mortar fire. More than once it had been a temporary hospital and morgue for both sides. The dying and dead were all comforted on its marble floors then buried in unmarked graves where Vick walked everyday. He said nothing to Doctor Lee whose angry black eyes frightened him more than any of the twelve in the hall.

The last portrait was the most recent martyr and Vick's mentor, Dr. Lucas Samples, who ministered his conservative white congregation through the civil rights movement and joined black church leaders to peacefully desegregate a town that hated the very thought of it.

But Samples prevailed and on a Sunday early in 1968 Dr. Martin Luther King Jr. traveled here to recognize Richmond's progress in a service covered by the national TV, radio and print media. Vick had a small part in the service, the Prayer of Forgiveness, which he sadly repeated in memoriam, four months later. In the aftermath of Dr. King's assassination Samples led a peace march through Richmond, Vick at his side.

"This is big, Lucas, and I pray you hear me. I've taken care of almost everything. We are going to be a national force once again. In every state your message will be heard," he said looking into his mentor's kind eyes captured in oil.

It was after Samples unexpected death in 1977 that Vick ascended to Senior Minister of Commonwealth Church. Since then he had completed terms as head of the Southeastern Presbytery, was often a key-note speaker in regional forums and had written a well-received book, 'Dixie Religion And Faith', which contrasted the region's African and European ministries.

Cool, calculating, and never without a comforting smile, Vick had been the perfect replacement to take Commonwealth Church through the prosperous '80s and '90s.

"Gentleman, I thank God everyday for your two-hundred years sacrifice and service but it's my duty to use that capital and my God given skills for the greater good." He walked slowly to the open end of the hall and turned.

"So watch as you always do, advise me if you can, but, gentlemen, no one will get in the way of our destiny, " he said to end the sermon.

"Him."

The hair on the back of Vick's neck straightened up. He checked his own thoughts too as chills and shivers crawled under his skin.

"Whom?" He asked the twelve.

"Him." Whispered the walls, the ceiling and the air around him.

"Justin?" He asked them and relaxed.

"Is that who you mean? He's more curious than the other social climbers but I can handle him. You must mean someone else? A politician perhaps?"

The walls were silent and he was done with them. "Fine gentleman, I'm off the mountains," he said and left them behind. His western North Carolina retreat was only a few hours away. It offered real sanctuary.

"But it's no vacation this year," he thought walking through the dark church. "Two presentations with investment bankers and a 3-day summit with my finance team. And I still don't have the production facilities wrapped up to start filming." He stopped at the water fountain.

"Lord? Why do I have to do everything?" he asked aloud after gulping down three pills for a pounding headache and another for sleep that would kick in thirty minutes. "In the next 7 days I have to shore up national and hammer out that production deal with our friends here at Channel 10."

"Jesus wept," Vick thought as he slid behind of the wheel of his Cadillac. "And what the heck could a whinny deacon like Mark Justin have to do with any of that?"

Chapter 5

The wisdom from above is first pure, then peaceable, gentle, open to reason, full of mercy and good fruits, without uncertainty or insincerity. James 3:17

There they were. They were always there. Etched in marble and hung on the wall in memory of a long dead preacher. Every Sunday Mark read and reread them. Each word had meaning and impact. Together they summed his hopes.

"Imagine having all of it. Peace from life. Life with purity. Reason with certainty. Gentle spirit taken in and turned out again." He marveled at the possibilities.

"No fear. That's the real prize, Marko. No damn fear. I wonder how that would feel?" He shook his head trying to grasp it but couldn't. He was always afraid of something.

The muffled thunder of 1218 fannies hitting the pew cushions jolted him back into the sanctuary's narthex where he sat daydreaming on the steps leading to the balcony. The 11:00 service had just started and he preferred the stairs in the narthex to the pews in the sanctuary.

"It's tough to whip the head bobbing sleep demons when you're a Sunday morning pew prisoner. Out here it's just my own demons," he mused. As the only Deacon not attending the service in the sanctuary, he was supposed to be walking the halls of Commonwealth Church making sure no one escaped.

Meanwhile inside the sanctuary Associate Pastor Jerry Tinsler was in the high pulpit reading the church announcements. In charge while Senior Minister Vick Springwell spent the week in Mountain Peak, NC, Jerry knew that Vick expected no complaints or incidents.

But Vick, or the fear of him, never really left this church. He was manipulating everything now. Beyond Richmond and Virginia his new media-based vision for the Christian masses was extravagant. With most of the pieces in place, two weeks ago

Vick revealed his grandiose plan to the church governing body, the Directorate, in their August leadership meeting.

Mark's thoughts wandered back to that meeting.

The agenda item was innocent enough, *Communications and Evangelics*, but Vick was on his game-confident, charismatic and unstoppable.

"I have prayed and seen a new mission, dear friends. This is God's calling for each and every one of us." He started his pitch to the gathered leadership.

"From this great institution we are going to create and operate a new, values based television network. It's called, Living In Faith Entertainment, the LIFE network. With the help of a small group of investors we are going to compete against the Falwell and Robertson media giants. And win."

Mouths dropped, glances cut across the table, stomachs turned, but no one said a word, yet.

"Dear friends, this is so very clear to me. We have a need in this country for a non-political conservative message delivered without a theological hammer," he said, extending his hands, palms up.

"We all know the problems crippling our community and every year we treat the symptoms with our generous donations of time and money. But we are not getting through. So, it is time to expand our mission," he proposed as Jerry distributed the two-page business plan around the table.

Smiling like a lawyer facing a friendly jury, he stood up, leaned over the table, and continued.

"Together let us establish programs that prevent millions of men, women, and children from reaching the crisis point we treat so righteously. To intervene and make it stick, our message has to be credible, fact based, and available 24 X 7. They have to see it, feel it, and know in their heart of hearts that we are delivering the light of a moral life. It will be our earliest point of communication and complements the crisis intervention we exclusively support now," he said walking around the room behind each seated officer.

"This is a media strategy with community roots built on expanding the influence of our church. Incredible as it may sounds, we are already talking about syndication in markets from here to Denver."

That turned heads.

"But, as you can see, it begins very modestly right here in Richmond, with a Sunday morning pilot program to be shown only in Virginia. We'll host *The Commonwealth Good News*. Not by me or some other preacher, that would just put us in the same old rut as the others. No, dear friends, I'm talking about a contemporary news program with stories of God's good work reported on location in our area. The reporters will be young, the production facilities are local, and the budget proposal is well within our means." He paused having walked completely around the conference table, and was ready for the big finish.

"Friends, I've prayed so much before bringing it here and I'm convinced we are *the* church to take on this mission. Let us not stand still any longer. Let's change the world. I'm asking you to give our children and all families a choice they don't have now. Together let us create a new LIFE for television," he paused for effect, raised his hands and added, "In Christ's name we pray to always be guided in His name. Amen." And paused again looking around the table.

"Any questions ladies and gentlemen?"

Mark remembered that moment and wished he'd kept his mouth shut.

"But your numbers seem low and there's no mention of our production partner. You sure we can fund this *and* our other commitments?" he asked so spontaneously that it had to be an uncensored blurtation from the Debating Society.

"In what sense, Mark? Are you suggesting this great church isn't up to the challenge?"

“Well, yes, that’s exactly it.” He tried to stare down Vick, but felt himself turning red and trapped.

“I’m only asking to take it to committee. Anyone voting with Mr. Justin to hold up on this?” They both knew there were no takers.

“Well Mark, you seem to be out there on your own so let’s make it unanimous. I expect you’ll enjoy adding this to your faith journey. And your broadcasting background is just what we need. Please don’t worry about the financing. There will be full disclosure before one penny is spent. You with us now?”

Vick’s confrontation with his senior deacon ended with a conforming nod and an embarrassed smile.

“Then, if you don’t mind I’ll flesh out the details with Finance in the next few weeks. We’ll have it ready for a vote then.” Vick sat back down at the head of the table. “Next on the agenda…

That meeting was two weeks ago but Mark’s thinking hadn’t changed.

“It’s just so wholly (holy, holy) bizarre. Vick’s taking Commonwealth on a power trip to build his own cable empire? It’s sheer fantasy, a farce, and would be comical if it didn’t bankrupt the church,” he thought shaking his head.

“It’s just reason number 666 to quit this deacon charade,” he concluded.

“Maybe so, but it pales in comparison to your insane treatment of poor old Mrs. Elkins *last* week. We’re surprised they haven’t kicked you outta the place already.” The Debating Society needled Mark everyday since the Elkins incident happened right here last Sunday.

The memory of it made him cringe.

He had been on door duty at the main entrance to the church, greeting, glad-handing, and door opening as the congregation arrived for the 11:00 service, when an idea occurred to him as he watched 85-year-old Dora Elkins use the hand rail to climb thc three steps on the front portico.

"You know, this morning I'm not parking her walker at the top of those stairs. No way, Jose. She's strong enough to walk on her own. Anyone can see it. I'll just leap over there and do a walker-ectomy before she hits that top stair. Then she'll stroll to the door on her own good legs."

As planned he grabbed the walker from the bottom step and placed it twenty feet away at the front door. When she reached the top step he was ready to wave her in.

"You don't need this, Mrs. Elkins," he said pointing at the walker like it was a game show prize. "You can walk over here on your own. I know it and I'm here waiting," he encouraged her with a smile and an exaggerated looping hand motion toward the door.

"Mr. Justin!" she shouted back, eyes narrowed and face scowled, still hanging onto the rail.

"I'll do nothing of the sort. Why you must be God's own idiot because I know you didn't think of this by yourself. Now git my walker over here and git me into this church right now!" She motioned with a finger pointed at her feet and continued scolding him.

"Such foolishness from a deacon. I'm shocked at you, Mr. Justin. I've *never* been treated such a way. Now, you'll see me all the way into my pew and maybe I won't report this to the boss deacon. You hear me?"

Mark trotted over with the walker and tucked it under her hands. Avoiding her glare, he tried to convince her again as they walked toward the door.

"Honestly Mrs. Elkins, one Sunday morning you'll make that walk again with only God's left arm for support. Don't you want to do that?"

But Dora Elkins liked walking on six legs and would never go back to two.

"Mr. Justin, you're a good greeter and you got a winnin' smile but you've got to let me and my walker be. We git in and out of this place pretty well. Have since before you were a deacon and will when you're gone, like all the rest. So no more of those shenanigans at the door, you hear me?" she harshly whispered as they reached her pew and seat, LL4-16.

"Yes, ma'am. I'm truly sorry about that. I promise it won't happen again. Please forgive me and enjoy the service," he whispered, easing her into the usual spot while positioning the walker against the pew. She began her prayers without acknowledging his apology.

He was crimson faced and embarrassed beyond words. Again.

"Think about it, Deacon Dimwit. What if she thought it was a first-rate idea and actually tried to walk on her own? She'd have said something like, 'Well you know Mr. Justin that's a mighty fine suggestion. Let me just give it a try.' Then she'd let go of the rail, take one step toward the door, fall flat on her face and break a hip. Merry Christmas."

That was a scary thought.

"What were you thinking? A miracle cure for arthritis then a little hike for Jesus?" The Debating Society asked and he shook his head not knowing why he'd done it.

"That poor woman could have died. Truth is you need to resign before you kill some one."

"Over the line, boys. I may not be fit for service but that's cruel."

Sitting in the narthex on the black marble steps leading to the balcony he realized the only thing he'd truly miss when he quit was this time to life-dream every week.

His favorite was the rock star fantasy left over from teen years as a guitar player for a standard three-guitar-and-a-drummer cover band that was popular in the small East Texas towns between Houston and Beaumont where he grew up.

In those days Mark dreamed about writing, recording and performing a catchy little tune that hit hard enough to earn some Houston air time. It never happened and the band died in 1969.

But not the dream. It remained a spiritual off ramp with a sign reading:

Exit 1969
Fun-Music-Satisfaction
Loiterers Welcome
Permanent Campsites
EZOFF
No Return.

"It ain't nostalgia if you never leave." He thought and noted that as the title for his first album.

"Yeah, and the past is just a crutch for a big-time loser," they replied.

He was reduced to a doubting deacon wasting time debating his own Debating Society, challenging his senior minister and coaxing old women to walk off a cliff. And his life was half over.

Then out of Unknown Zone (*as he named it*), a new song popped into his thoughts. It was a Dire Straits knockoff, melancholy but not slow, asking the question, "What Will I Do Without Me?" As usual, just a fragment arrived.

Where will I go when I'm gone?
How will I know where I be-long?
Who will I be? What will I see-ee?
What will I do without me?

Who will I know when I'm gone?
Will I still know how to sing this song?
Where will I go, above or below-oo,
Who will I be without me?

Again, the refrain, with a twist.

Who will I be? What will I see-ee?
Will I still beat off without me?

He grinned at the last line and the pipe organ in the sanctuary cranked up the third hymn. Mark lifted his glance from the floor to the wall and saw again the words etched in stone; James 3:17.

There they were. They were always there.

He read them one more time (*The wisdom from above is first pure...)* and then opened the large double doors on the front of the church.

Another wasted Sunday service. Stepping out onto the portico in the bright noon sun he remembered Madame Surgio's warning from the night before.

"Well Madame, I don't understand what you saw in the palm of my hand but as far as I'm concerned the big change can't happen too soon," he thought and turned to shake the hand of the first sinner stepping out the door.

Chapter 6

Shifting into autodeacon mode he smiled and waved goodbye (*Ya'll come back, ya heah?)* to the exiting flock. Like most summer days in the upper south the glare of the noonday sun was bright enough to have to shade or squint through.

And, like most accidents, no one saw it coming.

Mark was looking in the direction of the main street that fronts the church when he saw the station wagon moving too fast toward the crosswalk. He knew the driver didn't see Mrs. Daisy Hanover in the crossing and it was too late to keep her from walking directly in front of the speeding car.

The deep growl of skidding radials drowned out Mark's scream as the station wagon struck Daisy Hanover and heaved her five feet straight up.

She came down just slightly ahead of the lift off point, first smacking her butt on the flexible hood of the car, then bouncing down to the plastic cover above the collision-proof bumper and finally thumping to the pavement in a sitting position with her back resting against the station wagon's front license plate.

She wasn't dead or even unconscious when Mark looked into her eyes just seconds after she completed the jarring two-cheek landing. Daisy was staring straight ahead, stunned, unable to talk or move, eyelids rapidly blinking. But he had no skills to apply, no emergency training, nothing to offer her.

"Miss Daisy?"

Her eyes fluttered and her head bobbed in a sickly, loose way.

"Miss Daisy, can you hear me?"

But there was no answer, no hope of reaching her so in a purely reflexive response he picked up her hand, put his other hand on her shoulder and prayed loud enough for all arriving on the scene to hear.

"Lord, send the healing energy of your love into Mrs. Hanover. Let her live to nurture her family. Let her return your love seven fold and let us always know her as a miracle of your grace and mercy. Please do this here and now. Do this now."

The last sentence was a command not a plea or humble request.

Daisy heard every word of Mark's prayer but the rest of the world was gone. The gathering crowd, the screams for 911 and the screeching halt of traffic didn't register. Instead, she *felt* everything, amazed how the warmth of the pavement surged through her legs, her chest and flowed across the top of her head. Even though it quickly dissipated, a vaguely familiar afterglow lingered.

And then the world returned.

She was looking directly into Mark's sky blue eyes when the sounds and the light of the day came back.

"Will you help me up?" she asked him. "I think I'll be fine if I can just move over there on the grass and out of the street," she said, weak but audible.

"No ma'am, we can't do that just yet." He was certain someone had called the EMTs so he kept talking to her. "You shouldn't move until the rescue squad gets here. Mrs. Hanover, can you tell me if you feel me holding your hand?"

"Mr. Justin, I not only feel you holding my hand but I am grievously aware of a pain in my rear end and how silly I look all spread-eagle in the middle of the road for ya'll to gawk at. So let's get me over there and let the traffic start moving again. I'm telling you I'm fine," she answered in a much stronger voice.

There were smiles of relief, tears of joy, and one other victim; the driver of the car was in shock, hands gripping the steering wheel and staring blankly through the windshield of his soon to be famous 1996 Taurus station wagon. Two bystanders moved him into the shade of a large oak tree in the churchyard and he sat, near comatose, waiting for a cup of water fetched from the kitchen.

But the crowd had gathered around Miss Daisy. Dr. Bill Reston also witnessed the accident and gently nudged Mark to one side as he began a quick examination of her alertness, reflexes, and pain points.

"Ms. Hanover, I don't want to move you just yet but it does look like God was smiling on us today. You understand?"

"Yes William, I understand and I'll accede to your request but you know as good as I do that we could move this show about twenty feet thata-away and I'd be fine as fiddles," she said pointing to the shady area of the front lawn.

The West End Rescue Squad was less than a half-mile from the church so an ambulance screamed on to the scene in less than five minutes. DeWayne Logan and Sandy Burch jumped from the truck and parted the small crowd hovering over the elderly victim.

"Just give me some air and do what you have to do as fast as you can do it. I've got a family to feed," Daisy told them.

Dr. Reston quickly briefed them and Sandy decided they could move her to a backboard without risk of further injury.

"No broken limbs or hips and her pelvis is firm. No abrasions of any kind; only a sore rear. A bit unusual for an 80-year-old granny to skip away from one of these so, by the book, partner," she said to DeWayne.

As they gently fitted the Philadelphia collar around her neck, Mark let go of her hand.

"Thank you, Mr. Justin. Tell my family I'll be home shortly if doctors still have eyes and ears," she said from the backboard. "And, dear, you are such a fine deacon to take care of me like you just did. I'll never forget it."

As the siren blared down Grant Avenue, the cops arrived and wanted to talk to witnesses. Mark answered a couple of questions before putting the bizarre incident behind him and heading home for lunch. From start to finish the whole event had taken fifteen minutes.

"What did I just do?" he asked himself as he walked through the church parking lot toward his T-bird. "I prayed for her, didn't I?"

“You guys remember?” he asked The Debating Society.

Silence.

* * * * *

The police scanner in the ambulance crackled with reports of more violence in the city. Most of the victims were headed to the same destination as Miss Daisy. Thanks to a five-car pile up on I-95 and a drive-by shooting in the gang infested Whitehall section of town, the ER was full and chaotic. Shots fired into a home had wounded two children and the local news crews were in the ER for wall-to-wall coverage of the carnage.

Reporting from the hospital for WVTV, TV10 News, Dominique Johnson was directing her camera crew, framing the story, and interviewing witnesses.

After graduating with honors in mass communications, Dominique interned as a production assistant at the station but the real need was another reporter of color and she quickly moved into weekend on-the-scene reporting. Tall, young, beautiful, and articulate, she had the instincts of a veteran and used the camera with credible passion. In less than thirty days she became a local favorite and was now a Richmond *Who's Who* monthly regular.

“Looks like another godless day in the capital city,” she said to a cop fingering his Palm Pilot. She asked if he knew how the children were attacked.

He grunted “Maybe.”

“Jesus! He doesn’t give a shit about any of this. Children gunned down at home and all he can do is play with his PDA?”

She grew angrier.

“The violence in this city pisses me off but to this guy it’s just another day of niggers offin’ niggers. I ought to expose his ass for ignorance in the first degree.”

To Dominique every one of these crimes was a tragedy. So she used her anger to capture the pain, find the *heart* of it, and bring it home to the viewers.

She noticed that yet another case was coming into the ER.

“We got about a hundred witnesses all saying this blue hair got nailed by a station wagon out on Grant Street. The doc on the scene cleared her but the EMTs have her in transport here for more tests. ETA in under five minutes,” said the voice on the scanner.

Dominique’s curiosity peaked.

“Hey, what gives with the old lady they’re bringing in?” She asked the cop.

“Got it right here.” He smiled pointing to his PDA.

“Officer on the scene says she got prayed over by a deacon or maybe it was a priest but she ain’t hurt. No big deal. Bet it’s a scam, if you ask me.”

“No one’s asking, asshole,” she thought. “Thanks detective,” she said and kept mulling it.

“So, who was the church dude? Some bible beater giving her the last rites? No, it’s divine intervention, the power of prayer or psychic healing. Pick one without laughing,” she dared herself but then felt a familiar abdominal twinge.

(Itch, itch, itch)

“Don’t start with yourself down there. This is not real news so just stop it!” she yelled in her thoughts but couldn’t help rubbing the itch in her midriff.

The news bugs were some kind of gaseous critters in her stomach that wouldn’t stop scratching her gut when they got wind of a story. Other reporters developed a 6th sense or intuition or a nose for news but she was stuck with itching and twitching that felt like internal poison ivy.

“Listen to me. Let’s be reasonable here. The drive-by shooting is the story. This church lady about to roll in here is a sideshow. Come on now. You can not have a hard-on about this one,” she pleaded looking down at her stomach.

But a neck and shoulders tremor followed another belly twitch.

"Damn, you got friends in there," She said out loud. "Okay, okay. You win. We'll take a gander at the church lady with a station wagon attached to her butt and then we'll get some lunch. Does that work for you?"

She had long since stopped being embarrassed about talking to her belly button and had given up trying to get rid of them. When they got like this she just followed their lead.

"Alright. Quick now. We know an 80-year-old babe is no match for a two-ton station wagon so she's got to be bruised, broken or lacerated somewhere. Let's check, check, check…her fingernails. Hell yeah, her nails."

An attending was waiting with staff and they quickly lifted Daisy onto a gurney and began the examination even on the move towards the ER doors.

When the doors blew open Dominique got a better look at Daisy Hanover who was busy answering the doctor's questions (*she knows him*). He held one hand but the other lay flat on her stomach.

"Now hear this. Her nails are perfect. Even her pleats are still pleated." Dominique was shocked. "Isn't that special-hard to believe she was road kill fifteen minutes ago."

(Twitch, twitch)

The triage team moved in and blocked her view but she had seen enough.

"I'll talk with that attending here in a few minutes. Will that make you happy down there?" she asked her midriff.

(Itch, itch)

"I am so tired of being your roach hotel."

Dominique worked her way over to the waiting room where she could call in the story and chat with Daisy's attending, Dr. Louis Shotley, after his initial examination.

"Excuse me Dr. Shotley, Dominique Johnson with WVTV News. Can you give me an update on the church lady that met a station wagon the hard way about thirty minutes ago?" She said turning on the small recorder she always carried.

"Hello to you too Ms Johnson. The pleasure is all mine and just so you know, I have two rules for press relations. First, I'm the attending, so I won't answer any questions about my patient and, second, tape recorders are for weasels. Quote me please. If you want a story, check with Mrs. Hanover after she leaves the hospital. Right now I'm headed to the OR. We've got a lot of customers so please forgive me. I'm usually the perfect host."

"Yeah, right Doc, but don't you think it's unusual she's not at least dinged up a little. Seems a bit odd to me. And what do you think about an on-the-scene prayer by a deacon? Any thoughts about the power of prayer in a situation like this?"

Louis surprised her with a big toothy smile; he almost laughed, but continued walking down the hall.

"You got the name of that guy with the curb side service?"

"Does it matter?"

"Maybe. I'm a member over there and I might know the alleged silver tongue devil," he said still smiling.

"Cops questioned a guy named Justin who was first on the scene. You know him?"

"Yeah. Did anyone see him stop the station wagon?" This time he did laugh.

"Well no. What? The car hit her before it stopped and besides, he was at least fifty feet away when it happened. Why would you ask that?"

"Why'd you ask me about the power of prayer? You took a shot I'd say something you could use. So I've given you a clue and the rest isn't that tough," he said and looked directly at her for the first time.

"But it's not what you expect," he added and glanced at his watch. "Gotta go. Loved our talk but do check the rabbit hole before you follow this one in."

The last she saw of Louis he was smiling from ear to ear and looking at the ceiling as the elevator door closed.

The news bugs were doing *River Dance* in steel cleats.

"Yeah, yeah, I get it. You don't have to drill me a new bellybutton. The good doctor just about busted a seam when I mentioned his friend's name. He couldn't get away from me fast enough and that question about stopping the station wagon? I think he meant it but who hell knows?"

She walked back to the ER hoping to ask DeWayne a few questions about the accident but missed him. Dead end, for now.

"Okay guys, try this on. We've just ended one of the bloodiest weeks since President Lincoln strolled through here about 130 years ago. So what we need is something good and uniquely Richmond for balance. That'll be the idea behind *The Deacon and Miss Daisy.* It's a little story with heart, mystery, a dash of religion, and a happy ending. We'll tag it to the end of the broadcast. Whatcha think about that?"

Nothing felt. Dominique smiled for the first time all day.

Chapter 7

"Did you feel anything when you touched her?" Charlotte asked.

"Nothing felt and nothing moved that shouldn't have. I've done some wild stuff in a panic but not in a long time and never related to prayer or by touching someone," he said trying to replay it in his thoughts.

"You should have seen her; tossed like a blue haired pizza and denting the hood when she landed on it. That final landing on the street, it would've busted my butt for sure. Even after an overdose of Centrum 50 with calcium power crystals, no 80-year-old I know could take that shot and just stupor away from it. Dear friends, we have undeniable proof that Miss Daisy was in fact born with a rubber ass. Case closed," he said.

"Would you just tell me what happened?"

"Other than total panic, zero. No spontaneous bone knitting or organ mending hands-on healing. As cool as it would be, I can't do anything like that. It's not in the plan. And the best part is no one else thinks so either."

"Mighty fine, dear, rubber rump it is." And she passed him a sandwich.

They whipped through lunch and took off to one of the biggest flea markets on the East Coast. The afternoon was just right for treasure hunting among the one thousand stalls of junk at the State Fair grounds.

The phone rang. The machine answered.

"Mr. Justin. This is Tom Hanover, Daisy Hanover's son. I just wanted to let you know that my mother told us about your kindness and how much it helped her at the accident scene. We're at MCV now and she seems fine. They are running more tests but she wanted me to call and let you know she's thinking of you and how you helped. I've heard some of the details and this is a miracle from the Lord to keep her with us and (sniff) and I want you to know, oh I'm sorry, (sniff) how much your praying…(sobbing)". "God bless you, sir," he managed and hung up.

"Mark, hey, this is Tommy Robertson calling to check in with you. Sounds like you were a deacon par ex-el-lan-te with Mrs. Hanover in that accident and all. Very proud of you, son. By the way, she was fully off church property when this happened wasn't she? Can you get back to me on that last point? Don't want the lawyers involved, do we. Thanks again but, hey, don't let it happen again on our watch. Just kidding about that but check in with me."

"Mr. Justin, This is Helen Newman. I was there and I saw what you did. At church, I mean. It was so beautiful and caring and the way Daisy just woke up when she heard your prayer and how she wasn't hurt. Do you watch Ernest Angley? Anyway, I'm not saying it's like that but, Jesus be praised, I'll never forget it. God bless."

"Mr. Justin, my name is Myrtle Jenkins and I'm a friend of Helen Newman's. She told me about Miss Daisy and I wonder, oh, I'm sorry, this is imposing and please I know you're not one of those faith healers, but would you mind saying a special prayer for my father, Harold Reynolds. He has cancer, going through chemo, lot of pain. Would you mind adding him to your prayer list? I know you will do that for us. Now we all have some hope for our own little miracle. Thank you so, so very much."

"Praise the Lord, Deacon, praise the Lord. You are blessed with the spirit. Yea thou I walk through the valley of the shadow, I fear not a thing. You have a wonder-touch, Mr. Justin. It's real. Never doubt it. Praise the Lord. 'For whosoever shall do the will of God, the same is my brother, my sister and my mother.' That's from the book of Mark, but you probably know that. You are on God's right hand, deacon. His will be done. Amen."

"Mark, this is Joy Kirby and I was wondering if you'd mind speaking about your experience with Daisy Hanover to the Thursday Night Supper group at church. Just five minutes ahead of our feature speaker. It's so inspirational, we hope you'll share it with us. Call me at the church office to confirm."

"Mr. Justin, I'm Dominique Johnson at WVTV Channel 10 news and I was in the hospital covering another story when Mrs. Hanover was treated. I talked with Officer Sterns who told me you were first on the scene. We probably won't air it but I thought you could add some background in case we do. Call me before 5:30 if possible at 644-WVTV."

"Hey Mark. Jerry Tinsler here calling to let you know that Mrs. Hanover is fine and she wanted me to be sure that the church pastors knew how good you were to her after the accident this afternoon. What in Sam Hill did you say to her? Anyway, I want you to know how proud of you we are and Vick will be too when he hears about this. He'll be back in the pulpit next Sunday. Call me this week, por favor."

"Mr. Justin, it's Dominique Johnson again with WVTV Channel 10. I was hoping you'd call to answer a few questions for me. We've heard some more about the accident and understand that Mrs. Hanover has been released. That's good news on a bad news day so we've decided to do a 30-second feature at the end the show tonight. No names. Just our way of reporting something good in River City today. Please call me by 5:45 if possible at 644-9227."

"Mr. Justin, this is John Bishop, the driver of the car that was in the accident in front of the church today. No need to call me back. The lady, uh, Mrs. Hanover, well to me it's like she jumped up, twirled around and angled herself to sit on the front of my car and then slid off the hood. It stopped on a dime like it didn't want to hurt her. And it didn't so there's no need to get the insurance companies involved. What's there to report, anyway? Can't report nothing, right? Uh, that's all."

The machine reached capacity at 6:00. The phone continued to ring.

Chapter 8

Back to camera two as Dominique wrapped up the story.

"Was this a miracle of faith or just a lucky lady who takes extraordinary care of herself? Looking at the facts, we can't explain how she was so fortunate. Tonight we brought you the stories of a ruthless drive-by shooting and four more drug related murders but we also covered this one that ends with a thankful family and a grateful community. I found a huge measure of warmth, kindness, and caring in this small story about two extraordinary people. For many of us, it may be the best news of the week. So make it a good one Richmond and try to help someone have a better week when you get the chance. You might start a little miracle too. From all of us at TV10 news at 6:00, thanks for watching and please join us again at 11:00."

Dominique walked off the set and into the newsroom. The belly bugs were running wind sprints in the pit of her stomach.

"How about bringing the Deacon in for an interview? Could be a stiff, though, so why not the two of them, the elusive Deacon *and* the charming Miss Daisy. Is that what you girls want?" The itch ended abruptly.

"You are some spoiled little cucarachas down there." She rubbed her stomach knowing they had made her think through the next best step.

"I'll have to clear it with the other boss too. You know Seth calls the shots around here, girls, and you can crawl up his sphincter if you don't like it."

Seth Griggs, TV10 News Director, was cranky, old school and had a wall of awards to show for his twenty-five years of dedication to the news in Richmond.

"Interesting thing is that he's a member at Commonwealth Church and pretty cozy with the head honcho over there, what's his name. Oh hell, he's always on the phone with that preacher."

She flipped through the Rolodex on the desk next to hers and found a reference on the Commonwealth Church card.

Springwell, Victor. Arrogant. Agendas-hidden and not so. Careful.

"What in Jerry Falwell hell does that mean? A sinister minister? I'm going after the deacon. Seth can handle the big dog. Fat chance there's also a card on Justin but let's take a gander."

She flipped forward to the J's expecting the K's to click by but her jaw dropped when his card appeared. Then she had to sit down while reading it.

* * * * *

One of Dominique's 6:00 News viewers dropped the Sunday paper below chin level to listen to her final story of the newscast.

He summed it up in his own mind.

"This lovely young reporter is fresh out of some college journalism crib and blabbing about everything but the real story. Give her some credit for at least mentioning a possible faith-based intervention. But how much clearer can it be, people? This was a manifestation of Christian faith-a physical act of merciful intervention." He was getting angrier with every thought.

"Well little lady, The Christian Spirit Network is the only news org that knows the real deal here. You tell the tale but not the power of it," he said to the TV.

After thirty years in the field, as a missionary setting up hospitals on all seven continents and a CSN reporter, John Chambers had seen it all. But this kind of manifestation excited him the most.

"Next thing is to beat the bushes a bit, see if it's true. If it's network material we'll put a pitch together by mid week." He had worshipped at Commonwealth Church before and knew exactly how to frame it.

Picking up the phone and dialing the corporate office, he was sure Tom Frazier would drive a couple of hours to look into this with him.

“Tom, it’s Champ. I’m in Richmond and we’ve got a story. I’d bet your 401K on it. Just aired on the local CBS affiliate as a one-minute closer after their coverage of a God-awful weekend down here. It definitely raised my antenna.” He paused to listen and then responded.

“What? No, my news antenna, you heathen. Obviously I need to keep praying for you. Lookit, I’m going to swing by the site tomorrow but I want you to spend the afternoon down here and look into a spontaneous healing by a church deacon,” he said and recapped the incident.

Chambers and Frazier had worked dozens of stories over the years. Many started just like this with an excited phone call from John, the perpetual cub reporter. They agreed to meet at Commonwealth Church at 2:00pm and hung up.

Chambers wasn’t ready to give it a rest but his options were limited. On a summer Sunday there wouldn’t be church programs, socials or dinners tonight so there was no way to get into it before tomorrow unless he phoned WVTV to snoop the story.

“Call the cops, lame brain. There has to be a report, witnesses who would have seen the deacon do this wonderful thing,” he thought and then nearly yelled, “Oh yeah, John Boy. That is the testimonial ticket. Thank God for the police,” he thought as the 3rd Precinct phone rang.

“Yes sir. I’m John Chambers with the Christian Spirit Network. I’d like to talk with the officer that….”

And CSN was in the hunt.

Chapter 9

Mark heard the phone ringing as he turned the key in the large front door and pushed it open to enter the house. The answering machine hit capacity three hours earlier while he and Charlotte were wandering through the Giant Flea.

As always, Charlotte went to the phone to check messages. Mark decided to tote their new oriental statues into the back yard garden and began looking for the right spot to plant them. With only a small city lot to survey, it was quick work. "Not a bad weekend for you two homeless stiffs," he said to them as he headed back to the house.

Charlotte opened the storm door and practically leaped onto the deck, yelling for him to hear something.

"Uh oh, her freckles are gone. Bad news for sure," he thought as he looked at her. When Charlotte lost her freckles she was sick or terrified. He ran toward the deck.

"Mark, you've got to listen to the phone messages. You won't believe this. They've filled up the machine and you made the news and they want more prayers. They want you to heal them." She paused just a moment to collect her thoughts. "Don't answer the phone. This is scary stuff. I've never heard anything like it. They want a lot from you and they want it now."

"Recon I best git the shotgun, little lady. They'll rue the day," he said hoping for a smile.

"We may want to board up and head for the hills when you hear all this. It's not even a little funny."

"Daisy call? I expected she might. But you've got to take it easy on the melodrama. You know what those goose bumps do to me."

"Okay, Miracle Boy. Go listen to the messages and then we'll talk."

It took ten minutes to go through them. The religious nut case scared him but mostly he wanted to slap-silly a couple of the church guys.

“Hey beautiful,” he yelled to Charlotte. “You win. I got no idea how to handle this. They only train us to pass the plate.”

She came in to talk about the options.

“Yeah, right. Sorry I missed the show. You really pushed some buttons over there.” She looked at him with sad eyes he had not seen in a long time.

“Damn it, Mark. You had no business touching that woman.”

“Hey, I’m sorry but I didn’t think of anything else.”

“You didn’t think at all, you reacted. Besides, you quit praying years ago. Lost faith and all that angst. So, did you blast her with a healing ray? Is that what all those people saw?”

“People see what they wanna see. I can’t stop that.”

“Well, have you thought about Vick? He’s back from vacation in few days and you know he won’t be happy. But he’s not the immediate concern,” she said talking about the senior minister like he was a hit man on family leave.

“Then how about we consider this episode of the Twilight Zone over, make the calls and move on. Two calls, maybe, to those poor souls that mistook you for someone who can help. Just listen and refer them to Jerry. He’ll know the right church response. But blow off the reporter. She’s trouble.”

“So you think I should tell the believers I don’t do drive-by praying and, for grins, stiff most of the church leadership and a prime-time reporter. Is that the plan?”

“Make it go away, Mark.” She said concerned about the reporter and a lot more.

He’d done nothing like this since the summer ten years ago. It was pure ad hoc power that saved them when their car hit a deer on the Blue Ridge Parkway and skidded off a cliff. Air borne over the George Washington National Forest, he had glided the car and cushioned the fall on a 4-point landing in a blackberry patch clearing more than 200-feet below.

As far as she knew, when panicked he could do anything-no limits. But *she* would do anything to keep the lifestyle they loved. Nothing else mattered. Since it was the sworn duty of a church officer to help any member in need she understood what he had done and why two calls had to be returned now. She hoped the rest would wait until hell was chilly.

But the phone rang before he could pick it up.

"Hello. Yes, this is Deacon Justin but most people call me Mark. Who's this?"

John Chambers couldn't believe his luck. From a tip at the TV station and a cop with a half finished report, he was talking with the man who laid his hand on a dying lady only hours ago.

"Mr. Justin, I'm John Chambers from CSN, the Christian Spirit Network. I was in town and…"

Mark interrupted before John could finish his introduction.

"CSN? Now wait a second, whatever you're thinking. Just, wait a minute. Why are you calling me?" Mark was stunned. The Jesus network had picked it up some how and now God was calling. "Out of control," he thought.

Chambers sensed his fear and backtracked.

"You didn't see the story tonight on the 6:00 news? Please hang with me, okay? I don't mean to alarm you but I admired your response at the accident this morning and I thought it might be good for another audience. I just wanted to talk with you about it. Nothing else," he said wincing and waiting for the dial tone.

"Look, Chambers, here's the truth. There's no story for CSN or anyone else. Miss Daisy was in an accident and I just helped keep her calm while a doctor looked her over. Then the ambulance took her to MCV and I left and everybody left and she's fine. Not much to that, right?"

"Maybe, but the way I heard it a station wagon tossed her on the road like the morning paper. Did you see something different?"

"I didn't see much of anything. I just heard the car skid and ran a few feet to help. She was sitting in front of it when I first spoke to her."

"And what did you say?"

"What difference does it make?" Mark wasn't about to admit his faulty memory. "Look, it's been a long day and now you're trying to spin me into some kind of miracle man. I can't let that happen so this conversation is over. I won't participate in hype journalism. Sorry to be so blunt but I'm not a fan."

Chambers was ready for that one.

"But Mark we don't, we won't, spin anything. Just hear me out. Everyday we try to spread the word of God's work. Maybe you don't see it that way but don't you even care about your fifteen minutes of fame?"

He wondered if the Deacon had an ego at all.

"I had more than fifteen long ago and moved on. Maybe this will clue you in. It does not matter to me whether God intervened or if she was wearing a Teflon jump suit. It happened-it's over. But I am curious about one thing, Chambers, tell me more about that 6:00 report you saw," he asked feeling guilty about manhandling the reporter.

"Well, uh, they did, uh, a good job." Chambers was surprised but recovered. "No names and not much detail. It was just a feel good piece to offset the violence. You know, kids shot, gang murders and an old lady hit by a car, prayed over by a church deacon, and released from hospital unhurt. It had a happy ending and they went with it," Chambers explained but wanted to try again on his angle.

"Mark, we just want to cover the story. This city needed a Samaritan and like or not, you're it, at least for a news cycle," John said hoping to break through.

Mark didn't hear the last sentence. Instead, like a digital voice mail, his inner voice began speaking.

"*Lord, send the healing energy of your love into Mrs. Hanover. Let her live to nurture her family. Let her return your love seven fold and let us always know her as a miracle of your grace and mercy. Do this now.*"

His prayer for Miss Daisy was drifting by and this time he wrote it down before it disappeared back into the Unknown Zone.

"Mark? Justin? Are you with me?" Chambers pitch was dangling.

"Yeah. Did you ask me a question?"

"I was hoping to talk with you more tomorrow, maybe about a half an hour, just to hear your side, that's all. No pressure and no judgments," Chambers promised.

Remembering the prayer triggered a decision. Mark was going to finish what he'd started earlier in the day. "There is a *reason* for all of this and Mr. CSN is a player," he thought.

"Damn it! Why did this have to happen now?" It was maddening.

"Hold on Mark. Nothing's happened. We're just trying to set a time when we can talk." Chambers was confused by the sudden change in direction.

"So tell me what would you do if you were in my shoes?"

"Not my call. Either talk to me or not. It's up to you."

"Well that won't cut it," Mark said trying to draw him out. "Come on John. Tell me the CSN thinking on this."

"Lookit, Mark, all I can do is *tell* the story. You are an officer and a leader in that church and now you're an inspiration but nothing's settled. Why don't we meet tomorrow and just talk about it?" Chambers concluded and hoped his little vision was enough.

"How about my house for lunch at noon?"

"Sure, I can do that. But I'll be glad to pick up the tab anywhere you'd like."

"No, I'll introduce you to my bride and we'll have a sandwich. Our treat. That way I won't feel obliged if I decide to bag the whole thing,"

"Then it's a date. I'll be there at noon. Lookit, I know you think this is risky but, if we do it I'm sure you'll be pleased." Chambers was delighted but knew this guy was holding back-a lot. He could feel it.

"I'll see you tomorrow, John," Mark said and hung up. No need to tell him the address, he knew Chambers had it.

A wave of exhaustion swept over him. But then remembered the calls and messages from the afternoon. He had to return two of them tonight.

"This is going to be awkward and I don't have the energy to script it so let's hope the spirit still moves me," he said as he picked the phone and called John Trimmings whose wife was so ill.

He was careful not to bring up the prayer for Daisy. Instead he explained the church rules that require an Elder to accompany a deacon on any home visit.

"Mark, I'll not mince words. That's not going to help. I don't know *what* I had in mind but a lesson in church doctrine ain't it. Sorry to have bothered you," and he hung up.

No inspired words, no spiritual comfort, nothing for the Trimmings to lean on. His hollow church-speak had been worse than no call at all. He called Myrtle Jenkins with the same story for her father and got the same disappointed response.

"But this morning I didn't think at all-100% pure fear. We're lucky I didn't toss the car into a tree."

"That's not the point, Mark. It could be history right now if you'd hung up on CSN. You lost me on that one, dear, and I've had enough for one day. Good night." And she stomped upstairs.

"God knows what's going to happen next," he thought.

"God knows he knows," replied the Debating Society.

Chapter 10

Work was work. Hate it or love it, Mark was responsible for corporate communications in Whyecliff Pharmaceuticals, Inc. Every day had to be a good news day in the drug ad business. His job was to be sure that product, research and systems fed his office the latest on every drug in the pipeline and the market.

He'd been at his desk less than 5 minutes when Roger Stanley appeared in the door.

"Hey, boss, you got a minute?"

Mark waved him in. Roger was a former rep and the best spin-agent on the team and they had worked together for years.

"I saw your church on TV last night? The one with the traffic accident in front? Were you there? From the report it sounded like maybe a spontaneous healing, even a miracle."

"Hell no. It was anything but spontaneous. I was there and saw it all-definitely a scam. Sit down and I'll give you the eyewitness gospel." Roger almost fell over taking a seat next to the desk.

"The old lady was wearing inflatable panties and the car had a rubber bumper. Add some precision driving and the old woman and her lover put on a real fright show. But the cops will probably lock 'em up today. I can't wait to see the follow up on TV10 if they have the nerve to show how they were hoodwinked. Highly unlikely we'll see that one, don't you think?"

"Who was the deacon that helped at the scene, the one that said the prayer for the injured lady?"

"Just a Jimmy Swaggert wannabe and he fell for it like a dead tree. Prayed real good over her, I saw that. He even blessed the car that hit her and then directed traffic away from the scene," Mark replied with a straight face knowing Roger was on to him.

"It was you. You're the deacon that prayed over her, right?"

"Maybe, but it's no big deal," Mark confessed. "I didn't know what else to do so I just said a few words to calm her down.

That's it. Anything else you hear is pure fecal matter. We clear?"

"Sorry boss but *that* was a miracle healing, a true intervention from the Almighty. I don't know how you can sit here doing this mundane stuff?"

But Roger could see from Mark's body language that the discussion was over.

"Got it, chief, but I'm so proud to be working for you, a man of faith and dedication to the Lord. I know that's the only way you were chosen to save that poor dying woman. How about I buy you lunch and we can talk about it."

There was no arguing with Roger, saved 5-years earlier in a tent service, but he'd go absolutely charismatic if he knew about Mark's lunch plans with CSN.

"Sorry, you're out ranked. Got a date with my bride."

"Understandable. Upstaged by a nooner." Roger was devout but his sense of humor had stayed in tact.

"Boss, it's really important. We can't leave it like this for long. You owe me some face time, okay?"

"Honest your holiness, it is over. A one shot deal. Can we get back to the reason they pay us the big money?"

"Yeah, you got it but for the record, that whopper you just told was the worst lie I ever heard. Inflatable underwear? What a crock. Later." Roger disappeared from the doorway.

Out of nowhere another song leaped into Mark's thoughts. It was loud and complete when the first chord blasted to the surface. The words were his; the tune was a derivative of Bon Jovi's *Blaze of Glory* and the voice was Don Henley's.

Work sucks but it's necessary
And some days I feel so damn weary.
But I'm here from 8 to 8
Don't even think about being late
I'm the guy you love to hate.
I'm your manager.

A sustained and fading guitar note created a transition to the next verse.

I wish I didn't have to be here
And I'd love to be your friend,
But the money tree in my back yard
Won't grow a single limb.
So you owe me 8 hours of every working day.
And I expect you to respect me,
If you expect your pay.
I can make your day go really well
Or I'll make it into a living hell.
That's why I get the big bucks.
I'm your manager.

"I like it and it sure hits the message-managers suck." He stuffed the note with the verses on it into his pocket.

"Hey, deacon dipstick. Are you sure you want to trip the light fantastic with a reporter from the Caucasian Stranglers Network?" asked the Debating Society.

"Going through with it boys, but you have to wonder what song we'll make up for him?" he said aloud as he spun his chair around to work e-mail.

While the first message was opening, he flashed back on Roger's reaction a few minutes earlier and decided it would be best not to mix business with religion.

"This is my show and I'm *his* manager," he said with a smile and began an e-mail reply.

The morning flew by and at 11:55 Mark was pacing in his dining room, not just excited but on-air nervous about inviting Chambers to the house. The front door bell rang and he headed to greet Chambers, relieved to get on with it.

But instead of Chambers, a vaguely familiar young black woman greeted him as he opened the door.

"Hello. I'm Dominique Johnson with Channel 10 News. Are you Mark Justin?" she asked offering her hand to shake. He realized that he hadn't returned her calls and that she was dropping by to see if he was real.

"Yes you are and yes I am. I do owe you a huge apology. I meant to call yesterday."

He shook hands and noticed her strange grip that extended the index and middle fingers beyond his lower thumb and onto his wrist. She was taking his pulse and he needed a diversion.

"Say Dominique, would you mind moving the station van out of the driveway? Among other things it's blocking my escape route."

She smiled. He was off balance, soggy handed, and had a heart rate over ninety. So she obliged, motioning to the driver and he backed out of the driveway, parking about 50 feet down the busy street.

"How's that?"

It would have been great had another car not pulled into the driveway.

"This has to be Chambers." Mark said softly.

John recognized the reporter with Justin on the stoop. He never forgot a face and the Sunday 6:00 news story quickly played back in his mind.

"Oh, come on, son. Why invite us both?" he wondered as he stopped and stared a moment. "This is getting pretty good." He was all smiles when he joined them on the stoop.

"Hello Deacon, I'm John Chambers. Honored to meet you Ms. Johnson. Great piece last night-a thoughtful way to end a rotten weekend," he said shaking her hand. She did not take his pulse.

Mark had a sinking feeling in his stomach. "Chapter One: I Am an Idiot," he thought.

"Deacon, you with us?" Chambers asked as he took Mark's hand and shook it firmly.

"That's it. Be the deacon and go holy on them right now," Mark thought.

"Yes, I am, Mr. Chambers and I owe you both an explanation. Dominique left me several messages but I couldn't return them. That's why she's here and John, you caught me later. That's when he and I decided to have lunch today. I don't know how both of you found me at the same time but we are together now so please come inside and to break bread with me," he said but knew it was too lame for either to buy.

Dominique's stomach went insane. The news bugs brought their friends this time and they were all doing a Russian folk in spiked heels dance down there.

We love this story, she thought but wanted more than shared lunch with a CSN reporter. She would fall back and talk with him another time. The decision didn't quiet the riot in her stomach but it was her best move.

"Thank you both but I was just dropping by to see if there really was a Deacon Mark Justin at this address. I don't want to interrupt your lunch plans. But we can talk at the station if you can make it after work. I believe you know the address." she said smiling and offering her hand.

"If that will put a wrap on it I'll be there with bells on, Dominique." He could see that she had done some research and knew it would be better to talk there off the record there than on the record here with CSN here.

"See you about 5:30 and please call if there's a problem. I'll let security know they can reactivate your clearance," she said with an all-knowing raised eyebrow.

"And it's nice to know CSN has noticed our little story. Going to pick up it up?"

"Time will tell but it has been my pleasure, Ms. Johnson," and he bowed to feign respect. She's going to exploit another hero, humiliate him and his faith," he thought.

Dominique walked down the driveway thinking about what just happened.

"Hey, you guys clawing your way out of my belly. Listen up. You can shut it down. I believe you."

The itching stopped.

“John,” Mark started the transition. “We need to grab that sandwich. Got a 1:30 I can’t miss.”

Chambers took no notes. He asked Mark to repeat the prayer during the course of their conversation. Consistency was key to genuineness and the deacon didn’t flinch or reflect on his words. It was like he relived the event.

As he left, John quickly thanked the Justin’s but didn’t set up another meeting or mention any next steps. He didn’t want to spook them but odds were he’d bring a crew along next time. They were headed for national, maybe international airtime.

“This is great stuff. It’s enigmatic, inspirational and miraculous; a true story with dozens of witnesses. A manifestation of faith.” he thought and then said the title aloud.

“No sir, John Boy, an accident of faith.” He liked it so much he could not stop repeating it as he drove away to pitch his CSN partner.

Chapter 11

This wasn't going to be easy but all he had to do was stay cool, calm and deliberate. They weren't going into the studio or the control booth or on to the production floor so an interview in the newsroom should be a breeze but just being there made him as antsy as a groom at the alter.

He looked at the building for a moment and plunged inside. The lobby hadn't changed at all; brown speckled marble floors with centered white granite cutout of Virginia, the off-white ceiling smudged by endless cigarette smoking and the heavy paneled mahogany surrounding an updated security desk.

He was glad to see Dominique walking in his direction, smiling and perky.

"You want a tour first, for old time's sake?"

"Let's not. The nostalgia is suffocating already. Can we do this at your desk?

"Sure thing. Twenty years ago you didn't last long around here but there's no one left from those days. Whatever happened is history, no worries. We'll stick to this week's agenda."

He was relieved but not comfortable.

In the elevator an awkward silence took over, she looking up and he looking down. A bumpy lurch between floors lifted them both, almost weightless for an instant, and the hiccup that followed rattled the mahogany paneling around all four walls. Mark didn't look up but her eyes nearly popped out of their sockets as she grabbed him for balance and panic relief. In another instant the car settled down on 3 and the door jerked open with a loud mechanical thump.

"That's not changed either, I see. After you?" He extended an open arm to through the doorway.

"Maybe it works for you but my elevator ain't going to do that. Damn, anyone ever tell you that you're just a little bit creepy?"

"Only Ms. Justin and only when I'm smothered in coconut oil and pine nuts." He smiled for the first time and they headed for the newsroom. But he stopped in his tracks as they rounded a corner. The double doors of the studio were dead ahead.

"We must be turned around. That's not the way to the newsroom."

"Oh, we can get there from here. A short cut you may not remember. Don't worry we won't disturb the crew. They're prepping for the 6 o'clock in there. We'll sneak through without a sound."

Walking into the studio was a trip backward down a twenty-year wormhole. The set had been updated with green screens for weather maps and the anchor desk was a lighter wood but everything else, the heavy black lightproof curtains, camera dollys, and the control booth were all the same.

The on-camera jitters crawled over his skin and into his stomach like it was 1977. He reminded himself that it wasn't but the butterflies took flight.

They were half way across the floor when the lights in the control room flickered off and on. Mark stopped, they flicked on; he took a step, they flicked off.

Just as he heard a muffled, "What the hell?" from the control room, the green screen to his right lit up. The two studio camera guys were going thorough show prep, testing close-up to long shots, and both pivoted to point their cameras at the luminous screens behind the set.

"Keep moving," Mark pleaded with Dominique but she stopped to marvel at the screen now glowing like a Grateful Dead concert backdrop.

"Would you look at that?" She asked as a pulsing rainbow of red, blue and green swirled on the screen. The colors blended, rotated and separated rhythmically like a seamless kaleidoscope.

"Nice work in the control room – back to the '70s. Maybe in honor of your return? It's from your psychedelic era, right?"

The screen returned to green, then went dark.

He shut it down by sheer will as he took the last few steps out of the studio and into the broadcast hallway where his picture had once hung with the rest of the on-camera crew.

"Let me get you a cup of coffee. You look like you could use it."

He was sure it had been brewed in 1977 but drank and listened to her idea for a follow up before replying.

"So you want me to look into the camera and say, 'Hi ya'll, you may not remember me but now I'm a religious nut job. Put down that remote and lay your hands on the TV right now.'"

"That's *not* where I'm headed, Mark, but you gotta admit the religious overtones are flaming on this one.

"Only because it happened in front of the church and because I was the guy on duty. I was just shaking hands and keeping the doors from slamming small children. Any church officer would have done the same."

"Not a scratch, Mark. Not even a depleted pleat. Any chance God worked through you to heal her?"

"Any chance your TV reports caused the last gang killing in Richmond?"

"Ridiculous, but I get your point. Just one more. Do you think you were part of a miracle?"

"Do you think we can stop beating around the burning bush?" He had to smile at her directness. "Listen and believe. I'm not going on record about any kind of religiosity

"How about off the record?"

"Very funny. You know I don't have a clue and I won't add a layer of divine intention to the heap. That spin is all yours," he said ready to end the interview.

"Not just mine. CSN won't give a rip about your 3-bedroom-2-and-a-half-bath life here in River City. They are going to define you by this thing and once you're a Christian celebrity the crazies, the zealots and the poor fools that just want to believe will be knocking on your door."

"Thanks for the warning but you're both dangerous in my book. And besides, it's history, right?"

The news bug chorus line kicked her hard in the ribs.

"Not until someone explains how our victim walked away from a blind date with a two-ton station wagon. It's an itch that's not scratched yet, so to speak," she said rubbing her midriff.

"Then ask a doctor about it? I'm sure there's a medical explanation."

"That, Mr. Justin, is a fine idea. In fact, I've already had a few words with Dr. Louis Shotley. He sends his regards."

"Uh oh, bad choice. Lou's a pathological liar and female impersonator to boot. But before I deny all of it, tell me what he said." Mark realized that he and Louis had her in the middle.

"Nothing I could make sense of; just a strange brush off. Man, you two are a pair of jokers and I know when I'm being played so I think we're done for now. I've got postproduction on a real story. But hang around if you want to. Take another tour for old time's sake?" she asked still trying to draw him out.

"No thanks. I'll take the steps, exit stage right. Back to my world."

She smiled and picked up the phone to call Daisy Hanover as he went through the door.

Mark also made a call as soon as he got home.

"Hey, Dr. Yakenoff. Why are you talking to reporters about my business at church?"

"'Hey yourself. Remember, son? I owed you one from Saturday night. And besides, the news babe was itching for something so I threw her a bone. They'll probably lead off with it tonight 'Local surgeon exposes miracle man as space alien. Phlegm at eleven.'"

Mark didn't reply.

"Okay Marko, here's the deal. I was there and treated Daisy, if you can call it that. I examined her from follicle to toe nail and the findings were unremarkable, even the usual age related issues weren't presented."

"Shots, does that mean what it sounds like? She's eighty. There have to be issues."

"Did the lab work too and kept her a few hours for observation so it was a damn good look-see. But I didn't say a word about it to the news babe. Consider yourself lucky I'm a Boy Scout about that stuff."

"Thanks Lou. Seriously, there's more going on here than you know."

"Excuse me, bro. I'm the guy that told you two days ago this was going to happen so don't bullshit me."

"Yeah, you're right and that's why I called," he paused then asked in a much smaller voice, "Are, you sure this is it?"

"Well, little buddy, I've seen people totally uninjured after being shot-put from their cars, and I've seen 'em walk away from hellacious pile ups so it's in my experience to see outcomes like it but *my experience* ain't the issue."

"So it's more perception than reality?

"The reality is she's eighty, got suplexed by a station wagon, and should be dead. The perception is she wouldn't be here without some special help. Another pair of facts is that you're a deacon and you prayed over her at the scene. Right there on the street, man. Are they connected? Doesn't matter. Once that reporter made you, they are."

"But it's not cause and effect. It was just me; desperate and stupid me."

"We do some pretty amazing things when a killer dose of adrenaline jolts that ¼-volt of brain power I like to talk about. And personally, I can't rule out the power of prayer. Can you?"

"Not a clue, Shots. But I'm in pretty deep now."

"Ran right over your ass, didn't it? And you guys had better buckle up for the rest. I know less about what's next than I do about that pea-size brain of yours."

"Anything other than insults for me?"

"Only to let you know I'm not going anywhere. You listen to me whine when I kill a patient; I listen to you when you save one. Just remember the motto."

"Do your best and kiss my ass. Yeah, yeah, we are real tough guys."

"That we are burrito breath. Now let me catch a catnap. I'm on call and this is a busy town. Later."

Chapter 12

Driving his T-bird to Thursday night supper at Commonwealth Church, Mark thought that, all things considered, the week hadn't been too bad. The accident was just about history and both reporters had backed off. Best of all, there were no more calls asking for a miracle prayer.

Tonight he'd talk to Miss Daisy for the first time since the accident and he was looking forward to seeing her. His little 5-minute speech about the accident was a different matter, he should have declined, but it seemed like a good idea on Monday.

"It's only five minutes of torture. I can fake it for that long and there's never anyone here in the summer anyway so it'll be a small group," he thought trying to calm a case of the nerves.

His stage fright leaped to pit-drench level when he saw a near full parking lot and the TV10 News van parked on the front row.

Entering through the back door, he walked by the pastor's study and met Assistant Pastor Jerry Tinsler, a fellow Texan with a much larger frame and ten years his junior. They had been friends since Jerry's assignment to Commonwealth several years ago.

"Back door entrance. Trying to avoid your adorning public? Don't answer that but thanks for returning my call with the prayer you said for Miss Daisy. The whole thing was beautiful and you were so cool. I still don't know how you thought of it on the fly," he greeted Mark with an affectionate hand-over-hand handshake that swallowed Mark's hand.

"Oh yeah, pastor. Cool as July in Texas."

"Guess you saw your friends from Channel 10 are here. Vick won't approve but I don't give a deacon's patuti about that. It's good for the church and that's all I care about. Haven't been this many people here since Christmas," Jerry replied as they walked toward Fellowship Hall.

"You're right about Vick. He's such a control freak about the media. Let's not do anything that upsets his new LIFE vision for television."

They both rolled their eyes and laughed at the corny catch phrase.

"My little speech might add fuel to the fire. You sure I should do it?" Mark was hoping for a last minute reprieve.

"Hell yes I do." Jerry quickly replied and continued. "We've had calls every day about it and a full house tonight. It's usually dead around here; da-gone rare to feel this kind of energy in the old place. I do believe you've earned some prime time, deacon," Jerry said as they neared the hall.

"So, don't say anything that offends the average 80-year old and I'm also betting that reporter won't do anything but take a few notes. What do you think my odds are on those two?"

"Pretty slim, Padre. In case you didn't notice, the reporter brought a cameraman and, by the way, I'm not wearing underwear," he said and nodded toward the back of the hall where Dominique and her cameraman were sitting.

"The possibilities boggle the mind don't they?" he added and a bead of sweat popped out on Jerry's forehead.

They walked into the room and a small volume of applause began from one hundred ten Thursday night diners. Mark glanced at Dominique Johnson and she nodded back adding a "gotcha" wink.

Daisy was near the front and Mark quickly moved over to speak to her. The clapping reached its peak as he gave her a hug and shook her son's hand.

Dominique was impressed.

"This looks more like a hero's homecoming than a church dinner. Real nice setup," she said to Tommy who was already filming.

Jerry was surprised by the brightness of the camera spots and felt a wave of paranoia to go with a sweaty brow.

"Vick's going to raise hell for not calling him about this TV reporter and camera in here. Well, by God, he can kiss my West Texas butt. This was too hot to pass and Justin is a natural. He'll come around once I spin it for him tomorrow," Jerry assured himself as he took a seat.

The dinner line moved quickly and Mark shook hands with most of the gathered. It was just like greeting them at the door each Sunday but this time they knew who he was. He sat at Daisy's table and she was eager to talk with him.

"I was so glad to see our friend Dr. Shotley at the hospital I almost reached up and kissed him right there. He settled me down lickedy-split. You know him don't you dear?"

"Yes ma'am. He's a real sweetheart."

"Youd've thought I was a creature from Mars the way they kept pokin' all my various body parts and checkin' my fluids. It's not like I was a quart low or something." She stopped to take a sip of water then continued.

"But I need to talk with you about something I've done since then. I hope I'm not going to be a problem for you, Mr. Justin."

"I'm sure that's not possible, Miss Daisy." He couldn't imagine what she was talking about.

"Well, I got a call the other night from Miss Johnson over there and we talked about the accident and I wanted you to know that I might of gotten a little carried away."

He glanced up to see Dominique looking at him from across the hall and returned his glance back to Daisy. "You go ahead and talk about it all you want to."

"Well, she kind of tape recorded me in my kitchen."

"Oh," he couldn't hide his surprise but then recovered. "but she's such a cutie we'll be fine. Don't give it another thought, okay?"

He noticed that Jerry was standing up at the first table and tapping the nearest water glass. *It's show time*, he thought and smiled confidently at Daisy.

“I have a couple of introductions,” Jerry began.

“First I want to introduce Dominique Johnson and her cameraman to all of you. Most of you recognize Dominique as a familiar face from Channel 10 News. Now this means that you all have to stay on your best behavior,” he said as all heads turned in the direction of the WVTV staff.

“Also, we are privileged to have Dr. Ruth Duncan with us tonight to present her progress and challenges in one of the key medical missions in the Congo.” Dr. Duncan nodded and smiled to the crowd.

“But ahead of that and not on your program, I’ve asked Mark Justin to speak to us briefly about his Christian response to the accident involving Mrs. Daisy Hanover last Sunday. As you know, he was the first one to reach her after she was struck by a passing car and, by the grace of God, Daisy is with us tonight uninjured and as healthy as a spring chicken. We asked Mark to take a few minutes to tell us about what he did as first on the scene of the accident. Mark?”

Mark stood up and was suddenly very nervous as he began with a joke.

“Thanks Jerry. First, I want to recognize you too for *your* quick response after the accident last Sunday. Honestly folks, when it was all over Jerry took me aside, patted me on the back and said, ‘Mark old friend, what ever you said to Miss Daisy would you mind making a house call and saying it to my refrigerator?’” Some awkward laughter followed but quickly faded.

“Uh, sorry about that Jerry but you did say I had five minutes to embarrass you.”

“Yeah, but I didn’t think you’d be so quick about it.” Jerry said loud enough to be heard and more awkward laughter followed.

Mark looked around at the faces in the hall all looking back at him.

“Well let me get to the point, or, this case, the question I can’t stop asking myself. ‘What if we could always act directly from the wisdom from above?’ What’s amazing is that last Sunday, for just a minute, I think I did,” he said regaining his composure.

“More accurately, I acted *through* it. In that moment I was helpless, totally lost, no training and no clue how to help. I felt myself give up. And I prayed. Only when I abandoned myself could I help Miss Daisy. We were both gone but we both came back in pretty good shape.”

scanned the hall. “Would you look at this place? He’s terrible but he’s got them hooked now. He’s making a panic attack on Sunday sound like a divine little buddy club. Please...” she thought and listened in again.

“I’m still not sure what happened and frankly, it’s not important to understand it or repeat it.”

He noticed Jerry was pointing to his watch.

“The moral of the story is that you never know when a crisis will be in your face. So be ready for it, know it when it happens and give yourself up to the wisdom from above. You might even be amazed at what happens. Now I’d like to end by repeating that favorite bible verse of mine in the form of a prayer. Let us pray.”

Everyone in the hall, including the news crew, bowed their heads and he began.

“Our heavenly Father, please show us the wisdom from above...”

Seated at table four, Dan Campbell wanted to pray with the deacon but couldn’t stop the cough erupting from his chest and throat. He stifled himself as best he could but it echoed sickly through the quite of the dinning hall.

“I should have kept my fifty seven year old carcass in bed to suffer alone,” Dan thought as he rubbed his right hand. “I’ve got to get to the head. Once I’m in there I’ll clear my lungs, splash some cold water on my face, and get back in time to shake the deacon’s hand,” he decided.

Good plan. Bad execution.

He placed his hands on the table and was carefully raising himself to stand when he caught the back of his legs on the rim of his seat. Turning, he watched the aluminum-folding chair fall backwards with the slo-mo grace of a touchdown replay.

The crash of the metal chair hitting the floor reminded Dan of his favorite shotgun cutting loose with both barrels. But, as if hit by both barrels, he suddenly lost all feeling in his legs and they buckled under his weight. Plopping heavily on the floor ass-first, Dan went down.

"Oh Christ my lord and savior, I can't breathe. It's crushing my ribs," was his last thought before a spectacular sunset blazed across the room and then collapsed into black the way a thick ribbed theater curtain comes down when the show is over. Then, on little cat's feet, a blood red fog swooshed down and swirled around him until the chest pain stopped.

Dan Campbell's head bobbed just above table level and Jerry could see he was in the terminal stage of cardiac arrest. The cough, the blue lips, and backward rolling eyes were unmistakable.

Why do so many people die in church? He asked himself as he sprinted to the back of the room where old Dan Campbell looked to be headed for the last round up.

"Call 911. Call 911. Dan? Dan? Are you okay? Someone yelled from his table.

Dan was fine. The colorful mist pulsed and whorled around him and then vanished. He heard himself yell, "Hey Pa Paul, I'm going out for a swing."

And he did, at his grand father's house in Rome, Georgia. He ran out the screen door, across the wrap-around porch and leaped on to the tree swing in the front yard. The cicadas were in full song (*wee ahh, wee ahh, weeee ahhhh.*) and he arched far off the ground, swinging from the biggest limb on the ancient elm tree.

Jerry laid Dan down on the floor and opened his shirt. He wasn't breathing. He looked around the hall at the gawking crowd.

"No docs in the house." So he prayed. "Dear Lord, help me and Dan, here. We both need you. Your will be done," he whispered and blew the first breath into Dan Campbell's body.

Jerry completed the first resuscitation cycle when Mark squatted next him.

"Can I help?"

"You bet. We need a prayer, big time. I'm losing him and I'm not sure if the EMTs will get here in time. Lead us in prayer for Dan, here," he said and turned his attention back to Campbell.

Mark was surprised and weakly responded, "Sure." to the back of Jerry's head.

As Jerry bent over to continue the rescue, Mark saw Dan Campbell's purple face, eyes rolled up, frozen like a broken slot machine.

TILT! was his only thought.

Startled by movement behind him, Mark turned to see the entire clan of Thursday night diners walking in unison toward their dying geezer friend on the floor.

Seeing the ghoul on the floor and the ones walking toward him like a scene out of Night of the Living Dead pushed the boiled ham, mashed potatoes, and green beans up to the bottom of his throat.

"Oh God. I'm going to blow beets all over Jerry and the dead guy."

So he ran. Ran like the wind. Out of the hall, through the parking lot and into his waiting Thunderbird with its V8 growler, leather seats and premium sound system whisking him away from this B movie set and back to his quiet home a mile away. Charlotte was there and gave him a big hug as he walked into the kitchen. She wanted to know how the speech went and asked how Jerry was doing. It felt good to be snug-as-a-bug-in-a-rug in his modest home in his modest West End neighborhood.

Someone touched his shoulder and pulled him back to reality. Jerry and the dead guy were still there but now, so was Miss Daisy.

"Mark, let's ask God to be here with us now."

"I don't know what to say," he replied but couldn't look at her.

"Yes you do. It's here." She touched his chest with her free hand and smiled.

He turned and looked into her eyes to see the calm confidence of life without fear and nothing to be afraid of. That look eased dinner back into his stomach and he thought of the first line of the prayer he was about to say.

"Okay. We'll wing it again." He smiled. Still on shaky legs but now with a steady voice he turned and spoke to the crowd.

"Everyone take the hand of the friend next you," he told the group. Without hesitation, they became a human chain looking to Mark for what they knew would be a healing prayer

And the TV camera rolled.

"Lord, we ask for your love to surround us, to move through us and to smooth the way for our friend, Dan Campbell. Only you can move Dan's spirit but Lord he needs to come back to us now or go in peace with you. Please answer this prayer and let Dan be your servant in heaven or on earth. Amen."

"Amen," His audience responded in unison.

Sweat poured down Dan's face. The heat was unbearable. With his eye on the target he leaped from the swing toward the platform in the crotch of that ancient elm tree. Arms out like a bird of prey and trailing clouds of glory he was…was not landing, he was flying. Soaring past the tree house and far beyond his neighborhood,

He saw the surface of the earth come into focus but it was flat and lunar looking with small dark craters and the wind blasting in his face smelled like garlic and ham. Blinking at the ceiling and about to be sick all over the preacher on top of him, Dan Campbell returned to Commonwealth Church.

Jerry saw the life flare back into Dan's eyes and turned him on his side as soon as the first rush of air filled his lungs.

"Don't say anything Dan; you'll be in the hospital in a few minutes. The ambulance is nearly here. Just relax and concentrate on each breath. The Lord wants you to be with us a bit longer."

Jerry sat back on the floor and looked up to offer his hand to the Deacon. Mark shook it without saying a word and their audience responded with enthusiastic applause.

Dominique's flat handed air slash signaled 'cut' to her cameraman. She could barely contain herself.

The West End Rescue Squad quickly arrived at the church and whisked away another of its congregation to MCV hospitals. As he was wheeled out of the hall, Dan Campbell's vitals were weak and he was not especially glad to be there. He felt alone, not rescued.

The Thursday Night Supper flock lingered to congratulate Mark and Jerry. Jerry knew the buzz that started with the accident last Sunday would be a roaring rumor mill by morning.

Chapter 13

"You know this thing has a life of its own," Jerry said to Mark as they entered his small office.

"I just gave old Dan CPR and he responded-done it a dozen times so it's not that unusual and definitely not newsworthy. But when you add That Darn Deacon doing his second Oral Roberts impersonation of the week along with a freakin' on-the-scene news crew, let's face it, that's a hellofa story.

"What if I told you CSN is also working on it," Mark tried to ease into it.

"How's that? Did they call you?"

Mark nodded not looking at him.

"That's double trouble and you can't control it any more than Vick will when he gets back tomorrow. These guys create what their viewers crave. So after the murders and car wrecks let's serve up transcendence-proof of a two way street between heaven and earth, life-beyond-life right here in River City. With both CBS *and* CNS spinning it, you got tall tales and ugly gossip flying around faster than the LaBonte Brothers. Get ready to be a twice-anointed hero, Hoss."

"And *that's* quite a leap of faith, pastor," Dominique said as she walked through Jerry's open door, amused by his speculation. She dropped in to discuss the upcoming weekend feature and took a few minutes to lay out the plan.

"Sorry Dominique, I've got an exorcism and a ferret séance up next. Take a number."

"I think you'll find time for this. I've got a tape you ought to hear and I'd also like more insight into the last three days of your life."

Jerry interrupted. "I think you kids ought to work that out somewhere else. I've got my own problems. Would you like to interview our Senior Pastor? I'm sure he can find the time." Jerry hoped. Vick might even be able to use this to launch his upcoming venture.

“We’ll see, reverend. It ain’t in the can yet but you put on quite a show tonight.”

“Just a second. If your piece makes us a bunch of Christian kooks you’ll ruin my position here, screw my family life, and wipe out any of the little career I’ll have. Why not just let us speak for ourselves without sensationalizing Mark or Daisy or Dan or Commonwealth Church. We just want our friends to live, that’s all, and we did the only thing we knew to save them. You have a responsibility to report that part of it too. Don’t you?

“Fair enough, Pastor. You saved a life and we *will* honor that. CPR is considered a common technical skill but it’s not captured that often. If we run this piece I will highlight what you did for that man. I give you my word on it.”

“Thank you, Ms. Johnson. I hope you live up to that promise but right now let’s call it a wrap. I’m beat,” he said and began to consider how he was going to explain the week to Vick.

“There simply is no way to put lipstick on this pig.” He said to himself and closed the door behind them.

Dominique and Mark stopped under a bright streetlight at the edge of the empty parking lot.

“I take it that wasn’t your typical Thursday night supper.”

“We do have our moments and Jerry is prepared for any catastrophe.”

“So, tell me what gives between our friend Jerry and his boss. I’ve seen our card on him but sounds like Springwell is more emperor than righteous reverend.”

“Very perceptive but it’s more like a CEO with a twist of Henry the VIII. Jerry’s got some cause for concern.”

“For his head?”

“Well, not literally but figuratively, maybe. I don’t know. Depends on Vick’s mood. He dials up things as hot as he wants around here. Jerry’s got to survive the initial tantrum but he knows that. Now can we move on?”

“You bet. I want you to hear my little talk with Mrs. Hanover and your final thoughts before we begin editing. Even with that lame delivery, you got the message across. 'Get ready everybody, a miracle is coming for you too,' and when that poor man nearly croaked you got a chance to prove it *again* but *this* time I got it on film. It's freakin' unbelievable." she said smiling and shaking her head.

"So you are going to kookerize us." Mark was disappointed and afraid of her emphasis on him.

"No sir. But this is news. You want to help me with it or not."

"Sure. Over a cup of coffee at Lee's Tavern. You game?" Mark suggested through a slight smile.

"Mr. Lee's ain't exactly in my hood, you know, so let's make it the Starbucks at the Village. That's just about as close to your house."

"No, let's do Lee's. We'll have some privacy there and the walk home will do me good," he insisted.

Lee's Southern Tavern (LST) is a legendary West End fern bar and restaurant decorated with reptiles and expired license pates. Franky R. Lee runs the place and his two cooks serve hot buttered grits with all three meals. Marlboro cigarette posters decorate the bar and ashtrays on all tables encourage smoking. Few of Richmond's majority minority ever set foot in the place and Dominique wouldn't consider it but she needed the meeting.

"No problem. See you at Lee's in fifteen minutes and do not be late." she replied and disappeared into the parking lot.

Chapter 14

LST is a work of redneck performance art. The movie posters, the smell of stale everything, the University of Richmond coed waitresses (no waiters need apply to Franky), the stuffed baby gators guarding the bar and lard-based fried chicken all make it the West End dive of choice.

Dominique had already taken a back booth and waved Mark over when he swung open the front door. The hand held tape recorder was on the table and she was ready for business and nothing else, not even a 'hello'.

"I hate this place. It gives me the heebie-jeebies worse than the Confederate Museum down the street so just listen to the interview and we'll talk tomorrow," she whispered low enough not disturb the natives.

"Well if you're so uptight about it, forget the coffee and let's order some Rebel Yell." He tried to lighten the mood but she pointed to the recorder.

"And I want more background on your short happy life at The TV10. Gotta tell you though, after your little speech tonight I'm amazed you lasted three months on the air."

Before he could fire back, a blond twenty-something waitress arrived.

"Hi y'all. What'll it be tonight?" she asked in a genuine southern drawl.

Dominique waved off the menus. "Two coffees. That's it. Bye y'all," she said trying to hurry the process.

"Okey-dokey. Two cups of java comin' up," was the perky reply.

Dominique rolled her eyes and popped on the tape recorder. The quality was remarkable. Dominique's voice first introduced Daisy and then asked, "Tell me what happened Sunday when you were leaving church, Mrs. Hanover?"

Most of it was a personal rehash until she got to Justin's intervention.

"The next thing I recall Mr. Justin was in front of me. It was foggy, quiet and there was a lot of pain off in the distance. Then he put his hand on my shoulder and I heard his voice. He was very firm with his instructions to God."

Dominique interrupted her. "Was he looking at you or up in the air or down at the ground?"

"No, honey, he never took his eyes off of me. He's a kind man, but I'll never forget that tone he took with God. It was like he wouldn't accept 'no' for an answer. And then, Lord have mercy, the warmth of his hand and God's love were like a tidal wave breaking over me, washing away the pain."

The coffee arrived and they sipped in sync and stared at the recorder.

Dominique's voice asked another leading question. "Mrs. Hanover, you think you were part of a miracle healing don't you."

"Young lady, I can't imagine it bein' anything else. I'm old and in fair-to-middlin' shape but I don't see how I could practically get run over by that big car and walk away from it. I got some powerful help. How about them apples?"

"Maybe it was just your lucky day and maybe that car didn't hit you so hard. After all you've said that you don't remember much of what happened."

"You're right about one thing," Daisy answered. "It was my lucky day but only because Mr. Justin was there to grab God's ear long enough to get my life back. Maybe I wasn't going to die but I sure wasn't going to just jitterbug down the street neither. Can you understand that?"

"I just report, ma'am. Have to stay objective." she was surprised by the question and hated her pat answer. Daisy didn't care for it either.

"Sure. You'd rather not believe but go after them that does. Just a lot of empty talk if you ask me." Mark smiled at the dig and Dominique did too as they continued to listen.

"You're all nice and safe in your objectivity but it does not explain this and that's exactly why you are here." Then she intensified the argument. "So here's my beef with you media types. Because we believe, you make us out to be a bunch of rubes. But I'll tell you this, young lady. This was real and it was perfect. And I've said all I'm going to say. Turn that thing off."

Dominique pushed the stop button and peered at Mark. He didn't say anything so she laid out the plan.

"You and Mrs. Hanover are quite a pair. Don't be embarrassed about it. I have video of Bishop and his station wagon that hit her, the church, and Mrs. Hanover. I've also got your little speech and film of the dynamic duo at the church tonight. All I'm missing is a comment from you; just some straight talk a bit more about why you left TV10 twenty years ago."

Mark was sorting out his options, looking to turn the conversation around.

"What about Chambers and CSN? I haven't heard anymore from him or anyone else from their shop. They may want to talk with us some more," he said hoping to slow her down.

"They've probably lost interest. It's not a national story (*but it could be*). It's ours (*mine*). After editing it'll be a five-minute feature on multiple shows over the weekend. How's that sound?"

"I have no idea." Mark let his guard down for the first time.

"It's a bit late to reconsider and besides second time's the charm. How about noon at my desk."

"Nope. You'll have to come on by the house," he said certain that a trip back to the studio would trigger another supernat-attack.

"Are you okay getting out of here?" He asked suddenly feeling cornered.

"Yeah, I'm fine in your hood. Hit the road. The coffee's on me and I'll be by at noon. Bye y'all." She faked the accent without a smile.

Mark looked forward to the short walk home but as soon as he hit the sidewalk the repressed memory of his brief Richmond TV career ran his ass over.

He had been twenty-seven and left the Austin radio scene as soon as Hollywood discovered his partner. The Others landed the lead in a hit sit-com about an extraterrestrial living in suburbia USA and the rest was comedy history.

Done with Texas, Mark and Charlotte moved to Richmond after he won the TV10 audition-not spectacular but a routine start in a medium size market. Charlotte could practice anywhere and he didn't care if they paid him at all, which was exactly the attitude they were looking for in a Late News anchor.

The other fresh hire was Bobbie Jean Heckler, a twenty five year old former Miss Portsmouth, Virginia. She was a 5'5", blue-eyed blonde, with semi sweet personality hired to do most of the heavy lifting for TV10 weathercasting. After a disastrous first show she quit. Even after leaving TV behind he still felt guilty about her one-show exit.

"Hey idiot brain, wake up. This time you're not reporting the news, you *are* the news," The Debating Society brought him present "TV gave you a format, time slot, and script; total control of every show. But this just comes at you, Bozo. Zero control."

"Pathetic, boys. Bet you blew a neuron on that one. Got anything else?"

The answer came in the form of the lyrics, chorus, and music of a new song from the Unknown Zone. It was the voice of Buck Owens backed by The Buckaroos singing a catchy 4:4 country tune.

Oh, you're damned if you do
And damned if you don't.
What difference does it make

If you say that you won't?
Staying in the game it's the chance you ta-ake.
So, when your luck runs out
And it's time to make a stand.
To keep a dog in the hunt and faith in the plan,
Just call all bluffs and show the winnin' hand.

The chorus followed without missing a beat.

'Cause the devil's in the details
But an angel's in there too,
And every day's another day to win or lose.
Oh, you'll never know the answers
So be careful how you chose.
'Cause the devil's in the details
But there's an angel in there too.

He walked into the house whistling the chorus of The Devil's In The Details but stopped as soon as he crossed the threshold. Charlotte was waiting with a wad of notes in one hand and a pointed finger on the other.

"That must have been a hell of a speech tonight and you'd better be ready to do it a few more times. In the past two hours you've been invited to the DAR, the Women's Circle at the church, the Friday morning men's breakfast also at the church and the sustainer's luncheon at the Junior League next Tuesday," she said shaking a fist full of pink stickys.

"Don't you think this is getting out of hand? Where have you been, anyway? I could have used some help taking your phone calls," but she was most upset by the return of his celebrity.

"I'm sorry about that, but it's so damn complicated now." He quickly explained Dan Campbell's rescue at the church and the follow up at Lee's.

"That tears it. You've had two very public prayers for the dead or dying, church groups and nonprofits are calling for some reassuring deacon-speak, and two reporters are in prime-time feature mode. Do you understand what's happening?" She asked still shaking the pink stickys in the air.

"You know, I think I finally do. I believe it's faith blooming again and it feels pretty good. But the best news is that it probably has the life expectancy of one news cycle. And then it's back to our regularly scheduled programming."

She wasn't convinced and could tell he was thinking about the past.

"From here it looks like you're pushing buttons you don't understand and turning on people who *need* to believe in miracles. How long can you control where that's headed?"

"So what's your point? Let's not go off the deep end just because of a few phone calls."

"I don't have the answers and I don't want to piss you off but you've got the jazz going again that's for sure. I guess I just don't want you to be the miracle guy unless you're saving me, not the whole city."

"Comfortably numb," He replied in a near whisper.

Now that pissed her off.

"I think you like his shit too much and I don't think you mind losing us or yourself in it. Maybe it is faith on the comeback trail but to me it looks like some kind of cheap thrill with a big price tag. And while I'm venting you'd better know I'm not your personal secretary any more. So take the proceeds from what ever it is you're doing and find some help. I'm done with it." And she threw the stickys down the steps at him.

"Okay, okay, honey. I apologize for that one. Definitely a personal foul. Don't worry about the phone calls. I'll take care of everything before I hit the sheets. Will that make it better?"

"It's a start but how about this one. Sarah and I compared notes today and she said Lou really believes that Madame Surgio crap from the other night. That routine has been wearing thin for years. I cannot believe he's encouraging you like this.

"Yeah well, ah, we leaped to that conclusion together."

"For gardens seed, Mark, you're both losing it. He doesn't know what you're capable of and you don't accept it," she said and headed back up the stairs but turned around at the top to finish her thought.

"So here's the deal. You take care of today's mess. Tomorrow I'll consider calming down. And I don't want to hear about TV10 or CSN or any of your media hype. Let's agree right now; this shit has got to stop. For Christ's sake Mark, the next thing you'll be telling me is that *you've* got your own show again." She paused and looked down the stairs at him, waiting for a reply.

"I'll take care of these calls and you get some sleep. We'll talk in the morning," was the best he could do knowing that Dominique would be in the house tomorrow and that Chambers could reappear anytime with a film crew in tow.

Charlotte knew his evasion meant there was more to come, probably a lot.

"Oh just forget the stupid calls and come on up to bed with me. Maybe I can get through to you another way," she said frustrated but ready to make up. No matter what, they were going through this together.

"A tried and true torture method, madam. You can have your way with me all night long," he yelled to her as he tossed the stickys somewhere in the living room and took the stairs two at a time.

Chapter 15

John Chambers hadn't lost interest in the little story in Richmond but it was on the back burner until he finished a more pressing assignment in Central America. A Caribbean hurricane had slammed into Belize, tearing through most of that country before flooding Honduras and Guatemala.

Disaster is a priority at the CSN and their resources were already on site ministering and also reporting the rescues, relief efforts, and miseries of the affected countries. He was joining two other reporters and their crews working throughout Central America to make sure the world was an eyewitness to the suffering *and* the heroic efforts led by Christian relief organizations.

During the twelve hours of flights in route, he had time to organize his notes and sequence the production shots. On approach to Belize City he put the notebook, cassette and loose-leaf pages into a large envelope and addressed it to a colleague who was working the story with him. The envelope would arrive at headquarters tomorrow and he would be back home in three days. The deacon and Ms Daisy were too good to pass up but, like the rest of the news, their shelf life was only a few cycles. With a bold black Sharpie, he wrote 'An Accident of Faith' across the front of the envelope.

CSN had a helicopter waiting for him and a med-evac plane full of injured missionaries heading back to Virginia. He gave the envelope to the plane's pilot with instructions to personally deliver it. With a nod and a wink he knew it was as good as there.

John's chopper headed south with its pilot, a cameraman, a Guatemalan native for a guide, and Chambers all crammed on board along with equipment and supplies. Two hours after leaving the heavily damaged airport in Belize City, they were flying just below cloud level with a clear view of the flooded villages between Morales and Los Amates.

World aid was needed immediately and CSN would make sure the world knew the depth of human misery below.

The chopper was nearing the landing point just West of Los Amates when the first heavy tropical rain shower sloshed across them. Carlos Montecas, a veteran of the Mexican Air Force and born again Christian, had little room for error and corrected the copter's negative tilt as the altimeter leveled off at 300 feet.

"We're too low. The wind is picking up and I can't risk a 180 turn," he yelled into the audio system and quickly decided it was time to set the copter down before another squall pushed them into the trees.

"Hang on. We're landing in the nearest clearing I can find. Looks like we're a little early. This old hurricane es muy malo and we can't ride out another tormentoso in this canyon. Everyone strap in and gird your loins," he warned.

"Gird my loins? Sure thing John Wayne," Chambers thought as he and the others heeded the warning and tightened their seat belts. "And what the heck is a tormentoso? Probably local for, kiss your ass goodbye-o.

He looked around to see that the others were motionless, pale and looking straight ahead, terrified. So he loudly answered Carlos above the increasing wind and engine noise.

"Does that mean you're cutting off cabin service?"

Carlos flicked a quick smile and nodded his head while fighting the increasing sheer.

Chambers decided to say a quick prayer to "save my shorts from my own personal tormentoso." He was scared but his voice was steady. "Please protect us now, Father, we truly need to get this bird down in one piece and ask you to guide our pilot's hand with your hand and deliver us safely into the arms of our waiting friends. In your name we pray. Amen."

Three "amens" followed in unison.

Another squall hit the chopper and this time Carlos couldn't keep the nose up. They were only 50 feet away from a small, rocky clearing when the left pod clipped the last of the banana trees bordering the landing spot. Carlos jerked the controls back to the right but not quick enough to keep the rotor blades from hacking into a nearby cliff.

The ride ended quickly.

Joaquin, their guide, curled up against the right wall trying to be very small but was ejected and crushed dead as the copter partially broke open on impact and lunged forward in a one hop, rolling, upside down landing.

Carlos was knocked unconscious but stayed strapped into his seat while Toby, the cameraman, was cut to the bone by copter-blade shrapnel that slashed through the cabin. His leg was bleeding and he was unconscious.

Chamber's landing was altogether different. As the chopper pin wheeled and disintegrated, a large fragment of the blade slashed through the cabin, missing his neck by inches but slicing through his seat belt at the same instant his chair tore from the floor. The combination launched him through the side door that had opened on impact.

He felt the rain on his face as he lay on the bank of a swollen muddy creek forty feet from the destroyed helicopter. He wanted to yell for Carlos but couldn't make a sound. He tried again. Nothing.

"No point, not yet. I'm going to crawl over to see how the others faired. This is really bad, Johnny Boy. Do you hear anyone else?" He held his breath for a few seconds and listened to the sounds of the jungle, wind, and rain. He could hear everything separate and blended, and had trouble holding his thoughts.

"Nobody knocking on my door so here's the thing. Rain and wind let up and we're climbing out of this hole. Head into Los Tacos. No problemo, son. Old Carlos is buzzing the map and'll leap over here in a sec. Happy trails to you 'til we meet again."

And he passed out.

Chapter 16

"John? John Chambers. Wake up John. You gotta wake up right now," Carlos pleaded.

It was two hours since the crash.

"I hate to do this John, but I've got to throw some water on you. I need you to get up and help me with Toby. He's bled too much."

He tossed a cup of water in John's face and it did the trick.

"Carlos?" Chambers croaked almost in a whisper. He had been laying face up and his throat was parched.

"John, take it easy but try to move your legs for me then I'll get you some water to drink."

"Sure, whatever you say," John replied in a harsh whisper and tried to move for the first time since landing in the mud.

Nothing moved down there. He shifted his weight to the right but a bolt of pain from his arm almost blinded him and he fell back.

"Chingaua, John. I forgot to tell you. Your right arm looks broke. It's not through the skin yet so don't do that again. We'll set it as soon as you're up." Carlos said reacting to John's grimace.

"Sweet Jesus that hurt. Carlos, you've got to improve your drive-in service." John replied with an uneasy smile.

"Hey gringo it's time for you to move or I'm going to take your money and your women."

John focused on sitting up and hoped he wouldn't pull his back out. He lifted his neck and torso off the mud but his legs were dead. He tried again. Nothing.

"Oh no. Oh Christ, no. I'm paralyzed. I can't move my legs, Carlos. No, no, no. Please don't do. Please don't test me like this," he begged as tears quickly flowed down his cheeks.

Carlos put his arm under John's neck to lift him enough to drink some water but didn't try to raise him again. John had no control over the lower half of his body and chances were his back was broken.

He took a silent inventory.

"One dead, one dying, one paraplegic. The radio's in the creek along with most of the chopper. No choice but to button down the site and move out." He decided against moving John and instead to cover him with vegetation from the jungle floor.

"It may not save him from locals but it's better than dying in my arms right now. I can't handle that for sure," he thought and looked down at Chambers knowing it was the last time he'd talk with his friend. He'd seen at least three sets of prints in the sand around the creek bed.

"John, listen to me. You'll be home in a few days and we'll be eating some of those greasy tacos you make in your kitchen. You hear me, John? I am going to make that happen," he lied to give John hope.

He let him drink as much water as he wanted and then he buried John with dirt, leaves, bark, and lastly, the largest part of the aluminum helicopter skin he could find. When done with the camo-cover he stood back but took little comfort in barely making out John's moss covered head.

"John, my landscaping job is going to be your best friend for the next twelve hours. The problem is that the four-legged natives will be through here tonight so no matter what you hear, do not move. Not an inch. I'll be back with a crew ASAP. You sabe? Do not move."

"Sure Carlos, you're bringing back the cavalry and my mother-in-law. Vaya con divas," he said with a barely conscious grin.

Carlos leaped into the river bed and headed north.

In the deep of the night Chambers woke to the sound of continuous distant thunder and a rhythmic pressure against his forehead like a soft sandpaper facile. Slowly he realized the sound wasn't thunder and that the sandpaper was too wet and warm to be sandpaper. The truth struck him at the same time he remembered Carlos' last warning.

Don't move, John boy. Not an eyelash. Do not piss this thing off.

He was being licked by a large cat, purring as it enjoyed the salt of his brow and probably considering how to bite open his head to get at the real prize. But for the moment he was just being licked to death.

"Cats don't eat while the purr, do they? Sounds like a tenor, maybe a well-fed adolescent, I hope. Nice kitty, not too rough."

Paw across the nose, he went with it. A little turn of his neck and they were face to face. Cat-breath up his nostrils, purring, wet nose on his lips, and more sandpaper tonguing his forehead.

The cat, a jaguar, was so content John thought they might have struck a deal; he'd keep sweating while his new friend licked brine for a while and eventually trot back into the jungle. But then the sounds of metal moving a few feet away froze his thoughts.

It wasn't going to be that simple.

Across the wreckage field a bigger cat was following the scent of fresh blood and pawing through the twisted metal looking for the source. Even though Carlos had layered the larger pieces of aluminum against the cockpit to protect Toby, the cat swatted them aside and leaped inside the crushed remains.

Lying only a few feet away, John heard Toby's defenseless screams.

"No! God No! Stop, st--" Toby's last words were interrupted by a sickening bony crunch.

The big cat roared and roared again, announcing the kill. Terrorized beyond thought, John added tears to the sweat pouring from his brow and squenched his eyes tight, bracing for his own fatal bite.

Instead, he heard soft pads running in the dirt toward the chopper. He had been right about the age of the smaller cat that was now joining its parent at the kill site.

The high-pitched growl of his little friend mimicked the bigger cat's and John knew it was saying, "Hey mama, you gotta go over there. I found a real tasty one too." But she ignored her cub, for now, and they both worked to free their prey from the wreckage.

John listened to the pair drag Toby's body into the jungle. Grunting, growling, and occasionally roaring, it seemed the aftermath would never stop but finally all he could hear was the cadence of the jungle. Replacing the fear of immediate death, shock and loneliness consumed him as he lay sobbing in the dirt waiting for the cats to return.

He flashed back to his interview in Richmond yesterday with Daisy Hanover (*Was it really yesterday?*). In her neat little salt box home she *told* him to get ready for a miracle. "How you do it is your business but you best git ready to be a part of one cause you'll never see it comin'."

"Amen, Miss Daisy, but I'm a dead man unless there's a miracle that creates feline amnesia," he said aloud.

Not far away in the jungle the big cat roared again.

And John prayed for his miracle.

Chapter 17

"I got it." Mark yelled to Charlotte as he walked down the hall to answer the front door bell. Peeking out the peephole, he saw only a shadow standing on the stoop on the other side.

"Hey. We've got to change the bulbs out there. I can hardly see this guy," he yelled but she didn't answer. He hadn't heard from Chambers at CSN and this might be him ready to do a follow-up. He opened the door but his guest was a shadow among shadows cast by the front yard maple trees.

"Hang on. Let me cut on the hall light here. We've got a bulb problem," he apologized while his guest waited.

"Why didn't you pray for me?" the shadow asked.

Mark's blood froze. He knew the voice but hadn't heard it in 6 years.

"Dad? Is that you? It can't be. Who is it?"

"Why didn't you pray for me?" William Justin repeated as he stepped into the dim light on the edge of the stoop. Dressed in stained fishing coveralls and so sunburned that his skin, his face, was blistered red, barely visible under the rim of a sweat stained brown fedora, his father stared at him

"Dad. You can't be here, not now, not this way," Mark stammered and stepped back into the hall but his father didn't follow him into the house. Instead he reached up with a parched red hand and removed his old fishing hat letting his thick black hair fall in front of his face.

Mark watched in terror as his father silently reach into the weathered old hat and pull out the Justin family bible. He remembered how the family tree, beginning in the 1680s, was fully diagramed on the first two pages. But as his father opened it, the family tree had been erased and replaced with words scrawled in bright red ink:

There is no Goddamn wisdom from above

“You could have saved me. Now I’m burning in hell. Why didn’t you pray for me? Son, why didn’t you save me?”

Mark could not argue with his dead father so he grabbed the door to slam it shut but it was caught on something and wouldn’t budge. Now it was time to panic.

Running down the hall toward the back door, he screamed to Charlotte somewhere in the house, “Charlotte! Get out of here, right now! Charlotte!”

Charlotte answered from very close by, but he couldn’t see her.

He ran into the kitchen and looked back to see his father’s eyes had become white-light beacons searching the house for him. He yelled to her again.

“Get out of here now! We have to leave! Charlotte! Charlotte!”

“Mark, I’m here. For God’s sake, wake up! You’re dreaming. Please wake up!” She was shaking his left shoulder as he lay on his side yelling into the dark of their upstairs bedroom. He had startled her from a deep sleep and she wasn’t awake enough to know if it was his nightmare or hers.

Mark sat up but wasn’t awake yet and continued screaming looking directly at her. “Wake up, honey, wake up now!” he yelled.

“No, you wake up, I am awake.” she pleaded and began shaking him by both shoulders.

“No, you wake up. Please wake up right now,” he said also shaking her by the shoulders the same way she was shaking him.

“I’m awake! I’m awake, damn it!” She insisted and shook him one more time before dropping her hands to the mattress.

It worked. He wavered a moment then fell back onto the pillows.

“I am too,” He said in a quiet voice.

“And damn glad you are,” she replied curling up beside him. “What on earth was that about?”

He didn't want to talk about it. "I'm not sure. I think I had a nightmare," he said expecting the usual 'No shit, Sherlock but you owe me some change,' smart-ass response she coined in college. Instead, she snuggled closer, her head resting on his shoulder.

"Yeah, you're entitled to one of those but how about turning down the volume. You could wake the dead."

"Believe me they're up and on the move."

"That's nice, dear, but next time how about playing outside," she said nearly asleep again.

She smelled and felt so good and was so soft. It should have been safe to drift off and stay asleep until the alarm waked them.

"God I wish I didn't have to sleep, ever. One consciousness with lots of company is more than enough," he thought, eyes wide open, afraid to close them, again.

* * * * *

The noon interview with Dominique was done in less than thirty minutes and the crew was careful not to track up his house or move any furniture.

"So tell me about the Thursday prayer. What were you thinking as you hovered over a dying Dan Campbell?"

"It was a private moment."

"Private, my butt. It becomes highly public in front of a hundred witnesses and my cameraman. I'll probably use it," she replied not in a threatening way but just poking him for a response.

"Be my guest. But don't edit it into nonsense. Show it real and that's fine with me."

"By the way, how ya sleeping these days?" she asked but the answer surprised her.

"What kind of question is that from a beat reporter? You're not working on the health and personal hygiene desk are you?" Charlotte answered coming down the stairs next to the front door.

"I don't think we've had the pleasure Mrs. Justin."

"Let's not call it that yet but I do want to meet anyone my husband spends so much time with. And, we are sleeping very well. Would you like to know the secret?"

"No. I'll let you and Mark keep that one to yourselves but I would like to know why you think this is happening to you?"

"Oh please. Turn that one around, Mrs. Johnson. You are the cause *and* the problem here. It's all about your agenda, your ambition and your pure need to feed on us. I don't know how *you* can sleep."

"Whoa, ladies. Let's agree to disagree on that one and call it a day. Who gives a rip about sleep anyway?"

"I do," Charlotte and Dominique simultaneously replied and both smiled.

"So, you got a story or not? I really want to know when this is going to end and we can get back to normal around here." Charlotte asked.

"Until my viewers and I are satisfied you're not worth covering, we'll keep digging. Sorry if that upsets the state of affairs for you two but we go where the news takes us. Besides I think we're guilty of being too kind to the hero of our story." She had probably said too much but the news bugs in her stomach were doing field calisthenics.

"Frankly, I'm wondering if you're not a bit too prepared for all that's happening. Any chance you've had a warning?" she asked Mark.

"Yeah, we read it in the orange pekoe tea leaves," Charlotte answered.

"Right. Appreciate that but Charlotte, no matter what you think, it's not personal; it's news. Our mail is through the roof and my viewers are *very* curious about your guy. So, there's not much we can do about it, at least for this cycle-a feature for the Sunday shows."

And then she looked back to Mark for her final thought. "Get some sleep, deacon. You're a little baggy under the eyes; not good for your image. You never know when we'll be back."

And she turned to walk down the stoop wishing the news bugs would find another food source. But they were not going to drop this thing and neither was she. Now it was going to be an exclusive; a follow up more sensational than the original.

Hell, we might make a series out of it if he keeps this up.

As she opened the door of the van she looked over her shoulder to see Charlotte standing on the stoop staring holes through her.

“Ouch. Evil cycs rip my flcsh but this ain’t ovcr, honcy. I don’t even think we’ve gotten to the good part.”

Chapter 18

It was the last weekend of summer and the last Sunday with just a single service at Commonwealth Church. The Labor Day Weekend signaled the end of the summer's lazy, casual dress, assistant preaching, and relaxed atmosphere at the church. Although half the town was out of town, Vick was back and that was enough to prompt the Sunday crew to gather before the service and review their assignments. Mark had back door greeting duty before and after the service with the usual passing-of-the-plate in between. It was going to be an easy morning.

Standing outside the back door with only a half full parking lot and no one arriving, he let his mind drift. A song was forming, not exploding out of the Unknown Zone, but oozing out of the walls in his mind.

First the title, "Bertha's Butt".

"What? You're kidding. Now that is totally absurd." Without hearing the tune or words he knew the subject well.

On a hot summer night thirty years ago he and a beefy Bertha Sanchez climbed the Freeman, Texas water tower and overpainted the high school slogan, **GO PANTHERS** to read **NO PANTIES**. Great fun and the stuff of legends still told.

Then, in his own voice, a verse spewed through in a strange country ragtime tune.

I'd like to climb that water tower again
With a paintbrush and a beer in my hand,
When looking up was worse than looking down.
Now I wouldn't ask her to a movie or the prom
And she's not the girl I'd take home to Mom,
But Bertha's butt was an awesome sight to see.

It was hanging there like two full moons
Or was it oval shaped like water pontoons?
There was just so much to ponder,
When I couldn't see beyond her.
And polyester disaster was just one stitch away.

The back door of the church opened behind him and broke his concentration.

"Mark?" He instantly recognized Victor Springwell's voice. "I wanted to catch up with you real quick this morning. Can you drop by the office after the service? I'd like to talk about the events of the last week, if you don't mind?" Vick's asking was also insisting.

Mark coulda-woulda-shoulda made up an excuse not to meet him without more prep time but as usual he just did what Vick asked.

"Sure, uh, Vick, I can do that. And welcome back. It was quite a week and I'll be glad to fill you in." He could feel himself turning redder by he second, embarrassed by both the song and Vick's surprise.

"Great. I'll see you in the sanctuary during the service and afterward we can talk in the office. Looking forward to it," Vick replied and closed the door.

The dim-witted song about Bertha Sanchez's immense butt came back from the Unknown Zone with its catchy chorus and began an irritating loop. The mix of remembering the long climb up the water tower, the tension on those stretch pants (*barely*) and his disgust at the silly song made him feel nauseous.

"Better call in the reserves," the Debating Society offered.

His usual method of warding off tunes that wouldn't stop was to mentally play the theme songs from the Hogan's Heroes and the Andy Griffith TV shows. But this time it didn't work. Instead he was hearing all three songs overlaid and intertwined. 'Bertha's Butt,' 'The Happy Whistler,' and WWII marching music simultaneously blared in his mind.

"What a cacophony! Can't hear you. Sanctuary. James 3:17," the Debating Society screamed as he opened the back door and headed for the heart of the church where he hoped that prayerful analysis would replace the chaos in his head.

There they were. They were always there.

Silence.

"A week ago I prayed for Miss Daisy now I'm trying to unscramble my tune-happy brain. Where's the wisdom in that?"

He picked up a program and entered the sanctuary.

Immediately the organ prelude, a sonata by Bach, filled the air, and he tried to focus on it.

"Should be a friendly little chat with Vick so bug off, boys, and let's hear the man preach."

And all voices were quiet as he listened to Vick's newest offering. But this wasn't worship; it was chess and he was working on an opening move.

Just after the day's 724 sinners cleared out of the sanctuary and the crew cleaned up the used bulletins and donation flyers, Mark headed back to Vick's office. By the time he knocked on the door jam his anxiety meter had passed the butterfly-stage and moved into sweaty-underwear range.

"Come in, Mark, and catch the door please. I wanted a few minutes to cover your busy week. What'd you think about the service?" Vick was always courteous and forever disarming.

"Enjoyed it, especially your focus on spiritual renewal. After this week I think I could use a vacation myself," Mark answered trying to keep things light but Vick wasn't interested in much small talk.

"I won't waste your time, Mark, so I'll get right to the point. Everything I'm about to tell you is confidential and stays in this office. Can you agree to that?"

"Sure Vick, as long as long as we keep it legal." Mark replied without thinking.

"Nothing about this fiasco involves the law but it's still not easy, so here it is. Jerry Tinsler is no longer an assistant pastor at Commonwealth Church and I wanted to talk with you before we communicate to the rest of the Directorate and the membership. Since I returned on Friday I've covered the events of the week with the Elders and we believe that Jerry's departure is in the best interest of the church, even justified based the events of Thursday night." Vick paused but Mark was too surprised to respond.

"I informed Jerry last night and explained that the full Directorate would vote Monday to approve the decision. He understands our problem with allowing live press coverage during a service and that I have to swiftly deal with it. Simply put, it's become a firestorm that has to be extinguished. Our explanation is that Jerry is on administrative leave with full pay until he finds another church," he paused again but Mark still didn't respond.

"Mark? Are you all right?" He asked as he noticed Mark turning very pale.

"Yeah, Vick. Peachy." Mark's temper pumped some color in his cheeks.

"Please understand that this is very difficult for us and I prayed long and hard before making the final decision. You and I have a lot to discuss but it's important to get past this before we move on. Have I been clear on the matter?" Vick asked becoming impatient waiting for Mark's disapproval.

"Hell yes, you pompous overbearing egomaniac. You railroaded him because we got some press without your permission," Mark thought but checked his anger before it left his mouth and instead asked the obvious question.

"Did you fire him because he talked with a reporter? Because none of this was in your plan? That can't be right, Vick. Events moved too quickly. He just kind of kept them in play. I'm really sorry you're offended but this can't be for the best. It's way too harsh and I think your temper may have gotten the best of you." Mark said knowing he was on dangerous ground.

"You're dead wrong about that, Mark." Vick flared back. "It has nothing to do with the network. Jerry totally ignored our guidelines for media management and I'm furious the violation of our most sacred trust, the privacy of worship. I won't tolerate it and I did exactly what the situation called for."

"An old fashion tantrum took Jerry's head. Now what? At least he can't fire me from *my* job. Maybe I'll quit this 3-ring circus right now," Mark thought but didn't respond and continued staring down the angry head minister.

"Look Mark. I couldn't let this ride and it wasn't done out of anger. My responsibility is the trust of our membership and after this week I couldn't trust him with the church *ever* again. I'm truly sorry it came to this. We're all thankful, to Jerry for saving Dan's life but that news crew should never, under any circumstance, have been inside this church much less film one of our members having a heart attack. You have to agree with that."

"No, Vick, I don't have to. What's more, don't you think I'm to blame even more than Jerry? Maybe I should be dismissed too?"

"No, that's not how we see it but it is your choice. It may surprise you Mark but you're a key player in coming events and that's the primary reason we're talking now. I know what you did for Daisy Hanover and for Dan Campbell and I've seen the TV10 piece that ran last Sunday and the follow-up story airing tonight on the six and eleven o'clock news shows." He stopped to let Mark react.

"You've seen it before it airs? That means you've been to the station." Mark said and realized who it was. "Seth Griggs, of course, the Director of the News himself and long time member. Very nice, Vick."

"Yes, he asked for my input but that's not important." Vick replied in a gross understatement.

"Wow. You are way ahead of me, Vick, so why not lay it out there and tell me what you want."

"Good idea. First of all I want you to know that I think you've handled yourself extremely well *up to this point.* But it's more important for you to plan and execute a careful strategy as we enter what I believe will be a new phase of the event," Vick replied and stood up behind his desk.

"What's done is done and God's will be done. In fact we're stronger and in prime position to take advantage of it. But I have to control media access in and out of my church and you should at least consider the starring role I've planned for you."

“You keep coming back to that. You know I’m not on board with the whole ‘new vision for television’ thing anyway. I’m just not your guy and I never will be.” Mark couldn’t listen any more *and* keep his temper. It was time to leave.

“I understand but this is not something you can walk away from. And if you try you may be discredited here and in the community, maybe at work.”

“I can’t believe you’d threaten me, Vick. This conversation is over and I’m resigning. You can’t bully me like one of your associate pastors,” Mark coolly replied.

“I can’t stop you but let me make one more point. You know who sits near the front of our sanctuary each week and is one of our largest contributors? The CEO of Whyecliff, Charley Tobberman,” Vick said and raised his eyebrows for effect. “If I decide to take this to the pulpit, to characterize your interventions and press coverage as less than pure and for your own benefit, the consequences will be tangible. But I assure you I *do not* want to do that.” He motioned Mark back to the chair in front of his desk.

Unbelievably, Vick’s threat was real. Mark remembered that when he was elected to be a deacon, Charley pulled him aside at the next Whyecliff manager’s meeting and congratulated him.

“Really proud of you, Justin. Leadership at Commonwealth and Whyecliff are about the same to me. It’s all God’s work. I knew you were ready so I nominated you myself. Makes my day to see you advancing like that in our church,” he said with one of the most sincere handshakes Mark could remember.

And Mark knew Vick was capable of blackmail, maybe anything, to advance his network ambitions.

“Vick, what it the name of Christ are you doing?”

“I’m setting the stage, Mark. We have a lot to accomplish and a unique opportunity to do it. Our new vision for television is about to become reality and if you’ll give me one more minute I promise no more heavy-handed tactics. Will you do that?” He asked with an attempt at a friendly smile.

“Sure Vick, you’re holding all the cards so you might as well show ‘em.”

“There are two things we need to agree on. First, I’d like you to clear any more speaking engagements through my office. As an officer of the church I hope you’ll understand that request. If you don’t do any, that’s fine but the piece that’s airing tonight will likely generate more interest than the one last week. It’s very flattering and respectful of everyone involved. So be prepared for it and keep in mind that we work as a team. That especially applies to press interviews.” He made this last point with another raised eyebrow warning.

“Second, instead of resigning you’ll continue on the Directorate for another three-year term, but not as an Elder-more like a communications specialist. I can’t tell you the whole story now it will be leadership on another very public level. You are such an asset to the church and we’re just beginning to understand how to use your gift. You just need the right guidance and some polish. Can’t argue with that offer can you?” Vick had a wide smile this time and waited for Mark’s answer.

“I’m not arguing anything but I do know it should not have been handled this way. I need some time. And forget me for a second. How about Jerry’s family?”

“I said he’s being fully compensated and he has several leads already so don’t worry about that. It’s all taken care of. Besides you’ve got quite a plateful to deal with.”

Mark had to get out of there.

“You’re right, Vick. I’ve got a lot to think about and I need a little time. I’ll call you later in the week. One thing’s for sure, you’re never short on strategy are you?” Mark asked as Vick met him at the door.

Vick extended his hand and Mark shook it feeling like he’d just made a deal with the devil.

“I’m sorry about this rough start, Mark, but our plans for the network are in high gear and we have to make the most of every opportunity now. Nothing should get in our way. It’s so close. I know you’ll be guided by prayer (*and my foot up your ass*). Just remember, you and I are going to make good things happen out of all of this."

"I thought I already had," Mark replied and walked out the door, defeated but glad it was over.

"Mark, before you go there is one other thing I forgot to mention," Vick said and stepped into the hall.

It wasn't over.

"We heard a pretty bizarre story from Dora Elkins about an issue you had with her walker a couple of weeks ago."

Mark's stomach plunged to the floor as he turned to meet Vick's eyes. But Vick raised his hand indicating that Mark needn't try explaining whatever happened on the portico two weeks ago.

"Don't worry. Mrs. Elkins was actually amused by your sudden attachment to her walker and remarked how she'd never seen a deacon move that fast. Actually she thinks it was a warm up for the *real* miracle with Mrs. Hanover. Sounds like you recovered pretty well so don't give it another thought. I'll see you later this week and we'll get into more detail about the network," he said ending the conversation with a dismissive wave of a hand before locking his office and leaving through the back door.

Mark was alone in God's house. Walking through the empty church he struggled not to scream every cuss word he knew. It crossed his mind to slump into an empty pew and take a few minutes to cuss it out but decided to keep walking and calmly assess his predicament.

"So boys, that went pretty well. Don't you think?"

"Yeah, the old woodshed looks a little different from the inside, don't it? Simmer down, we'll recap." He was actually glad to hear from the Debating Society.

"Satan just fired the good guy and post-edited the follow-up story airing tonight on Destructo TV. You're headed for some warm up speaking gigs in the next few days *before* he puts you in a cage to appear on Clown TV. Also, there may yet be some residual interest from the Christian Slander Network (*What happened to Chambers?*). And as for your pesky prayers, better find a suppository for those things. That about cover it, Slick?" The Debating Society always enjoyed center stage.

"Nicely done, synap crap. But here's my take. Vick is the man with the plan and that's what the last ten minutes was all about. Scary thing is he probably has the influence to get me canned. That makes this a very high stakes game, boys. And we all know that little chat was calculated down to the last humiliating cut. He wants me embarrassed (done), defensive (done) and afraid to call my mama without permission (over done). Well, maybe not mama but certainly Dominique and Chambers."

He stopped to be sure he was walking toward the exit but found himself in front of the memorial in the narthex.

There they were. They were always there.

But this time he hated them and kept walking

"Screw you. I've had enough of this joint and *your* fake religion," he said to the dead preachers as he past them on the way out.

Then it hit him like the bright afternoon sun.

"Man, I've got the rest of my life. All I have to do is bob and weave through the next rounds this week and I'll be fine. Even if Vick is threatening me, his network fantasy is a freakin' long shot. He has to know that. It's not going to happen. Fact is, Marko, normal is just a week away, maybe two at the most."

He put on his sunglasses and let the T-bird drive him home.

Sitting in the driver's seat of his car, Vick picked up the cell phone from the center console and made another call to Atlanta. After listening for a moment he smiled and "God blessed" the banker on the other end of the line. That part of the funding was approved.

"Now there's just the local media and a Commonwealth contribution to seal the deal. Then it's 'lights, camera, action' for Springwell TV. Just like it's meant to be, Lord."

He put on his sunglasses and let the Cadillac drive him home.

Chapter 19

On the short drive home Mark decided to keep most of what just happened to himself. Charlotte would go ballistic, no mercy for either him or Vick, if he mentioned, even hinted at, Vick's threats. After a week in the wake of it, she was tired of the whole thing. The too-busy phone, her preoccupied friends, and the general loss of sleep all added up to an irritable Miss Charlotte. Domestic tranquility was already on thin ice.

"Not to beat the proverbial dead horse but have you thought about what happens to us if this repeat performance makes you a religious nut case, or some zealot or a publicity creep looking for some hype? You're not any of those are you?" she asked as they ate lunch.

"Naw, but this grilled Palomino sure is tasty, very tender after so many beatings." He wasn't happy to have the subject up for discussion again but tried to sooth her concerns.

"Look, honey, I'm just playing it out and I do think the reporter has an angle: ordinary people doing extraordinary things to care for each other. With all the murder and other violence around here, it's the contrast they're going for," he replied trying not to remember Vick's hellacious grin. "Let's look on the bright side. Nothing has happened that'll change the course of our happy little life here in River City and I'll bet the mortgage nothing is going to change that."

"Well that's a lousy deal. You don't have that kind of cash but I'll take it, anyway," she said offering her hand palm down to him.

He took it and lightly bit her index finger knuckle, kissed it and then, in almost a single motion, kissed his way up her forearm and bicep until he was leaning across the end of the table and planting a long and sincere kiss on her lips.

"I should bet with you more often. Double or nothing?" she asked offering the other hand, but then took it away and cupped his face with both hands to be sure he was listening. "We both know you're never far from wrecking our little oasis so don't let this thing be the one.

He smiled, amazed at how perceptive she was with so little information. He took her hands and kissed them again. "Whatever you say pretty lady," he replied and turned his thoughts back to the 6:00 broadcast.

"Hey, I need to call Roger Stanley and be sure he's watching the news tonight. He tried to talk with me all week and I blew him off. He'd be really pissed if I didn't let him know this was going to air."

"Yeah. You'd better check in with your fan club," she said, instantly regretting how bitchy it sounded. "Sorry, It's been such a weird week and I'm sure the piece tonight will be fine. I'm just glad Vick took it so well. A rare win for our team, huh?"

"For sure. He wasn't fazed at all. In fact, I'd have to say he's got the big picture and likes it. No doubt about it, today is my lucky day," he replied with a classic misinformation maneuver and got up from the table while the getting was good.

"I'll call Roger and then head out for a *Slurpee*. Got an urge for an icy cold one. You want to walk with me."

"In this heat? I'll fry before we get there but bring me one back. Make mine the blue goo."

* * * * *

Boubah Pakasandra loves his name but hates his job. Until he and his cousin, Talc, have enough righteous jing, as Talc calls the $3,000 they need to move north, Richmond is their lay over between New Delhi and New York. He knows when he leaves Hicksville USA no one will ever remind him that his last name is the same as a ground cover that grows in the better gardens of the redneck southern United States. In fact there are days it seems that every West End matron and garden fairy come out of the woodwork just to insult his Asian heritage.

Today, like every day, he's just doing time doing time behind the 7-Eleven counter in this hellhole of heat and hayseeds. Add the half broken Slurpee machine to his problems and he figures it will be another humiliating afternoon before his shift ends at 6:00.

"Merciful Holiness, spare my psycho self from another shamming," he prayed after lunch in the tiny office behind the front counter and so far the afternoon is a lazy one, too hot for most Richmonders to venture out.

Opening the glass panel front door sends a cool 70-degree gust out into the summer sauna and returns a 98-degree blast across his front counter. For Boubah it's just another irritant; for Mark it is instant relief.

"Hey Boubah. How's it goin'? Killer heat. Over the sweat line for sure." Mark says walking past the front counter on his way to the Slurpee machine.

Boubah gives him a quick nod-up. "You are also across the dork line my friend, from which there is no return."

"Only one way to stay below the sweat line on the trek back to the hacienda and there you are," Mark speaks softly to the machine waiting in the corner.

But seeing the blue bubblegum flavored side is dead, not swirling, he knows Charlotte will be denied the 'blue goo'. But the Coke side is twirling and sloshing, ready for business.

"My lucky day continues. Nice of you to keep one lane open."

Twenty oz. cup in place, he pulls out the go-spout expecting the brown glop to immediately fill her up.

"Burrrrrp…bup," Slurpee answers flaring a large brown bubble inside the plastic tub but not a drop for his waiting cup.

"Ah, come on darlin', you can squeeze one out for me." He's sure there is a Merle Haggard tune in that line but ignores it and pushes the go-spout slowly back into the stop position for another try.

"Probably frozen up a bit are you?" he empathizes and grasps the butt end of the spout where it joins the tub. "Maybe a little body heat will set you free. You do know we have to work this out, don't you?" he warns the machine.

"Ouh la la. That must feel fine for the slurpeemabob," Boubah muses, "But unless you jam it up your Panini for about an hour there is no goo for you today." Another clogged spout caused by feedback up the tube from the warmer and more humid air in the store. "Constipation too happens, my dorky friend." He smiles and continues watching out of the corner of his eye while ringing up a sale.

Mark's fingers are nearly frozen when he pulls them away from the butt of the spout. "All right you hog nosed slushheap. Time to give it up and I do mean right now," he harshly whispers and yanks the go-spout to the open position expecting his body heat and the sharp jostle to free up the brown sludge.

Instead, the machine answers with huge twin bubbles breaking to the surface on *both* sides of the Slurpee brain.

"Burrrrrp! Bup! Werrrrrr…" is heard across the store as the brown *and* blue goo suddenly fill the whole tub with frothy slush. Inexplicably, the stainless steel mixers have been supercharged into a new gear.

"That's what I'm talkin' about, but take it easy in there. This won't hurt," He ignores the radical change in the machine and jams the go-spout in and then yanks it out one more time.

"What are you doing, man. Can't you see that thing is shorted out," the guy behind him warns and begins backing away from the counter.

"It's okay," Mark nods back toward the machine and smiles, "I think it's ready to play our game now."

Weieirrrrrrrr… It revs even higher.

"I'm serious, buddy. She's gonna blow." The guy replies and, seeing the brown and blue sludge in a frenzy, turns and sprints down the isle.

But Mark stands his ground and hangs on to the go-spout, a test of wills between a changing man and the telekinetically charged machine.

"No need to turn tail 'cause this one's not going to blow. It's going to flow. Right now."

Exploding with the force of two highly torqued stainless steel mixers, the Slurpee mix blasts the plastic top away from the tub and sends it rotating like a tiny UFO toward the counter where Boubah is watching.

"Great Buddha moola. Dick! Everyone dick yourselves!" he screams ducking behind the Scratch Off lotto rack just in time to see the plastic top sail over the lotto tickets, bank off the cigarette display and fly though the open door of the popcorn machine to jam under the lid of the oil stained kettle. On contact with the hot coconut oil, the plastic Slurpee lid begins melting and a bloom of acrid smoke billows from the popper.

Just behind the top, like two gallons of cold sweet projectile vomit, the Slurpee machine spews its entire contents over Mark, covering him from head to toe with both tubs of brown and blue icy goo.

But the machine isn't stopping. It has a life of its own.

Weeerrerrr...

"What the hell? Boubah, give me a hand back here. Clean up on isle nine! Shit! Why is that thing still running?"

Boubah can't speak, much less move. Seeing the empty Slurpee machine vibrating down the back counter like a screaming legless banshee and the popcorn machine belching poisonous smoke, he crouches lower, looking through a peep hole between shelves, waiting for a cease fire.

The grinding whirl of the revved up mixers hits a deafening pitch when the empty machine finally vibrates far enough down the counter to bend its electrical plug out of the wall socket.

Zipcrik! Pop!

Sparks fly from the wall as the machine shorts out with enough electrical surge to tip the tub over and launch its twin mixers like miniature spinning missiles.

"Holy crap. It's alive!" a man yells from the bread section and grabs two bags of hamburger buns just in time to deflect one of the flying mixers into a barrel of international crackers.

“No shit!” yells the woman next to him as she dives head first into the chip rack to avoid the second mixer cruising by her head. It clears the collapsing chip display and smashes into the front glass sending other customers to their knees just as the jarring crash of the plastic tub echoes through the store.

“Call 911! 911!” scream two hysterical customers running through the thickening smoke and out the front door.

Boubah still can’t move from behind the counter. But just as most of his customers are running out of the store, another walks in, runs to the popcorn machine, yanks out the burning plastic top and throws it outside in the parking lot.

“Boubah thanks you very much. You are a cool hand Luke, Doctor.”

“What’s the matter with you? This place could be burning down, for God’s sake,” Louis scolds him and looks toward the back of the store where Mark stands covered in melting slush, still staring at the counter.

“The possession of the Slurpee machine is finished and no one seems to be needing my assistance. There is no need to insult Boubah.” But Louis ignores him.

“Are you very fine back there?” Boubah yells to the large woman removing herself from the destroyed chip rack. Red faced and wobbly, she walks toward the counter.

“I’m a lady so I won’t tell you what I think about your yellow-belly behavior but you got one hellofa electrical problem back there. And for what it’s worth, I’ll probably sue you and your damn store,” she warns and flips him the ‘bird’ as the door closes behind her.

“Is it my fault the devil is possessing this store?” he asks out loud and then realizes the Slurpee machine could just be the start.

“Oh Buddha moola, please don’t let it take the cash register too. If the money catches on fire they will throw Boubah away without a key.”

Mark never saw the attack of the Slurpee machine. Blinded by the slush and half in shock, he still can’t move as Louis approaches with a smile and a handful of paper towels from the coffee counter.

"You want to explain this one, slush bucket?

"I just tried to draw a Slurpee, man, and it goes berserk on me,"

"Yeah, that kind of thing happens to all of us from time to time."

Louis smiles, assessing the broken machine on the floor. "Looks like you gave El Slurpo one hell of a jolt. You're coming out party, perhaps?"

"Thanks for the napkins. I don't want to talk about it."

"But what about my Slurpee, mister? You killed the Slurpee machine." Louis kid-mimics and hands him some more napkins, snorting a bit trying to stifle his laugh.

"Lick me, Dr. Hackenberry. It *is* my lucky day, damn it." Mark replies, stepping over the expanding pool of melted slush and trailing some with each step toward the door.

"Oh Boubah, I won't be paying for that Slurpee if it's alright with you."

"It is very fine, my friend, but the machine could be out of bounds for some days. Please, you will try another of our fine stores next time?" Boubah avoids eye contact by busily picking up the scattered cigarette packs.

"Sure thing, Boubah, but I'm warning you. I'm coming back for those cheesy nachos as soon as I get on my apron and goggles. See you in a few." And he and Louis exit into the heat.

Immediately behind them, Boubah runs to lock the front doors, turns the open-closed sign over, and runs back to the tiny office to make a phone call. So excited he can only speak Hindi, he explains to Talc that, jing or not, they are leaving for New York within the hour.

* * * * *

Just as Vick said it would, the follow-up story aired on the TV10 Sunday News at 6. From the studio anchor chair, Dominique began with a recap.

"In a follow up to a TV10 exclusive, your e-mail and phone calls prompted us to catch up with the people, places, and events we barely mentioned last week in the story about a lady, a deacon, and a prayer. As you'll see, it was even more heartwarming than anyone could imagine. Naturally it's our "Good News Of The Week".

The piece ran 4 ½ minutes and opened with Dominique on the Commonwealth Church front lawn describing the scene of the accident. The story continued with Mark's interview followed by Miss Daisy's powerful revelation, then thirty seconds split between the EMTs and Dr. Louis Shotley, followed by a statement from the leader of a local atheists group. "Taking these perfectly explainable events and spinning them into some big mystery then calling it divine intervention is irresponsible and reckless….".

The story cut back to a thirty second of voice-over of the Thursday night supper rescue. With its dim lighting and muffled sound track the video looked more like a geriatric version of Ring Around The Rosy but Jerry Tinsler's CPR heroics were gone.

"What the hell happened to that shot? He in it, for sure."

The piece concluded with a 45 second interview with Vick Springwell. "God's grace and His role in our lives was clearly evident this week at Commonwealth Church. These events that have inspired so many to call upon us for guidance and prayer. We'll be adding programs for even more extensive outreach into the community."

She had strongly argued against that last minute interview with Springwell. It changed the story's center of gravity. Anyone could see that. But her boss and TV10 news director, Seth Griggs, would not air the piece without it. He was adamant and now, there it was; the story refocused on the church, not the people who lived it.

But something else had happened. Beyond those eleventh hour changes the on-air version had been altered since editing and approval by her producer. Justin's interview was longer, so was Springwell's, but Tinsler was cut out, surgically removed.

"I promised him fair treatment but delivered nada. Crapola."

So along with her TV audience, she was seeing the finished piece for the first time and she was livid as it neared the end.

"Who screwed my story?"

The red light atop camera one lit up. Caught off guard, she stared directly into it creating a moment of dead air. Reflexively she looked down at her copy and began reading the first sentence of her wrap-up. She looked back to the camera after recovering enough to read the teleprompter.

"I'm sure of one thing. The spirit of this story is just as real as the senseless violence that overwhelmed us earlier in the summer. But get this. For the past seven days no murder has been reported in the city and other crimes are down too. In fact, we haven't covered a shooting, stabbing, or any violence this week. Maybe the love in these events has spread through River City like a welcome summer breeze. Coincidence or not, we'll take the safer streets, quiet emergency rooms and peace for our children. Keep it up Richmond. The story doesn't have to end here. Take care of each other. That's the lesson of the deacon and Miss Daisy. So make it another good week and I'll see you next weekend. From all of us at TV 10, good night."

Camera one pulled back while the credits ran until the final cut over to the network news feed.

"What a freeze up. Afrodeer in the headlights!" She thought as the camera pulled away toward the back of the studio.

"How dare anyone make changes after post editing? Who has that kind license here-the same guy that twisted my arm to add a last minute interview ("for the pastoral perspective") and the only one with a reason to go to bat for that hypocritical minister? Seth, you scumbag! You actually ran it by Springwell. Bite me, damn it."

The studio lights dimmed further and interrupted her thoughts. She realized that the guys in the control booth were gone and that she was alone.

"God, it's warped. I've got to talk some reason into him and then his kick nuts into another orbit." She smiled at the thought of her 6'4", 260-pound news director in agony bent over holding his crotch.

Walking back into the newsroom, the silence was deafening. It was empty. "Last Sunday every available reporter, camera tech, and editor was in here trying to decide which murder to lead with and now, get this scene. It's beautiful. Time to take my own advice and slow down," she thought and then felt a sharp scratch inside her stomach.

The news bugs clawed another rut in her gut. Censorship in the name of the church had arrived at TV10 News.

"You guys are so intense," she said to her midriff. "I don't need a new belly button. We'll take 'em tomorrow. Give it a rest tonight. That's an order," she told them as she approached her desk in the back of the newsroom.

A yellow sticky note was stuck to the back of her chair and the stomach patrol pole vaulted into her throat. She slapped her midriff with one hand and picked up the note with the other.

"See me first thing in the morning. I can explain---Seth."

The cryptic message was in the familiar sixth grade scrawl of her news director. "I ought to return the favor with a little sticky of my own. Something like, "See me in the editing room first thing. I'll be on the floor picking up the better parts of my story," she said out loud.

A familiar song turned on in her mind. Marvin Gaye asked the right question, 'What's Goin' On?' She walked out rubbing her stomach and remembering every note of the classic and a modified line from another.

"Tomorrow's another day, scumbag."

Chapter 20

Charlotte didn't wait for the TV10 story to finish airing before pulling the plug on the phones. She wanted no disturbances during their back-yard party tonight. But unlike last Sunday, the answering machine was the least of her worries this week.

In less than thirty minutes traffic control was needed on Chaparral Street in front of their home. On this warm Labor Day Sunday evening, when the sun set at 8:03, the six o'clock news story brought out a few dozen curiosity seekers and others more hopeful of a miracle. Mark's name was mentioned four times in the story and since there was only one Mark Justin in the phone book, they were fair game.

Louis and Sarah used the back alley short cut to stroll over to the Justin's back yard patio. He was looking forward to the Bar-B-Q as well as gloating over the Madame's Saturday night prediction and his first TV appearance.

Charlotte saw them coming and read the doctor's mind.

"Lou, you camera swine. I hardly recognized you out of drag. Has the Madame booked Vegas yet?" she asked opening the back gate and giving him a hug.

"No, Atlantic City first. The drunks there are more our type," he feigned a nonexistent celebrity as they walked into the Justin's small back yard.

Because the front yard wasn't visible from the back, neither the Justin's nor their friends could see the crowd gathering out there. Obstructing the narrow sidewalk, ten curiosity seekers were already lined up along the split rail fence.

Chaparral is a primary East/West route carrying traffic to and from many of the West End's shopping and restaurant districts so the curious crowd invited others to stop and look at the home of the praying deacon on TV. No one had ventured onto the lawn so they were leaning on the fence like passersby at a car wreck.

From behind the back yard fence Mark was the first to hear the murmur of a small crowd in front and opened the gate to take a look. He slammed it hard enough to shake the whole fence line and hung his head.

"Hey, what's up with---"Charlotte heard the mumble and changed her question. "Who's out there?"

"I don't know but it probably has something to do with the story."

"No shit Sherlock but you owe me some change." She had saved that one.

"It's not that many, just a couple of joggers leaning on the fence. I'll go and talk to them for a minute. They're just curious. Probably. No doubt they'll go away if I just step out to say hello and goodbye."

"Yeah, that's good plan for the first minute. Let me know if you need any help in Amen Corner and what ever you do, honey, do not pray for anyone. They'll leave if you don't encourage them," she said dismissing the undismissable and turned back to their friends.

"Wow. I'm impressed, partner" Louis said. "Our fan is here. We'll *both* go out there and give 'em more than they paid for. I love it. A guest shot already." Louis put his arm around Mark and opened the gate.

They walked up the driveway looking at the gathered looking back.

Mark walked ahead and made a point to keep the fence between them. But it visibly swayed with their weight, not made to take that many leaners.

"Better to face them than be sued by them when the fence tumbles down," he thought as he greeted and invited everyone onto the manicured front lawn.

Now it looked like a yard sale with nothing for sale. People milling around either talking to each other or hugging someone they knew. And they kept coming as the sun began to set.

Eventually the small front yard hemmed in twenty men, women, and children. Some wanted just to see Mark, (*like the 5-legged calf at a county fair*) others wanted to *feel* something new (*as if the peace in the city emanated from there*). They wanted to talk about the TV story and ask if he had really prayed for those people; if he'd healed them. Some asked if he'd be their preacher.

Thinking that a dose of reality couldn't hurt, Mark also introduced Lou and together they were a hit. Louis had forgotten how desperate the general public was for a house call. Everyone had an aliment and expected instant diagnosis so, he followed Justin's lead and did his best to refer them on the spot. No one would feel rejected by either the deacon or the doctor.

In twenty minutes it was over and Mark was surveying the lawn for divots as Louis waved to the last of the hangers-on.

"So Marko, it's a good thing you had me here to keep the peace but we'd better pray for rain tomorrow, you think?

"Oh yeah, Dr. Delirium, you settled the masses with that little quack show. A true bonus here at Psychosis Am Us. Good thing you've got deep pockets." Mark winked at his friend and added, "Give me a minute out here will you and downplay it with Charlotte. Just tell her it was a couple of joggers and an old geezer with hemorrhoids."

"Right, your worship, but you absolutely have to avoid a repeat performance. This kind of blind devotion is sure to turn ugly when they find out you're a phony. Just don't molest anyone else without me," he said walking toward the driveway.

The twilight was spectacular, blue-to-pink-to-orange sky above his tall maples and the lawn never looked better.

"Will you pray for us?" asked an approaching voice.

Walking down the driveway from the street, a young man, his wife and their daughter approached the fence. Mark hadn't seen a human aura since he volunteered in a local hospital twenty years ago. It only happened mostly in the cancer ward and even then he thought it was just the lighting.

But when this little girl walked in front of the sunset, there it was again, dark and unmistakable.

"Please don't ask me that," he thought and a wave of nausea nearly crumpled him as he *saw* the shadow of death that surrounded the little girl. She was a pale blur inside of it.

"Come in the yard and let's talk about it, sir," he weakly replied.

The child's death-aura disappeared with the shadows and Mark saw the dark circles under her eyes, her snow-cold color, and the gray wool hat over her bald scalp. She was cancerous, ill from the disease *and* its treatment. You don't forget the shroud of hopelessness around the walking dead and it's almost unbearable to see it suffocating a child.

"You know why we're here. All we want is a simple answer and a small bit of your time, sir." The father seemed to read Mark's thoughts.

"Yes, I understand but let me shake your hand first and introduce myself to your family. I'm Mark Justin and I'm glad you're here," Mark hated his reply but smiled as he searched for better words.

"Why would you be glad, Mr. Justin? Me and my wife and our daughter, Mary, here, are the saddest people in the world and you say you're glad to see us? Well sir, I think you should be as sad to see us as we are to be here," Jason Andrews barely contained his anger.

His wife's eyes were bloodshot, out of tears, but crying nonetheless.

"I just want to know if you'll pray for Mary and help her. We been down at St. Gertrude's for another treatment. They say she's not responding but I seen you on TV. Can you really do something with those mighty words of yours?" Andrews was pissed off and desperate for something more than chemotherapy to treat his daughter.

Mark didn't answer but squatted to talk face to face with Mary. She was three feet tall and eight years old.

"Hello Mary. I'm sorry you're not feeling well and I'd like to help if I can. May I hold your hand while we talk for a minute?"

She held out her right hand and forced a smile.

"It's so cold. It's actually colder than the air temperature. How is that possible?" Mark thought as he wrapped both of his hands around hers.

"Mary, you're taking medicine that makes you sick aren't you?"

"Yes sir and it tastes bad and then I have a belly ache for three days and then my hair falls out. Can you make it stop, mister, please? Just for a little while?"

Mark felt the strong pull of her dark aura but refused to be drawn in. Instead, he gave her the wrong answer.

"I wish I could make you feel better and warm all over, Mary, but I don't know how to do that. I'm so sorry but I want you to know that you'll be in my prayers every night and that I'm going to ask a whole church to pray for you everyday. Believe me, there will be a lot of us trying to help you, I promise,"

"That's okay. Will you ask the doctors too? They don't help me either."

"You got it. And we'll pray for your Mom and Dad too," Mark replied with a smile but felt worthless, heretic.

"That's not good enough." Andrews said as he stepped in front of his daughter and pulled her hand away from Mark's.

Before Mark could stand, Jason grabbed his shirt collar and hauled him up to eye level. The pressure around his neck was immediate and turned his reflexive scream into a high-pitched wheeze. Suddenly unable to breathe, Mark was looking into the eyes of a lunatic who wanted to kill him. And was about to do it.

"You're a fraud, a goddamn fake, and I'm sick of you little turds and your empty words," he snarled as his strangle-grip held up Mark for more punishment. And with a bend of the knee for thrust he threw a gut punch that lifted Mark off the ground. Andrews dangled him for a moment, then let him collapse, wind gone, stars out, weakly coughing.

"No, Jason, please don't hit him again! Oh God, please don't do this!" His wife screamed.

"Daddy, no! Don't hurt him too! Stop it! Stop it, daddy!

Mark was leaning forward on his knees, grasping his stomach, gulping for air when Jason followed up with a thundering right fist, connecting just above his left ear, driving him into the ground.

With his wife and daughter crying and screaming for him to stop, Jason bent down over the helpless deacon and whispered a final message.

"I'm going to let you live, you worthless piece of church crap. That's a better deal than my little girl gets. I hate your guts, Mister, and my advice is that when you advertise yourself as God's gift you'd better deliver. The next guy may not be so generous," he said in a low voice only he and Mark (somewhere in the distance) could hear.

Andrews stood up and was deciding whether to kick Mark's lying mouth or just stomp on his ribcage when his wife pulled hard on his arm.

"Jason, we have to go right now."

"You're right darlin'. I'm through with this turd anyway. Look at that wimp lying there. Says it all don't it. Let's get the hell out of here," Andrews replied as he picked up his crying daughter.

"Better pray for yourself, asshole," he said to Mark and began walking quickly up the driveway toward their car.

Charlotte thought she heard someone screaming from the front and quickly left through the gate. As she ran past the front of the house she saw a man, woman and child getting into a parked car.

"Is everything okay? Is someone hurt?" she yelled to them.

"No, everything's fine," Andrews yelled back and added, "We're on our way to Disney World and just wanted to stop by and chat. Thanks, for asking." And he gunned the engine to drive away like they were about to miss the last flight for Orlando.

Charlotte looked up and down the street for something that could account for the commotion and realized Mark was nowhere in sight.

"Mark? Where are you? What's going on out here?"

He was able to respond only by clinching a fist full of gravel from the walkway in front of the stoop but it got her attention.

"Mark? Oh no, Mark! Please don't move, honey. I'll get Louis."

She bent down to see that he was still alive and then ran down the driveway.

"Call 911! Call 911! He's hurt. Mark's hurt. Louis!"

But the doctor was already running up the driveway to help his friend.

"Oh God, Louis. I think he's unconscious but he moved his hand."

"Let's take a look-see. Pulse is strong but it's easier when the patient is conscious. Mark, can you hear me?" he asked leaning down close to Mark's head.

Mark blinked awake and moaned. The world was a blur that smelled like dirt and slate but he was coming around.

"He hit me all over," he whispered.

"That's good. I mean not good but better than stabbed or shot. You may be bleeding internally and from the looks of that knot blooming on your head you might have a concussion too. Just take it easy and don't try to move. We'll have you at St. Gertrude's in few minutes for a good going over," Louis replied and nodded to Charlotte.

"I'm fine, really. I just need to stay here for a little while until I can see and breathe again," Mark whispered without moving.

"That's a fine plan, Marko, but Charlotte tells me this spot is reserved for another assault later tonight so you gotta go for a little ride." Louis replied as a siren sounded in the distance.

“You hear that? It’s your cab ride to the local health spa. Just let the EMTs do their job and I’ll line you up a sponge bath after we check in.”

“Lou is that your tennis shoe? Can’t hear much through the buzz down here. My stomach burns and I taste blood. Is that okay?” Mark asked in a stronger voice.

“Yes it’s my shoe and no it’s not. It’s the number one symptom of getting you’re ass kicked so let’s cut the chitchat and save it for the ER. We’ll be there in less than five minutes,” Louis worried about the rate of possible blood loss but it appeared to be an ordinary beating, the kind wives, children and drunks take every day.

“Lou, I can’t believe this. It’s exactly what you said last weekend. Exactly. Is he going to be okay? Did you see that too?” Charlotte asked while wiping quick forming tears from under her eyes.

“I think so. Looks like a sucker punch by one of his fans. And remember his Life Line splits, it doesn’t end, so… Oh, hells bells, forget about that stuff, Charlotte. He’ll be fine. Doctor’s word.” He hugged her shoulder as she bent down to comfort Mark.

The rescue squad siren blared from less than three blocks away.

With another crowd beginning to gather, the ambulance turned the corner and pulled into the driveway. The EMTs quickly loaded Mark into the back of the vehicle and sped away to St. Gertrude’s ER less than a mile away.

Chapter 21

Dan Campbell was also in St. Gertrude's and had been listed in 'critical but stable' condition for the past seventy-two hours. He could feel his reanimated heart giving out, doing what it wanted to do three days earlier at the Thursday night supper. He was feeling weaker each hour even if the doctors were talking full recovery with treatment and time.

Lying in his semi private room, Dan had just seen the TV10 news story that featured his near death experience.

"I wish they'd let me die. Is that asking so much?" He asked Dominique as she signed off.

The night before his brothers pleaded with him to go with the bypass surgery. He refused.

"But you'll die with out it, Danny. Don't you understand?" his youngest brother, Andy, begged.

"No chance, squirt, but listen up. I'm liable to get out of here and kick your scrawny butt again so let's put a better face on it, okay?"

"Yeah, I will, but don't try to bully me. We're gonna talk about it some more," Andy replied wiping tears away from his face.

Now his room was bright with the Sunday setting sun that tinted everything. It wasn't as bright as the one in the church dining hall three days ago but he saw it as another signal from above.

"How 'bout that, fellas? Your big brother made the TV news on his last day in this skin. Gotta love that but I'll tell you and that news lady something, I'm not coming back this time. Maybe the docs will try but they won't have that preacher and his prayin' deacon to bail them out," he thought as the light of the sunset intensified in his room.

"I do wish I could see you one last time, Andy, but I'm on the edge now. No tears, no fears, no money grubbing doctors, no worries. It's like being on a ledge and falling up. I'm just going to close my eyes and head home.

* * * * *

"You are their keeper. The heart of the center. Stay and love them. Stay and heal yourself. Love your life. Love their lives. Love life …."

Mark's prayerful chant finally disturbed a chaotic sleep and he stopped. But he wasn't lying down. Gaining consciousness he realized he wasn't even in bed but was sitting beside one, head bowed, hearing the electronic pacing of life monitors, and shivering in the night chill.

"Am I naked?" He asked and snapped opened his eyes. He was still in the hospital but not in his room.

"Okay Marko, don't panic. You've been sleeping in a chair with your head on the foot of your bed so just stand up and crawl back under the sheets."

He moved and lightning flashed through his head as blinding pain from the concussion spiked and a wave of nausea gagged him.

"Easy there, dick head, don't hurry this. It's not dark, you aren't naked no one is looking. Just slide into bed real slow," he thought and was glad to see shapes in the room come into focus.

Suddenly, the door opened and the bright hall light beamed into the room blinding him again.

"Who are you?" asked Nurse Kendall, "and why aren't you in your room? Do you know Mr. Campbell?" She harshly whispered running into the room.

"Mmm nam ur mar," Mark replied unable to speak clearly.

"Who's there?" Dan asked awakening from a light sleep.

"It's all right Mr. Campbell. Somehow this mute patient has wandered in here."

"What ward are you from?" she signed to Mark.

"Mmm nock a moot," Mark was still dazed and raised his hand so she could read his wristband.

“You lost your boots? And you must be chilly too,” she signed.

“I’d better talk or I’m headed for the pyschward.” Mark focused.

“I am not a mute. Please take me back to my room,” he said slowly and carefully as she read his wristband.

“He speaks? Fine then Mr. Justin, but you’re three floors from home base. How did you get past me?”

“Mark Justin? I don’t believe it. Why are you here? Did you pray for me again?” Dan asked and they all heard his heart monitor abruptly chirp faster.

“I don’t know Dan. I got beat up. Unconscious. They put me in a room. Here I am,” Mark said hanging his head.

“You know each other? Well, at 2:00 a.m. I don’t care if you’re long lost brothers. This little reunion is over. Mr. Justin is going back to his room then we’ll get to the bottom of this disturbance,” she said picking Mark up by the shoulders and leaning over to push the service button.

“Mr. Campbell, I’ll order a weak sedative to help you get back to sleep. I’m sorry for this commotion but I assure you that Mr. Justin won’t be sleepwalking any more tonight,” she said as Mark walked with her toward the door.

“Justin, I have to know if you prayed for me again.”

“I don’t know any other reason I’d be here, Dan, but I’m not sure. We’ll talk later.”

“Not on my watch,” Nurse Kendall said as she escorted Mark into the hall.

Dan heard her voice fade down the hall as she interrogated Justin. He also heard his heart beat return to normal.

Another nurse swished in with the sedative and a cup of water. He decided to stash the pill between his cheek and gum, drink the water, and spit it out the moment she was gone. She smiled and closed the door behind her.

"I'll kick his ass if he messed with the natural order of things. I was on my way. I was almost home again, damn it all," he said to the darkness.

"Where's that pill?" He had swallowed it.

"Love what? Love life? What does that mean? Damn it all. It means I'm not coming back home, PaPaul."

* * * * *

The tune was new. It began with a far away guitar echo of a distorted minor chord bent and increasing in volume (Boston style) until it broke over him and into an undulating set of harmonic major chords.

The voice of James Hetfield, Metallica vocalist, sang the lyrics as the volume and distortion changed into a softer tune.

What do you want from me?
What do you expect from me,
When I don't even know who I am.
I can see you want more
but like I told you before
I'm not going to be your savior.
I'm not a preacher, a teacher or the man of your dreams
I'm just here for a flash,
Passing through to pay dues.
That's all it really means.

A quick transition into a three chord break and then back for the power lyric of the song.

I can't see what you see, it's your life not mine,
I'll never be your savior.
How could you be so blind?

Mark was stage left, leaning over his favorite electric 6-string slung low and bouncing off his right thigh as he played their hard driving tune. He was a member of a super band. His hands knew the chords and the lead riffs poured out of the Les Paul guitar that seemed to play itself.

He looked over to give James a nod but Metallica had turned into Nirvana and Kurt Cobain was draped over the microphone swaying back and forth, waiting to pickup the lyrics after Mark's solo.

The stage lights flashed brighter and brighter as the song hit a crescendo. The glare was so strong he couldn't see Kurt or the stage but the crowd called his name. "Mark-y, Mark-y, Mark-..."

"Mark, honey, Mark honey. You need to wake up. It's time to wake up and smell the coffee. Marky? You in there?" Charlotte was gently coaxing him back to reality but she wasn't getting through the crowd noise yet.

"Mark, honey, please wake up," she watched him breathe and thanked God again that he wasn't badly hurt. She was surprised when he reacted with a smile. Just a grin at first but it spread into a wide smile.

"Thank you. Thank you very much," he mumbled and moved his free hand up to cover his eyes. The world was a bright blur when he opened them. He had no idea where he was.

"What year is it?"

"It's 1997, honey. You're in the hospital. Someone attacked you last night but you're going to be fine. You've got a really bad headache, though. Are you back ready to play our game?" Charlotte asked and returned his smile.

"Hi there. It's you and I'm not Eric Clapton, right?" he said and squinted at her.

"Well, no, but you fooled somebody. Ginger Baker is in the gift shop waiting to come up.

"Great. I'd better get into my leathers. Always glad to see one of my groupies," he replied and smoothed her hair away from her eyes.

As he tried to sit up his smile turned into a grimace. "Ow, that hurts like hell. Does the railroad spike ruin my hair?" He asked and lightly touched the knot above his ear.

"No, not at all. Blends right in there," she said but then her façade crumbled. "Just relax, honey. You'll be better tomorrow.

Great timing though. Getting beat up on a holiday weekend you won't miss any work," she said and couldn't hold back any longer.

"Damn it, Mark." Tears streamed from both eyes as she lean over and gently hugged him.

He couldn't cry through the pain in his head and stomach so he just tried to comfort her, softly rubbing her back.

"I'm sorry, I'm so sorry this happened. I'll be back to normal, we'll be back to normal soon, as normal as normal can be. Just get me back to our normal home and we'll be fine."

But they both knew normal was fading like a missed exit on I-95.

Louis had been making rounds most of the morning and was polite enough to knock before entering the room. Charlotte had talked with him earlier and excused herself so that he could discuss Mark's recovery.

"I got a couple of things for you about this ass whipping. First, the guy that did this wasn't trying to kill you. He just wanted to punish you and it's a hell of a message. Let's read the handwriting on that noggin. As your doctor and friend I advise you to get out of the savior business or hire a bodyguard if you're going to continue. Sorry to be so draconian but there are a lot of pissed off people looking to take it out on somebody. That is an ugly fact, partner, and you can't change it." Louis said as he had rehearsed it all morning.

"Check this out." He handed Mark "Section B" of the Richmond Times-Dispatch. The first article in the "Local Briefs" section was circled. 'Local Church Figure Hospitalized' was the small headline followed by a three-sentence summary of the attack and Mark's condition.

"Louis, I didn't ask for any of this."

"No you didn't but you did put yourself out there. Come on, man, it's the law of unintended consequences. You know that. It has weight, its own gravity, and you can't play around with it. That's all I'm trying to say."

“Okay friend, you got me on that one and I’m not in any position to argue about it, that’s for sure. But it’s my turn for a little speech.” Mark looked up and also raised his hand up for Louis to grasp the way arm wrestlers clasp for a match. “Thanks for taking care of us Lou. Once in a blue moon you’re right and I don’t know what I’d do if you weren’t there to gloat over it.”

“You can count on that,” he replied as they shook hands and then quickly dropped their grasp.

“Now I also want to consult with you about your little midnight stroll to Dan Campbell’s room. For this part of the show I brought some props, do you mind?” he said taking some MRI scans from a manila folder.

“I’m not going to ask how you got past the nurse’s stations and various other on-duty staff. Security is working that pretty hard and will talk with you after they analyze the surveillance tapes. Not to worry, sleepwalking is a hobby around here but invisibility isn’t so they’re trying to figure out how you hacked the system. Their problem not mine,” he said grinning because he knew they’d find nothing on the tapes.

“I’m here to cover Dan Campbell’s puzzling recovery and I’ve only got five minutes so we’ll hit the high points. Now in doing this I’m violating doctor-patient privacy rules so you have to keep this confidential, okay?”

“Well, Dr. Shotley, I think I can but I’m not so sure about you,” Mark replied with a smile.

“Right, good point. So to make it legal, for the next five minutes you’re a pro bono radiologist. You got that?”

Mark replied with a snappy salute and Louis separated the scans.

“Now look at this. It’s his heart at admission. Look at the arterial occlusions here, here, and here. His infarction indicated a clot at this point and with, all that other blockage, his heart just quit pumping,” he said pointing to areas of Dan’s heart scan taken three days earlier.

"Well sure, any pro boner radiologist can see that," Mark joked.

"Hey, I'm trying to figure it out so stay with me. Now today those occlusions are gone, vanished. This, he said pointing to the most recent picture, is amazing stuff. So, being the crack staff we are, we followed up with catheterization and EKG to be sure. In those tests the dyes showed normal oxygen and blood flow. They also show there's no dead muscle. In fact this morning he's pumping strong enough to drain a small swamp," he said pointing to the last set of graphs and x-rays.

"Well, this is a world-class hospital, Lou. Isn't that supposed to happen?"

"You're right about that, stink weed, but hear me out. The CKs showed a significant spike at admission so we know he actually had a heart attack. Yesterday's blood assays showed a loss of strength in both ventricles but today's are near normal and the early angiographies showed enough build-up in his arteries to choke a goat. Where did all that muck go?"

"Don't ask me doc. I'm just here for the masseuse and room service. Why not give yourself a pat on the back for a job well done?"

"Because I'm not that good."

"And neither am I."

Louis gathered up the Campbell file and made the decision.

"Well one thing is certain. This morning our friend has some new pipes and plumbing and I sure as hell can't explain why. So, that leaves us with only one option," he paused looking at Mark.

"The hospital will take credit for it," Louis said with a smile and then added. "But you, sir, are bad for business so I'm discharging you at noon. And Mark, he said heading for the door, you ought to talk with a shrink about that sleepwalking routine. Hey, ever wake up in your neighbor's Volvo?"

"Hey, you ever cut off the wrong member?"

“You’re fired. I’ll call and irritate you at home tonight. Stay off your head for a few days.” Louis replied and disappeared through the door.

“Wait. Lou, when are you letting Dan out?” Mark shouted and winced at the pain it caused.

Louis stuck his head back into the room. “Probably tomorrow. Later.” He said and vanished.

Just before noon Charlotte wheeled Mark to the front desk for checkout and the nurse on duty stepped from behind the large counter to talk with him.

“I believe in you, Mr. Justin. Please keep up the good work. We need you praying for all of us,” she said extending her hand for him to shake.

He was embarrassed but thanked her and shook her hand.

“As normal as normal can be,” Charlotte’s said and wheeled him out the door.

Chapter 22

The front door bell woke him.

It would stop if he ignored it but a persistent visitor kept irritating it. He peaked out the peephole but the full afternoon sun blurred the figure on the porch.

"Hello there!" he yelled from inside and the pain in his head punched back.

"Hello. Yes. I'm looking for Mark Justin. Is that you Mark?" said a vaguely familiar voice.

Mark opened the door to see Bobbie Jean Heckler. The TV10 weather reporter was a true blast from the past. Twenty years after her on-air disaster and vanishing act from Richmond TV she was still petite, endowed, brunette, beautiful, and pissed off.

"Bobbie Jean? Is that you?" (Oh Mabeline, honey will you be true?)

"Yeah. It's me. Can I come in?"

"One condition. Tell me you're not a reporter."

"Will you let me in anyway? It's important. I wouldn't be here if I had a choice so give me a break. It's urgent."

Still not bashful she sat on the small Victorian sofa, only a foot from his side and close enough for him to smell her perfume. He was struck by how gracefully she'd aged, like a frustrated beauty queen.

"You look great, BJ. You must be in front of the camera somewhere."

"Wish I could say the same but you look like crap so just listen to me. I know your story but this is why I'm here," she said pulling a large envelope out of her portfolio size purse. 'An Accident Of Faith' was written in large black letters on the front.

"I'm just going to blurt out all of this so please don't interrupt."

He nodded agreement but another alarm that sounded like a distant chain saw cranked up and idled in his ears.

"It's a trap, meathead. Rip off her dress and run outside," The Debating Society was delirious and he tried to listen to Bobbie Jean over the idling chain saw.

"John Chambers sent this to me before he disappeared on assignment in Central America. His chopper went down somewhere near the Guatemala-Belize border before they made it to base camp." She looked at him more angry than sad.

"Search parties are all over the place down there but there's no word. Any questions before we come back around to you?"

Mark said nothing, stunned by another personal tragedy this week.

"Anyway, John's brief on your story wasn't complete so I've pieced together the rest of it. I'll spell it out and keep in mind you're less than full speed after what that God-fearing Christian did to you," she said sitting up.

"Just like your attacker, CSN isn't buying the whole miracle story so I'm here to give you a heads up and get a reaction.

The concussion was taking its toll. He couldn't process the threat and just stared. "Her forehead has no wrinkles."

"Really, I'm sorry you were cold-cocked but we know the truth about your exploits and aren't fooled by the locals fawning all over a couple of Samaritan rescues. It doesn't pass our sniff test."

"BJ, what happened to you?" He interrupted. "You barge in here from a self righteous little network, attacking and insulting me. I don't get it.

"Okay, okay, you're right. I'm rude, obnoxious and pissed off and I wish John had left me out of it."

"Rude? It's a frontal assault. You can't hang me now, twenty years after you had a bad air day. I was in the back studio pacing and practicing my own lines, too scared to watch. What happened?"

“Dead air would have been merciful. It was worse than that and you know it. Let’s check memory lane a second.”

He nodded; glad for a cease-fire but knew where she was going.

“They reduced me to a babbling, confused, embarrassed… shit, you name it. You can’t understand how awful it felt, how it still feels. Those sadists in the control room sabotaged my very first weather show-no graphics, no teleprompter, no maps. No nothing. Just God-awful rainbow colored static spewin’ into every home in the market.” She stopped and stared, turning red and angrier.

“But it was interference, BJ. That studio gear was ancient and you know those guys wouldn’t do that to you. But you vanished, I never saw you again. Something else happened, didn’t it?”

“Damn straight it did. After we faded to black I hunted down that good for nothin’ news director and told him to go find himself another weather whore. That night I packed my stuff and drove home to Virginia Beach, crying at 80 mph down I-64. And that’s it. You got it now?”

“Yeah, I do. After you left I covered some of your spots but *Weather Wise* was history and me too just after you left. Crummy pay, cheap equipment and ratings you could count on one hand.”

“Well, you could have called or looked for me or something. I was devastated. I needed you.”

And he was ready to confess. The rainbow interference had been his fault; generated by nerves he reigned in before his first show but he had been frantic hours when she began hers. Nothing good was going to come of this now-she had to leave.

“Just tell me how it ends, BJ.”

“Alright, bottom line-your story is a scam, a lie constructed by the secular media. We’re ready to go on the air with that,” she replied like a determined prosecutor looking for a confession.

“A godless scam? Are you serious?”

"You bet. Any comment?"

"Yeah, quote me. What are you guys smoking? This sounds more like meat for a Christian talk show. Is that what you have in mind?"

It was but she didn't respond and he continued.

"Tell your CSN pals that none of this was planned. Chambers knew it and you ought to be ashamed." He winced as the chain saw revved up inside his head.

"But it is unraveling, Mark. They're turning on you because they know. We don't think the charade should go another cycle without an objective response. I'm here as a professional courtesy before we run it."

He was about to tell her where to run her story when a noise at the back door startled both of them and broke the tension. Charlotte was home, struggling to open the door with both arms full of groceries.

"Hey hon. You up? Whose car is that in front of the house?" she yelled while walking to the front.

"Charlotte dear, you may remember Bobbie Jean Heckler, ex weather whore at TV10. We worked together for a short time in '77."

"Whoa there Mark, you'd better have a seat, honey. Are you okay?" she noticed his lack of color but offered her hand to Bobbie Jean to be polite.

"Hello, Ms. Heckler. Sorry but I don't recall much about those days and I apologize for Mark. It's been pretty tough around here. So…, are you still on the air somewhere?"

"Yes. As a matter of fact I'm with CSN now and I'm following up on the story filed by John Chambers." Bobbie Jean replied coldly.

"Where the heck is John? We've wondered about him all week."

Before Bobbie Jean could answer, the doorbell rang again. Charlotte got it and led Dominique Johnson into the living room.

Mark looked at her, rolled his eyes, and sat down heavily on the sofa.

The chain saw cranked to a higher pitch that was going to take his head off if it didn't stop. He was thankful Charlotte continued the introductions.

"Dominique from TV10, this is Bobbie Jean from CSN. I just got here too and I can't believe our luck. Mark, I thought the celebrity panel arrived tomorrow. But no problem, ladies. I'll put on some coffee," Charlotte said barely managing her temper and turned toward the kitchen when the doorbell rang again.

"Well this just has to be today's mystery guest," she said looking back at Mark but didn't notice how he'd changed.

She answered the door and led Vick Springwell into the living room. Mark tried to stand but couldn't make liftoff and awkwardly fell back on the sofa. He was unable to speak with them and Charlotte quickly finished the introductions.

"Vick Springwell meet Bobbie Jean Heckler from CSN. I think you know the rest of the panel. Now excuse me while I get that coffee going," she said and walked quickly toward the kitchen wondering if Oprah or Billy Graham would be next.

In the kitchen Charlotte leaned over the sink and turned on the water to mask the sound of her harsh whispers.

"Damn this thing. Damn it to hell. Reporters and ministers, newspapers and television. I just want them to go away. Get the hell out of my house and leave us alone," she said nearly blind by tears and anger.

Back in the living room Vick broke the silence.

"Ms. Heckler, you're from CSN. How interesting. I'm the pastor at Commonwealth Church and here to check on my deacon. He's recovering from a brutal attack yesterday right here in the front yard. Mark, I know you're not feeling well but…" He looked toward the sofa and lost the thought.

Rocking back and forth, face in hands, fingers rubbing his forehead, Mark could not hear them. The chain saw screamed and a fiery sun cut through the living room windows. There was no way to talk through the blinding pain; he was passing out and welcomed it.

The light, the buzz and the pain took him.

In the kitchen, Charlotte tried to regain her composure. In two minutes the coffee was brewing and she would be ready to apologize to her preacher and the two reporters. She had known Vick for fifteen years and usually greeted him with a proper hug and a smile. She was embarrassed for rudely dumping him in the living room.

"Time to turn on the charm. Whatever's happening in there we'll get past it. Be polite and take a few questions. One thing's for damn sure. They won't write about a lack of Southern hospitality in this house," she said out loud.

She turned to walk down the hall but stopped in her tracks at the sight of Vick backing out of the living room entrance and stumbling into the front foyer. He looked horrified; face contorted and mouth open, half falling as he lost his balance. In a total panic, he reached for the front door, threw it open, leaped onto the stoop, and ran down the front stairs.

"Vick?" She yelled to him but he was off the stoop and running down the front walk toward the street.

She took one more step toward the hall and stopped to watch Bobbie Jean stagger out of the living room, hand over mouth, and stumble into the hall table hard enough to send the collection of brass candle sticks crashing to the floor. After falling to one knee and catching herself on the table, she leaped up and ran out of the house through the open front door, trailing Vick by only a few feet.

"Mark? What in God's name is going on? Vick looks like he saw a ghost and Bobbie Jean is absolutely spastic. We're in enough trouble without…" She stopped in mid sentence at the living room entrance.

Mark was sitting on top of the sofa back; feet flush on the seat cushion, looking into the room. But his eyes had completely rolled up into his skull and only the whites showed. He looked hollow and corpselike, hardly recognizable.

"Oh God. Mark, honey, what's happening to you? Please don't do this. Damn it, Mark. Stop it! Stop it right now!" She begged but he wasn't in there.

Unlike the others, Dominique couldn't run away. She was laying face down on the carpet in a pool of her own vomit, sputtering for air between coughs. Lifting her head off the floor but still looking down, she began babbling.

"No way that just happened. It couldn't. It didn't. I know it didn't," she said and then heaved the last of her lunch on a corner of the oversized Oriental rug that decorated most of the living room floor. Another coughing spasm shook her.

But Mark was not breathing. Rigid, lifeless and staring into his brains, Charlotte grabbed him by both shoulders and shook; shook the daylights out of him.

"Mark, wake up. Wake up right now, damn it!"

Still nothing.

"You cannot leave me. I won't let you!" she screamed and leaned him forward enough to then slam his back against the wall. The impact shot through it like wrecking ball thunder and oil paintings on either side of them plunged to the floor splintering plaster frames in all directions.

"Look at me, Mark. Breathe, damn it. This instant!" She slammed him against the wall again, this time hard enough to knock the curtains down on top both of them and send the table lamp crashing to the floor, splattering shards of Chinese porcelain across the room.

"Now, Now, Now!" She repeated and continued shaking him even with the curtain draped across them.

Finally, the chaos and violence reached him. He reflexed wildly with both arms, flinging her off the sofa and onto a side chair that tumbled backward and fractured under her weight.

"Mark?" she asked, lying on the floor, stunned by the hard fall.

Eyelids fluttering, he flickered back to life and sucked in a long deep breath. Still sitting on the top of the sofa he teetered forward but fell heavily on his side onto the sofa cushion. Only his expressionless face showed from under the fallen curtain. He was still unconscious but his blue eyes had rolled forward.

Curled up in a fetal position, catatonic but breathing, at least he was alive. "Now it's time to page Louis." She struggled up, wobbly but able to handle the phone and paged their friend with a '911' behind the return phone number. If not in the middle of surgery he'd make double time and bring an ambulance.

She brought a damp rag from the kitchen and began rubbing Mark's forehead as he panted for air and stared into space.

Dominique was still on all fours, not yet strong enough to stand.

"Are you okay?" Charlotte coldly asked.

She nodded but was still nauseous and dazed by what had just occurred. It was unanalizable.

"I've paged a doctor. Use the bathroom to pull yourself together." At that moment Charlotte hated her.

"For Christ's sake, Mark, what is happening to you? What's happening to us?" she softly asked. "Come back to me. Please come back. Remember our motto, 'No shit too deep'? Well, I'm drowning here. We'll fight our way through it if you'll just come back to me," she said swabbing his head with the cool rag.

Dominique had found her legs and walked back into the room with a pan of water and a fist full of paper towels from the kitchen.

"He kind of passed out but then, then, it was unreal. He was taken or transformed or something. Right in front of us," she mumbled and began cleaning the rug.

Charlotte cut a glance at her but didn't say anything. Her concern for Mark stopped the urge to walk over, kick the reporter in the ribs and drown her in her own puke. Instead she continued swabbing his head and quietly begged him to come back.

Louis arrived in less than five minutes. He quickly examined Mark but a candy stripper could make the diagnosis.

"His heart rate is really up there and his respiration is too quick. Unless he has a history of seizures we don't know about, it looks like the concussion created a kind of delayed, trauma-induced shock. Let's get some oxygen going until the ambulance arrives." he said and strapped the mask over Marks face.

"I'm sorry Charlotte. I shouldn't have released him this morning," he was looking down at Mark and shaking his head. "Mark, old bud, didn't I tell you to stay off your head? My bad for sure." He confessed and then looked around the room for the first time.

"Looks like you had a street fight in here and it smells so rancid." he asked and then noticed Dominique on all fours cleaning the carpet. She was in her own kind of shock.

"Never mind. If *you're* here I know what it's about. You finally pushed him over the edge. Hey, are you happy now? Think he's had enough?" he asked loud enough to get through to Dominique.

"You have no idea what he's become or what he's done. It *was* a seizure, Doc, but not the kind you treat. I'm half in shock myself, blowing chunks and damn near choking on it. So no lectures right now, okay? Just get him back."

"Right. No lectures but I've got a free lobotomy for you anytime," Louis replied losing some of his usual cool.

Scrubbing the rug, Dominique felt empty, drained and numb. Emotionless. Suddenly she realized the itch was gone. Her news bugs were missing.

"Hey, wake up down there. You should be trying to dig me a new belly button after this."

But there was no itching or scratching from the inside out. She even swirled the residue in the pan to be sure they weren't swimming laps down there.

"Where are you? Did he do something to me? Holy mother of God," she mumbled and stood up, still on shaky legs.

"What did he do to me?"

“You?” Louis responded to her question. “Take a look and remember that face. It’s what’s left of my best friend-comatose and wasted. This is *exactly* what you wanted and it damn near killed him this time.”

For the second day, a West End Rescue Squad ambulance screeched into the Justin’s driveway and left with the head of household on a gurney. During the short ride, the oxygen brought him partially back to reality so that when they wheeled him into St. Gertrude’s he was mumbling about pain from every muscle in his body.

Chapter 23

Scared men do scary things but Vick wasn't down to scared, yet. The images of Justin or what had been Justin or what Justin was becoming replayed endlessly. Trembling hands and unsteady legs couldn't keep him straight in traffic and he was going to be pulled over by the first traffic cop along the way. The thought of babbling nonsense to a uniform amplified his desperation.

He and the others were terrified. That had to be the purpose of what they had just witnessed. Beyond belief, there was no measure, no understanding it but what scared him the most was the direct threat against him and the new network.

Then he became aware of the wetness in his crotch and down his leg. In the past 5 minutes he had lost all control.

"Add it up, Victor. Justin is doing everything possible and impossible to pull the plug on Living In Faith Entertainment. So much is on the line. We can't let that happen. Time to end it," he thought.

Reason returned but it wasn't reasonable. Or was it?

He pulled into the James River Memorial drive way and stopped after the first turn took him deeper into the cemetery. Memories of so many services for the freshly dead flooded back and took the place of Justin's horrifying image. Head stones of familiar names were everywhere. He helped them live and die and then rested them in peace.

Thinking again, he picked up the phone. "First things first. Stop any word, even rumors, of what just happened-muzzle Dominique Johnson. A quick call to her boss and the story will resemble a palmetto bug in a room full of loafers." Seth had wanted to squash the Justin boondoggle from the start so this would be a short conversation.

Vick changed some facts, left out others and told a thoroughly convincing lie about the illusion in Justin's living room. Seth nearly came through the phone after hearing the latest on what was turning into an outrageous hoax. His newsroom was being played.

"That son of a bitch is done. He's a heretic and maybe the antichrist for all I know. I swear, Vick, it ends here and now. I'll even bring in the legal staff if you think he's crossed that line. Nail him every which way possible."

"I feel the same way Seth but a legal move would also bring the church into it and times are too sensitive for that. Let's make sure it is over. Close the Justin file for good. Besides, you and I have to focus on the TV10 and LIFE launch. That's our priority. Justin is a speed bump. Right?"

"Indeed. But we flatten his butt right now. Talk with you soon," he told Vick and hung up.

"Damage control continues. The little blond from CSN was hysterical, nearly wrecked her car leaving the house. They won't run with it-too bizarre even for their fanatics." Made sense for the moment and he dismissed her.

"But what about Justin? He's so unpredictable and dangerous."

Vick opened the center console and pulled out the business card of a consultant with his Atlanta based financing syndicate. He punched in the number with a steady hand.

"Hello, it's me. This is not good news so I'll get right to it. There's an unexpected problem. Things have changed up here, you know, with the deacon I told you about. He's, well, he's out of my control now and I'm not sure what to do." He wished he'd not made the call, in this condition, without more thought. But there was no other possible action. He was turning it over to Atlanta.

"Well, he's threatening us," he said looking at the headstones of a husband and wife he'd buried five years earlier.

"Christ have mercy on us. Forgive me but I don't know how to deal with this," his heart raced, eyes welled up. "I'm only a man of the pulpit. What do you suggest we do about Justin?"

He listened for a minute and then hung up. Feeling as dead as all of those he'd buried out here, he realized that he'd sold his soul to network television.

* * * * *

Dominique left the Justin home in better condition than Vick but, still shaking, she headed back to the safety of the newsroom. Fortunately she hadn't vomited into her purse and ruined the tape recorder hidden inside. It was gold standard proof of the improvable.

"First the church supper film and now catching this on tape. He scared me sick. And that warning to ease up on the sleaze was very real. Pace yourself, kiddo."

Arriving at her desk, she saw a yellow sticky on the back of her chair with a one-sentence message written in a familiar scrawl.

"See me <u>now</u>. Seth," was all it said.

"Uh oh. There's another come to Jesus meeting in my immediate future. Fine by me. I just had a close encounter with the real deal and *this* tape is taking *this* story into the stratosphere," she thought walking to Seth's office with tape in hand and knocking on the door jam.

"Shut the door and have a seat," he commanded and pointed.

"Seth, you won't believe…" She started but stopped when he raised his hand like a traffic cop at a busy intersection.

"I know," he interrupted and stared her down.

"You know? You know what happened on Chaparral Avenue?" Dominique was dumbfounded but then realized Springwell had cut her off at the pass.

"Well, what took *you* so long? I got a call about it thirty minutes ago."

"Never mind that, Chief. Do you want to hear the tape of it?" she asked thinking he'd be curious.

"No, I don't want to hear it because it's not relevant. The story ends here and now. No more interviews, no more featurettes, no more debating religious locals. This is the type of hype that's nothing but trouble; run it and we'll look like we're piling on to make sure all the other stuff we've done look credible. Fact is, it ain't news anymore," he said the last five words tapping his fingers on the desk to make the point. "So, we won't run anything else on Justin or anyone connected with him. Period. End of story. Thirty. Understood?"

"Well, boss, what should a reporter do after witnessing *and* recording something impossible but as real as drug murders in Barton Heights? And don't raise that hand at me. I need to be heard on this." He didn't move so she continued.

"Seth, I've seen what nobody alive has *ever* seen. Now, you tell *me*, your number one street reporter, to walk away from it?"

"Listen to yourself, Dominique. You are raving. Now give me that tape and head down to Barton Heights. The usual violence in this city is back with a vengeance and your crew is ahead of you-double murder in an apartment. They are waiting on you. This city is waiting on you. Are we clear?" he replied with a slight smile and held out his hand to take the tape from her.

"Yeah, I heard about it," she quieted down and looked him in the eye.

"So tell me, chief. What's the real connection between you and Springwell?" she asked handing him the tape. "Is there some reason you're steering me away from Justin?"

Seth stood up so fast that the back of his legs slammed the chair against the office wall. For a moment he looked like he was coming across the desk to slam her against the wall too, but regained his sense of authority.

"Before I kick your ass out of my office let me tell you what this is really about. I'm a Christian and I happen to believe in the unbelievable. What you saw isn't so impossible if you know the Lord and know we are all his servants. But it has no place in this station. We aren't the zealots at CSN or the hayseeds at Radio Farmville. We deliver news. Our viewers expect car wrecks, politics, and murder. They want bad guys, good guys, and interviews with innocent bystanders. And they want it all in bite-size chunks. That's what we do and *you* do it better than any reporter in the market."

He pulled the chair back under his huge frame and sat again to finish the lecture.

"So, kiddo, your epiphany doesn't count here. Figure it out on your own dime. The bad guys are loose-dealing drugs, stealing cars, and killing fair citizens. That's your story. Any questions?"

She was on his last nerve and should have walked out but decided to stand her ground.

"Seth, you didn't answer the question. If I dug into it what would I find?" She asked in a quiet voice.

He avoided looking at her but answered.

"Vick Springwell has been my minister for twenty-five years. I've served him on committees, dozens of projects and we've been on international missions together. You see a lot in all those years." He had let his guard down and instantly regretted it. "So go do your damn job while you still have it."

She had heard enough to respect his threat.

"Yeah, boss, I will. Barton Heights calls. I'll have film at six for you," she replied and walked out with more questions than answers. She didn't know what Springwell had on him but it was material for certain.

"Maybe pictures, maybe witnesses, maybe worse. One thing's for sure, we don't want to dangle off that cliff again. He's pretty close to the edge," she thought as she picked up her purse and headed for the van again.

On the crime scene she developed the backstory of the Baton Heights murder victims through the eyes of their friends and neighbors, establishing the chain of emotions and facts by quiet conversation and instant trust. Somehow it seemed easier and more fluid with her emotions better controlled. But she missed her itchy-scratchy news bugs. They had made her the top grit-and-hit reporter in the city hadn't they?

“Not an itch or a twitch and I keep replaying that performance by Seth. You guys should be kicking the hell out of me on that one. We *know* there’s more to it. Man, I got no game without my cooties or…”

She thought about it for a moment.

“Or do I? “What did Justin do to me? To all of us?”

Chapter 24

Mark woke up the next morning with no sense of himself--conscious but unintelligent. Blank. He looked at the clock on his VCR-6:15. With that bit of information he came back to himself, identity and history intact.

"God I hate booting up like that. What a core dump--memories, emotions, and connections off loaded to God-knows where. What day is it?" He asked and then remembered that too.

"It's the Tuesday after Labor Day. Back to work, back to school, back to life between holidays. Living for the weekend. This is one of the most depressing days of the year," he thought as we swung his legs off the den couch. The TV was still on.

He thought about yesterday's visit to the hospital. Immediately after check in, he was answering all Louis' questions and only the headache with its irritating buzz remained after he came to. The MRI showed no brain change and X-rays showed his stomach was on the mend. Otherwise, he was bruised some and slightly dehydrated.

None of the test results explained the seizure. Louis chalked it up to the concussion and the stress of the press. After a saline IV, more observation, and a long nap, he was armed with a prescription for sleeping pills and Louis released him, again. He left St. Gertrude's in a fog but physically no worse for ware.

Charlotte hadn't disturbed him so, after 8 hours of deep sleep it was time to go to work and file the weekend's baggage deep in mass storage. Most of it was already there. He needed to go to work.

The shower helped but shampooing was painful. He would have to play through that and the whirllies-about the same as a moderate hangover but no funny fuzzy-navel memories with this one.

Just to be sure, he'd check with the doctor's opinion about going to work on a used concussion.

"You're going back to work? After what happened yesterday? Tell me you're kidding-it's a really bad idea. How can I get through to you? This ain't a muscle pull; you bruised your brain and I'm beginning to think it's a fairly small target." Louis scolded him.

"Just the facts lady and spare me the editorials. What's the problem with going to work for a few hours?"

"Try this on. You'll likely have a dizzy spell or two or maybe blackout without warning. You shouldn't drive for a couple of days or tax the precious few brain cells still operating up there. You ought to nurse this thing as much as possible, vacate the premises. Watch TV. The headache maybe gone but you're still hurt. You with me?"

"Loud and clear, Lou, but this was unexpected. I'm not covered at work."

"It was an unexpected *ass kicking*. As your doctor I'm telling you to take some time. The risk of a financial collapse may jump some but we shareholders gladly accept it. Are you going to listen to me or am I just wasting a valuable consult?"

"I hear you but I need to go in to set the rest of the week and I'll be out of there before lunch. How's that for a plan."

"It sucks but I'm not your nanny. Get Charlotte to drive you. You're a public nuisance on the highway. I'll stop by and harass you later. But my official advice is to stay right where you are, road hazard." and he hung up.

Mark ignored the doctor and headed to the office in the T-bird after Charlotte left for the morning. He lied to her about Lou's concerns and they agreed to meet back home for lunch. They both needed him to do something normal, if just until lunch.

Work is work but mainly it's a living and no one wants to work the day after Labor Day. Roger Stanley didn't hide any enthusiasm as they sat down for the usual staff meeting. Roger was a charismatic beam of joy after seeing the TV10 follow up and Mark asked him to keep it to himself until the meeting was over.

In thirty-five minutes the week was set,but his headache was back and that annoying buzz saw drifted in and out of his mental office.

As he adjourned the meeting he remembered Louis' warnings about a quickie blackout. Suddenly he felt hurt and isolated.

"This is not good. I hate it when Lou's right. So we'll keep this our secret but gentlemen, we need to get out of here. If I can check in with the boss, return a few calls and talk with Roger about filling in, I can get out before I pass out," he thought and rubbed his head. The pain increased another notch.

"If you pass out or do some kind of Jeckle & Hyde act in this building, it's the end of the world as we know it. So relax, focus, and get the hell out of here, hero." The Debating Society had taken a direct hit and was respectful enough to frighten him.

"On it, boys," he thought looking down at his desk.

"Boss, you all right?" Roger stuck his head in the door and saw his manager talking to a coffee cup on the desk.

"Yeah, yeah, never better but I've got to take a couple of days off. We need a quick level-set before I head home for a message and pedicure. I've got a headache that won't quit,"

"You were in the hospital over the weekend. I read about it. Some lunatic attacked you and they had you in for observation. I tried to call but couldn't get through. You have a concussion."

Mark opened the top drawer of his desk, dug four Advil out of the paper clip tray, and swigged them down with black coffee.

"Not a good move, chief. It's a contusion and that's a blood thinner you just chugged. It'll make things worse. Let's wrap it up and get you gone," Roger warned as he sat down in front of the desk.

"Thank you very much, doc. I'll have the MRI sent to your office. Wouldn't want a misdiagnosis."

"And I'll ignore that. You know we know the drill. So, just go home and let your grizzled veterans take charge. We can handle it and I'll call at the first sign of a renegade news letter or labor shortage," he kidded but Mark didn't appear to be paying attention.

"Really boss, you could have teleconferenced in and you'd be back on that couch watching Beavis and Butthead about now. You're heading out, right?"

"Just as soon as *I..I..I talk..talk..talk to..to..to Phil..Phil..Phil....*"

Mark heard the echo but didn't know where it came from. It was his voice reverberating through a Fender Champ amp in his brain. He wasn't sure if he talked or thought the words but the reverb-voice made his stomach fall straight to the floor and the little color he brought to the office drained out of his face.

"Mark, Mark, hey what's going on. Are you okay? Lean back for a minute. What's wrong with your eyes?" Roger reacted to Mark's new look and voice.

"*Close..close..close the..the..the door..door..door*," Mark's voice told him but Roger couldn't move. He had no idea who was sitting behind the desk.

Mark felt himself slipping away and tightened both hands around his chair's hard resin arms. "No floating away in here, have to stay put, no matter what," he thought without an echo.

"*I..I am..am..am here..here..here but..but..but not..not..not for..for..for long..long..long,*" he heard himself say or think but then focused on the next sentence.

"I..I..I won't..won't..won't let..let..let this..this..this happen..happen..happen again..again..again. Not..not..not here..here..here, not..not..not now..now..now." He willed himself and simultaneously felt the chair lifting off the floor.

He pressed down on the chair arms trying to stay grounded. As he felt his feet lift off the carpet he pressed his arms down with all his upper body strength.

And that was enough stress to cause his right wrist to pop and a blinding pain shot through his right arm and shoulder.

"Ow! Damn! It's broken!" he yelled and grabbed his wrist and stood up behind the desk. He turned to look back at the chair expecting it to float away but realized the reverb voice was gone as the chair banged off of the wall.

The fit was over. But Roger was staring at him, mouth agape, ghostly white, unnerved by whatever had just come over his boss.

“Je-sus Christ, almighty. Now you tell me what’s going on or I’ll have to call 911. Are you having a heart attack? Is that why you’re grabbing your arm like that? Can you talk to me?”

“No, really, I’m fine now. Well, not fine. I think my wrist is broken and my head nearly exploded but I’m good, really. No need to call anyone, I’ll do that in a minute,” he said rubbing his wrist and sitting back down. But Roger moved closer, unconvinced.

“Honestly, I need you to back off, doc. Just a little after-shock from the concussion, that’s all. It’s passed. I’m going to make it,” Mark said forcing an uneasy smile.

“Well you may be aces chief, but I’m not. I’ve got to go change my shorts after that performance. What the hell happened? It looked like you were going to rip the arms off your chair. And just what did you mean when you said you won’t be here much longer? Your voice was so distorted so, so…” he searched for a word, “evil.”

“Just take care of things for a couple of days and please keep the pressure on. We will get our collective asses kicked if we don’t finish on schedule. And catch the door for me.” Mark wanted to recoup alone.

“Okay boss. I’ll go back to my foxhole and I’ll be praying for you. By the way, I’ve had a concussion, two actually, courtesy of some homicidal linebackers. Had the headaches, whirllies, nausea but, just now, whatever that was, didn’t come from a concussion.” he said and thought about it.

“Whatever that was, boss, it does not belong here,” Roger warned and closed the office door as he left.

Mark stared at the closed door for a moment, realizing how right Roger was. He thought about changing his voice-mail greeting to say that he'd be back on return to this dimension but decided to leave the standard "Call someone who cares" message.

In less than five minutes he was out of the building and in the T-bird that whisked him home through light traffic. Charlotte was still out and he crawled into bed with one last thought.

"Don't want to float away in my sleep so I'll use my belt and strap my arm to the bedpost."

He turned over and yanked his belt off and struggled to warp it about the head post before falling asleep.

Two hours later he awoke in the same position, loosely tethered to the bedpost by an unbuckled belt.

"Hey, dog breath. You're supposed to be a pipeline for the wisdom from above," the Debating Society lectured. "We got nothing but a zombie tango here. Time for a new plan. The truth, whatever it is, is the answer. Wisdom flows from that river."

"Prophetically obtuse, boys, but you're barking up the wrong synapse," he answered as he swung his feet over the side of the bed and sat up.

Instantly the nausea and headache symptoms swept over him forcing a quick retreat back into the three pillows piled high for a soft landing.

"Looks like the truth will have to catch the next chopper out of the fire zone," he said closing his eyes and drifting away with visions of a war movie playing in his mind's eye.

The next time he awoke the whirllies were gone and his headache had subsided enough to head down stairs. He needed orange juice and peanuts in the worst way.

At first he walked past her and into the breakfast room. But stopped and backtracked into the hall. There she was, a striking brunette dressed in black sitting on the living room sofa, Bandit, their white cat, asleep at her side.

"Relax, home boy. Little Bandit can't sleep through a silent vowel so there's nothing to be afraid of here. And she is adorable."

Bandit stretched and purred, tail-flicked him, and curled back up.

"Ask her what her sign is?" the Debating Society advised.

She looked at him through large dark eyes, waiting for him to start the conversation. He was sure they'd met but he couldn't place her yet.

"Okay stranger, let's begin with who you are and how you got in here. Did Charlotte let you in?"

"It's just me and our furry friend here but I do have a message for you. Update your security. This place is not safe anymore."

"I can see that. But first, let me guess. You're either the Not-So-Grim Reaper or a very charming alarm salesman. Either way, it's time for you to go. Not a good morning for your pitch."

"Yeah, that's a killer headache, tension everywhere. I saw your aura on TV, all red and streaky, so I wanted to see it for real. TV distorts everybody but that's no secret."

"And how am I live?"

"You are still one very intense rainbow. Electric, beautiful, and sexy. I especially like the warm spot in the middle," she said walking around him to look 360.

"Thanks for that. So, have you ever *seen* Tom Cruise?" It was coming back to him.

"Yeah, I have. He's bright white and spiky. Energy from every orifice,"

"Lucky him. Anything else before you go?"

"Yes. I know you won't understand this but you're missing a wrapper and that's not good. You still beacon your power all over the place. That's how they will find you and it's also why you have fits like the last couple of days," she said hoping he would believe. "Hell of a signature, rainbow, and you've got to control it, especially when you're stressed out.

"It's you! You jumped in my van after the beach trip. I was hurt and depressed and was going to…" He stopped, embarrassed by the memories of the day twenty years earlier when he was about to drive his van off an I10 bridge near Houston.

"That was half a life ago, rainbow. But today, this day, the people near you need deadbolts and an alarm system in this house. Do not skimp and get it taken care of now. The outside too, all four sides, not just the front. Your lives are at stake," she said walking toward the back of the house.

He looked at the cat, now awake and looking back at him, then followed their mystery guest into the den. But she wasn't there and, assuming she was completing a security tour, he headed back to the living room.

"Bandit, where's your friend?"

Bandit just blinked, long-paw stretched across the sofa and curled up to catnap again.

"Right, not your problem."

"Hey, grape nuts, that's a real nice upgrade on your usual hallucinations-psychic stripper is a classic. But she is right, not real, but absolutely right; security sucks around here. Somehow she got in and out and so will they. Now, do exactly what she told you to do."

"But who is she?" he said out loud already thumbing through the phone book.

"'Who are they?' is the better question," The Debating Society warned.

Chapter 25

Charlotte answered the phone, cold and indifferent. Mark's double hospitalization had turned her into the Dragon Lady and nothing got past her.

But Dominique couldn't sleep, eat and hadn't thought of anything else in the past forty-eight hours. She had to talk about it. She had to see him.

"But I really need to talk with him. Will you let him know I'd like a few minutes?"

"You've had more than a few. Didn't you get the memo? Stalking him isn't news anymore."

"But you don't understand…"

"It's okay honey. I'll finish it," Mark interrupted after picking up the other phone. But it wasn't okay with Charlotte.

"Dominique, you are a leech, not worth his time or attention so, Mark, get this over. I mean it." And she hung up.

"I can't take another interview, Dominique. I just don't have the energy and Charlotte doesn't make idle threats.

"And that's not why I called. I'm just glad to hear your voice. You were in pretty bad shape the last time I saw you. It's not all my fault, Mark. I wasn't the only one."

"What difference does it make?"

"Because it's personal, not TV. It's about you and me, not the stupid story. That died a wicked death Monday afternoon in your living room. I really need to talk to you about what you became. You know, what you did to us."

"In that case we don't have anything to talk about. The last thing I remember was Vick walking into the living room. After that the world went white and a chain saw took off my head," he said recalling the blank space in his life and rubbing the left side of his head.

"I came to in the hospital with a killer headache and thirsty enough to chug the James River. All I know is that Vick and BJ ran out in a panic and you left a lovely parting gift on our living room rug. You want to tell me what happened in between?"

"You have no idea. It's driving me crazy," she said.

"Must be guilt. That rug will never be the same."

"Careful Mark. I'll change my mind and let you figure this out by yourself. Be nice. But, just one business question. Have you heard any more from CSN?"

"No, nada, and I'm getting the silent treatment from everyone else. I've heard from all of the groups that invited me to speak---"

"And they all cancelled." She finished his sentence.

"How'd you know? So, can you tell me why I've been banned in Richmond?"

"Yes I can and a lot more if you'll meet me at your front door in thirty minutes?"

"Sure. I can't wait to be enlightened but do not bring the TV10 van."

"I promise. The story is as dead as your speaking career. Took you a total of ninety seconds to kill it the other day. Check your driveway. I'll be in my own very ordinary Honda." She hung up.

During the drive over Dominique decided it would be the last time she'd set foot in his house. In fact, it would be the last time she'd ever talk to Justin. Off her chest but not out of her life, there was no getting past it; he had turned her inside out.

To reach the family room they had to walk past the living room and just a glance was enough to make her shiver; the ghost in there was too real.

"I will never set foot in this house again," she swore to herself.

"Mark, we both know the story imploded. It's too unbelievable. You really don't know how incredible you are, do you? Did anyone suggest hypnotism or other techniques to make you remember what happened?" she asked as they sat on a comfortable overstuffed couch.

"Nope. Only the three of you know and I'm beginning to think I'd better off if we called it a night right now. Was it really so bad? Did I flash Bobbie Jean or moon Vick?"

"I wish. That would be news. But you were more creative than that. First you dazzled us, then scared us and, in the end, we believed."

"Believed what?"

"You'll see. I'll tell you everything then I'm leaving; out of your life for good. I'm only going to do this once so listen up."

And she began describing the details of what she and the others had witnessed in his living room two days earlier.

"Your face, my God, Mark, your face. You had no eyes, only white orbs glaring at us like a zombie. You were unrecognizable, transformed and possessed, like a devil or an angel." Now she was crying but continued.

"We were terrified. And then you spoke in a voice that made me know you are not evil, Mark Justin. You are not a demon."

She told the rest of the story through tears, body quakes and a trembling voice.

"Quiet yourselves and free your minds. Listen perfectly," Mark had said facing them.

Then, cradled and lifted by invisible hands, he slowly rose above the sofa. Still in the same sitting position, without moving a muscle, he floated to the center of the living room.

"Don't fear me; fear what you have become. Each of you has reach, influence, but you harm so many you profess to help," the specter of Mark warned.

Slowly floating up, turning his gaze to Dominique

"Stop exploiting them for your own celebrity. To rein in the violence you hate expose the source. It can be stopped. You know how to purge your vermin. Do it now," he commanded.

Dominique had felt a sudden wave of nausea break over her throat. She dropped to her knees and heaved lunch on the living room rug. She tried to get up but another convulsion spewed more of the contents of her stomach on to the floor. Gasping to recover, she looked up to follow Mark's levitation.

Floating higher and looking at Springwell

"Your plans are ruinous. Cleanse your spirit and ego. You will not be warned again."

A dark streak appeared on the minister's pants and ran down his right leg. The warm and wet sensation of his own urine jolted him out of a stupor and he began back peddling toward the hall.

Hovering just below the ceiling and turning his head toward Bobbie Jean.

"Your revenge is pitiful. Contempt surrounds you. Let it go and regain your life. Your friend is your charge," he said to her.

Gazing down at all of them

"Leave this home and family. Lead with love," he said and began to descend back toward the sofa, posed in the same sitting position, eyes still turned backward.

"And as gently as a feather, you floated down onto the back of the sofa," she said to end the story.

Mark just starred and didn't respond.

"Yeah. Stunning ain't it. That's why I tossed my lunch all over your living room rug. You were powerful beyond words. Beyond us," she said as the memory overwhelmed her again.

"I'm shaking, Mark, I'm shaking so hard I can hardly stay in my skin. Give me a moment."

She took five Lamaze-type cleansing breaths and then continued.

"What I saw was not you. I mean it could not have been you in there. I mean … I think the Lord took you," she said in a quiet voice as tears streamed from both eyes.

"Remember your little Thursday night after-dinner speech? Your point about helping Miss Daisy by giving up yourself?

Well, I didn't have a bloody clue what you were talking then but now I do. I get it real good now," she said smiling and wiping the tears from her cheeks.

Mark returned her smile not knowing how to answer.

"And just so you don't think I'm a total hack I got a little news flash for you. It is all on tape."

"You recorded it, Mr. Butterfield?"

She nodded but didn't understand the Watergate reference.

"That's fantastic. Play it. You owe me that, Dominique. I mean, even if I can't believe it, I do want to face it."

"I know it's weird to hear me talk about you when you weren't you but that's what happened and I want you to face it too. That's the only reason I'm here." Her voice was breaking up but she continued.

"Now just sit there and let me play this thing," she said. "I've been too afraid by myself but I think I can take it if you're with me. It took me two days to get up the nerve," she was trembling.

"Where was it? I never saw you turn it on."

"In my purse near the top. You were a little busy terrifying us at the time. I duped one for the boss but he refused to play it. He and Springwell shut the whole thing down. I bet this is the first time anyone's heard it," she said hesitating, rethinking her next move.

"I gotta warn you. I may have to stop it or leave the room or something. I don't know how much I can take."

She pressed the play button.

Silence.

More silence.

They looked up from the recorder but didn't speak. Finally, the first sound.

"Uh, uh, oh no." It was Dominique's voice followed by gutturals, "huwaa… aah… bluwaa… bluhaa… gup,gup... huwaa…" followed by splattering and more gulping.

She grabbed the recorder and punched the 'off' button but didn't look up.

"Now *that* is Pulitzer Prize material. In a world of nonbelievers, this changes everything," Mark's sarcasm rang through his old radio voice.

But she wasn't fazed.

"Don't you see? This confirms it. The Lord's voice would never be recorded. Everybody knows that," she said like it was a *Reader's Digest* factoid.

"That's absurd, Dominique. I guess He only shops retail and everyone knows that too. It has got to be my turn now?"

"Sure, try to spin me but it won't make any difference. I know what I saw and know what you did. Nothing changes the truth.

"But do you honestly believe I channeled the Almighty, became a white-eyed levitating Archangel and made you barf on my rug?"

"He used you to save us."

"But what if I told you that I've done something like this before. Under extreme duress I sometimes manipulate, kind of collect and direct forces I don't understand. Would it make more sense?"

"Hell no. Now who's being absurd? What a stretch. I'd have to believe in *you* instead of God."

"But truth doesn't depend on belief, right? What I'm saying is that I had no other way out. The three of you were attacking us, Charlotte and me. My head whirled and buzzed, and suddenly I actually felt my life pour out on the floor. The next thing I know I'm in the hospital. But in between something unbelievable occurred. I can explain it and you can't."

"Oh yeah. Like I'm supposed to believe that when the shit hits the fan you become some kind of time-space distortion wizard? Is that supposed to be the truth?

“No, not time and space, just matter. You know, bodies in motion changing without apparent cause.”

Mark had never confessed before, never told anyone the first word about his power but it was time to see how it played.

“Well, you were about to get grilled. That’s for damn sure. We were coming after you,” she said and looked into his eyes for a clue.

“But if you were unconscious how did you control the show? And you’re voice. It’s been recorded hundreds of times but not this time. Can’t explain that can you.”

He couldn’t.

“So, I’m going with God on this one and getting the hell out of here. But you accomplished the mission; zero threats, no accusations and the nosy reporters are all gone. Nothing left but me tossing cookies on a tape and two worthless eyewitnesses,” she said pointing to the recorder.

“You win, Mark. And the Lord wouldn’t have it any other way.” She smiled, more relieved than she thought possible.

“You’re safe because of truth unbelievable and unreportable. Not bad.”

She stood up, ready to exit and never come back.

“So what’s the lesson, Dominique? Knowing which West End take-out to avoid for lunch?”

“Not funny but I do thank you. I’m so much more corrupt than I ever imagined and you and God were crystal clear. We have to change or face the consequences.”

She stopped just outside the front door and turned back to point a finger in his direction.

“And if you ever do remember, don’t call me. I came over here to clear my mind, to get over it. I’m moving on-not coming back under any circumstance. You got a problem with that?”

“No ma’am. And I’ll make it easy-you are now officially blocked.” He pointed a finger back.

"Goodbye Mark. And by the way, you bet your ass it would have been a Pulitzer if I could report it," she said and walked down the stairs to the driveway.

As he watched her drive away a new tune popped up from the Unknown Zone, slow and clear with major guitar chords, an orchestra led by the violin section, and the voice of Moody Blues singer, Justin Hayward,

Just because you say it doesn't make it so.
The truth is that the truth is not for you to know.
So spare me the facts you say are indisputable,
What's true for you ain't true for me
I'm not that gullible.

The violin interlude filled and then faded.

So spread your lies and hypnotize those who hear your song.
Paint them a picture so right it can't be wrong.
Make your fame off pain and shame,
For you it's just a show.
But just because you make it,
Just because you fake it,
Just because you say it,
Doesn't make it so.

"That's a good one, boys."

But right now he needed Charlotte's reaction to Dominique's wild tale and she listened without interrupting except for a delightful laugh when he explained what was on the tape recorder.

"That's certifiable. All of it. You can't believe it," she said.

"I really don't know what happened but that doesn't make her a liar. Truth doesn't need belief, does it?"

"No, dear, but I do. I *have* to believe something about all of this. I'm the one that slapped you out of a coma when it was all over. So, even if I was making coffee and missed something, I sure as hell don't believe that yarn," she said and sat up to make her next point.

“Sounds like she had food poisoning with attendant hallucinations. Really, she couldn’t tell the difference between a bright light and chunky soup. I know you and a levitating oracle is not your style,” she said and put her arm around his neck to pull him closer.

She gave him a long goodnight kiss and settled back in bed knowing Dominique’s story was finally, officially over.

“Hey, deacon dumbass?” The Debating Society chirped up, “You are never going to know if you’re a demon, an angel or just a worthless hole card. Conscrew it anyway you want but truth and reality don’t know aces from deuces. Find them and look ‘em in the eye. Everything else is noise. Vick and Bobbie Jean were there. They know the facts and that’s truth without insulation?”

Too tired to understand what they meant or to argue the point, he shut them down and buried himself under the covers. But he was afraid again. Afraid there s no way back to normal or worse, no way to stop becoming the thing he had dreaded all his life.

When she was asleep, he slipped out of bed and crept downstairs to sleep on the couch. Deciding not to turn on the usual TV weather blather, it was nearly 4:00 AM when the vintage sitcom themes and visions of a simpler time finally lead the way to sleep.

Chapter 26

Even on a busy street their house was an easy mark. Contractors in white panel vans on Chaparral Ave. were as common as city sparrows and the crew from Atlanta shot all the necessary film from a near by parking spot. The patterns and habits of the targets were the usual working couple routines set in stone through years traversing the American middle class.

But there was celebrity to consider with the Justin's. Accidents and daytime hits were messy and obvious followed by publicity, investigation, trial and, usually, conviction. In this case, disappearance was the outcome of choice-mysterious and clean.

Their additional security, internal alarms and basic trips on the outside, was likely a coincidence. A minor concern in any case. It never ceased to amaze him how security companies could install inside touch pads near glass doors or windows-easy pickins for a high-resolution camera filming the punch-in code. Security was a state of mind anyway and this couple had invested badly.

The interior would be like all the rest in this old neighborhood but he scheduled a Pest Terminators survey to map the particulars. Now they knew the house inside and out.

Their objective was to subdue, kidnap and dispose of the targets. The Great Dismal Swamp was the final destination; a short drive with easy access to the wetland home of so many hungry hosts. The locals would put their best Missing Persons team on it and the media would have a field day but the evidence would point in no direction at all. Nothing from nothing leaves nothing, simple and effective. For the sleeping targets the price for screwing around with the Lord was about to go up.

At 4:00 AM on that moonless Wednesday night two figures sprinted out of the shadows, crossed Chaparral under bright streetlights and leaped a tilty fence onto a manicured front lawn. The cicada *wee-ahhs* overwhelmed all sounds and the giant Maples cast shadows across the property. Was there ever a better cover? No, but the brick, still hot from the summer sun, prevented their heat sensitive field glasses from seeing the targets inside. Always trade offs-never perfection.

The new outside laser-trips were invisible to the naked eye but had nearly blinded the technician wearing sensor goggles during the survey the night before. They blazed across the front of the house, webbed in neat squares, but only one slim beam was set up on the driveway side-a fatal oversight that established their entry point.

The porch light had been red-flagged by the survey team and Pest Terminators had loosened the bulb that afternoon. But it was shining bright now. Someone had noticed, tightened or replaced it. A minor problem unless that someone was waiting inside, armed and dangerous, observing their approach,

It was a burden to think of the world as full of assassins. Had this been his home, the team would be dead, detected and killed a few seconds after they stepped into the yard. But the targets were a danger to someone else, not this team. He stood on his partner's back and flicked the porch light half-a-twist to put it out and they retreated back in the shadows to observe the house. Nothing moved and the cicadas still sang.

But there were risks inside-the alarm system was not the worst of them. Creaky oak floors were impossible to silence. The crew knew there was a good chance the targets would hear them, even scramble out of bed to call the cops if time allowed. It wouldn't. They were using tasers and tranquilizers for a quick and numbing strike.

There was no gun in the side table drawer, not even a baseball bat by the bed, no weapons at all. So after they jimmied the deadbolt and disarmed the alarm, he would sprint up the stairs and electrocute both occupants before the cobwebs cleared. No bloodshed and a 30-second getaway once the house was secured.

Go time.

The door unlocked with ease and a bit of WD40 kept it from creaking. The thing he had most worried about, a change in the alarm code since filming, hadn't happened. They were inside, in the middle of the house, without a sound.

But they had been felt.

Mark wasn't armed but he had been underestimated and rolled off the couch on to his hands and knees, connecting with the invaders instantly, sensing their movement 20 feet down the hall. He heard a rush of quiet footfalls running up the stairs but also a quiet footstep remaining in the hallway.

"Two to kill us," he felt more than thought.

Panic so intense he couldn't hold back the scream, a bloody murder scream, swept him away. He leaped over the island counter and into the kitchen on the dead run.

"Ahhhhhhhhhh! You sons of bitches! Charlotte!"

Something grazed his head, and a stunning pain shot through his body but it also lit up the hall enough for him to aim and launch his 190 lb. frame into a surprised invader.

The target became a missile and body slammed the would-be assassin with the force of dead weight times thrust. It sounded and felt like a small bomb had detonated as they crashed into the hall table, crushing it against the wall below the staircase. The brass candlestick collection added metal to the chaos of splintering wood and bodies thundering onto the floor.

Upstairs, standing in the bedroom doorway, the leader fired his taser into the sleeping targets at the same moment as all hell broke loose down below. But he had no time to consider why they weren't convulsing in super-charged spasms or what had gone wrong with his quiet assassination.

"Get out of my house!" Charlotte screamed and rammed him on a dead run with a huge pillow. She didn't stop pushing until he tumbled off the first tier of stairs.

"Shitabrick!" He yelled, ripping the pillow from her hands just before slamming into the wall of the upper landing, sending another quake through the house. But the old plaster didn't budge, it hit back hard and he collapsed to tumble down the flight of stairs he had just run up.

Mark couldn't move but he didn't have to. As he twitched from the effect of one taser probe delivering its shock through his right ear, images of burning buildings, a firestorm engulfing a town, people running, screaming, clothes on fire, covered his vision.

And the hit team was with him. From beside his withering body in the hall, the assassin he had crushed began crying out in pain.

"I'm on fire! God, I'm on fire! Sssshhhiiiitttt! Help me, Tommy!" He screamed as if awakening in a crematorium. Getting to his feet he began jumping up and down touching the ceiling with each crazed leap. But there were no flames, just the searing pain of burning alive.

From the landing at the bottom of the stairs, even through the pain of a broken arm, Tommy felt the flames ignite, cover him and smelled his flesh burning all so suddenly that had no sense other than screaming and running for his life.

Both assassins slammed into the front door of the inferno, shrieking about fire and help and God, grasping for the handle while Mark lay on the floor still twitching.

Through the flames Tommy twisted the deadbolt and opened the door. Nearly dead, face melting, hands charred into black nubs he leaped for the outside, running through the night screaming incoherently for God to have mercy on his soul. His partner ran behind, flailing and wailing-no words for the pain.

Just as Tommy burst through the fence, running right through it, the getaway van skidded to a stop in front of the house and the panel door slid open. No one exited but both assassins dove through the open door and it slammed closed as the van peeled out. It turned the corner at the end of the block and accelerated; the engine noise fading beyond the neighborhood in a few seconds.

The entire confrontation lasted 45 seconds, exactly what the crew had practiced for entry, control and abduction. But somehow the assassins had become the victims, screaming and rolling around on the floor of the van until it was miles away from the house.

Regaining their senses and realizing they were not charbroiled, both men cried like babies until the crew tranquilized them with the needles meant for Mark and Charlotte.

As professionals their careers ended that night. No workman's comp in this business; both were capped shortly after the failed job.

Mark groaned.

The high-pitched head ringing was as bad as the old chain saw but less threatening. He stopped twitching and began to relax.

"Are we winning?" He asked as Charlotte removed the taser probe from his ear. It had torn through and seared a small hole mid lob.

"Stay down a second and let me check outside."

As calmly as she could, Charlotte walked onto the front stoop to be sure their attackers were as gone as the quiet night implied.

"Everything okay over there?" Neighbor Jack called from his stoop next door.

"Yeah. What the heck was that? Animal control?" She yelled back, nearly in shock, leaning on the rail.

"No clue. Sounded like 2 hyenas in heat. Probably a couple drunk kids from party central over there." He pointed toward the University and then waved good night stepping back into his house. Neither had seen the Justin's splintered fence boards, scattered on the sidewalk, lost in the shadows.

She helped Mark to the living room sofa where he had nearly died three days ago. He was alert this time but the daily assaults were taking their toll.

"Was that an assassination attempt?" She asked as they sat.

"They didn't want to kill us with those things. Damn it Mark, they were kidnapping us. That is *totally* insane. Why would anyone do that?" She asked the unanswerable.

"Hey beautiful." He looked at her with clearing eyes. "You knew."

“Right. If I had known don’t you think the cops would have been here and tasered their ass? No, I just hated the porch bulb being loose. That was part of the set up but this was plain luck. I got out of bed to check on you and there the asshole was in the doorway trying to kill me. So I shoved his hit-man ass with a pillow and watched him bounce off the walls.” She was surprised how good it felt to remember it.

“But what did *you* do? Send them to hell?”

“That was the idea. The taser dropped me like a boat anchor and I guess I did what any basket case licking the floor would do.”

“I doubt that, dear. Those guys were pros; planned this down to the second and you turned them into screaming weenies. That’s a new one,” she said and stroked his wounded ear.

“You’re getting stronger.” She felt more secure than she had in a long time.

“I’m also wising up. No cops, okay?” Mark didn’t return the smile.

“No blinking lights, no news vans, no stories. We handle this one. Those guys won’t come back but that doesn’t mean we’re safe. We need a plan,” he said rubbing his ear. “You think it’s going to leave a mark?”

She looked over at the smashed table in the hall and shook her head.

“Guaran-damn-teed.” Charlotte felt the change in both of them.

“This is our war now and they have surprised us for the last damn time. But we do need one more recruit,” he said looking at the stain in the Oriental rug.

Chapter 27

The Chippendale style card table stored in the basement made a return appearance in the hall and the clean up was done in a few minutes. Then Mark left a semi-controlled voice-mail with the security firm about the gap inside their patented 'ring of protection'.

"So, how do we take it to them? By land, sea or air? And exactly who is it we're taking it to?" Charlotte asked over a fresh cup of coffee.

"There are only two groups we've crossed that are rich enough to hire a team like those guys and that's another reason to leave the cops out of it. They won't believe either CSN or Springwell's LIFE Network are behind this. But I've seen his numbers; they're going for a national market. He's fronting some big bucks and big wigs and they don't take kindly to strangers threatening their project."

He saw her shiver, as if a bug crawled up her back, and held her closer.

"And there's no doubt that CSN was gunning for us too-doesn't matter they've gone silent. If Bobbie Jean convinced them I'm the anti-Christ they might try something like this. Seems extreme though, even for them. It means the network leaders decided to put everything on the line, commit a high-risk crime, imprison us and maybe film or document the deprogramming of an unholy deacon? Hard to believe but fanatics run on passion and those guys believe in their work."

"So we're going after both of them? You sure we want to do that?"

"Nope, but some conversation won't hurt. Let's see who's most surprised to see my mug in their portico. And there is one person we should tell about the hit."

"We said no cops *and* no media, especially her." Charlotte read his mind.

"She can't report it but she will help smoke 'em out. But, first things first. I gotta see Vick."

* * * * *

"Good morning Mr. Justin. I'm so glad you're feeling better." Virginia Bartell, Vick's gatekeeper, coffee fetcher, and appointment secretary, answered with genuine affection and continued.

"I know your calling for Dr. Springwell but I just have to tell you. I witnessed you praying for Daisy. I felt the power too, tingly, like a surge of love, or something like that. It was a miracle. I don't care what they say. And I hope it changes others around here too." She stopped, realizing more than one line had been crossed.

"Oh just listen to me, I'm sorry. I need to mind my own beeswax. He's in his office. I'll ring him for you. God blessed you, Mark."

"God bless you too, Mrs. Bartell."

The transfer took more than ten seconds. "He's thinking about it."

"Mark? I'm between meetings and I don't have much time but I do want to know how your recovery is going."

"Well thanks, Vick. I'm feeling some better but the concussion is keeping me out of work for a couple of days. Nothing I can't shake off but I would like to discuss our Monday meeting. Can you spare about thirty minutes later today or tomorrow?"

Silence.

"Vick? I just want to understand what happened. It won't take even thirty minutes, get your insight and that will be the end of it."

"You, uh, don't know? You don't remember?" Vick's usual strong voice had a tremor.

"No, that's not it at all," Mark lied. "But I've talked with Dominique and her version varies some from mine so I wanted to talk it over. You were so upset and left in such a panic. I want a chance to make things right, that's all."

"That's kind of you, Mark, but I'm hardly the issue here. We agreed to manage press relations together and I was shocked to see those two reporters in your living room. Besides, I understand they've dropped the whole thing." Vick found his footing at the mention of the media.

"Yeah, looks like they have; like someone was going to yank their FCC license if they didn't." Mark fished for a reaction.

"Oh? That's quite a rumor. How did you hear about it?"

"Just a hunch, that's all and there have actually been some fresh inquiries." Mark lied again to keep Vick on the defensive. "Can I tell you more about it tomorrow morning?"

"I'm not sure I have anything to more say. It's old news but there's no reason I can't talk with one of my deacons so let's make it early. How about 9:00?"

"Sounds good and, for the record, this will be our final discussion about it. As Charlotte reminded me, 'It's time to move on.'"

"Good advice, Mark, so let's do just that and more importantly we'll discuss the other leadership options I've been working on for you. It's time to get into the LIFE project and we have some opportunities that need your commitment. I've prayed a lot since Monday and I know you're the right choice. So get some rest and we'll talk for a few minutes in the morning. Good bye." Vick hung up leaving Mark looking into the phone.

"Other options? For what, Elder of Perpetual Irritation?" Vick had frustrated him again but The Debating Society had an answer.

"Hey, fireball, remember the punks you nuked a few hours ago? If *he* sent them, you're talking to a steely-eyed stone cold killer. If not, he just tossed you a fig leaf or an olive branch. Whatever, somehow we are back on track for VickTV, the fresh little network that's taking the moral high ground to a new low. So, get a grip. You got fanatics coming out of every orifice."

“Great imagery, boys. Always good to hear from a bunch of synaptic split ends. I gotta lie down.”

“You know we’re always here to help in the little ways we can. So bottom line, miracle boy, you can either bind, gag and beat a confession out of him or lube up and sing Onward Christian Soldiers in his network fantasy. Bad options. We think you’d better find door number three.”

“You don’t get it. There is no hole to crawl into. This is our fight and we take it to him tomorrow. But we really need a plan.”

“If we’re gonna to stick it to the man,” they whispered back.

He was exhausted from all of it-the healings, the beating, the transfiguration, the tassing, the Debating Society; only Charlotte was real and she was likely drilling and filling at the moment. With that reassuring thought he crawled on all fours to the den couch hoping he would sleep into the next century.

* * * * *

The phone rang and startled him out of a numbingly deep nap but by the time he reached the phone he at least knew who he was.

“Mark, it’s Bobbie Jean. Figured it was time we talked. You got a minute?”

“Whoa there a second. Out of thin air you call to check my pulse?”

After an awkward silence she spoke up.

“It’s not like that at all and please don’t fight with me. I don’t have the stomach for it. You terrified me and I can’t take it again. I called to finish the story, okay?”

“So how’s this for suspense and drama? Does CSN want to kidnap and torture me into some kind of confession? Is that your headline?” He had no pretense left.

She began sobbing. “Please, please don’t attack me. You said revenge is killing me and I believe you. For God’s sake, Mark, I just want to be what you told me to be!”

She was sincere and about to dissolve.

“No killer here, boss. Check your phone log under Springwell,” the Debating Society stated the obvious.

“I’m sorry BJ. I know you’re afraid and I won’t do it again, I promise. In fact, let’s start over. What can I do for you?”

“Just listen to me. I’m kind of desperate here,” she said swallowing hard to regain some composure.

“What you did, what you became, was right out of the scriptures, New Testament, Luke and Mark, testimonials of Christ’s post crucifixion appearances. I’m serious, directly out of the Bible. I found them, they’re in the King James Version.”

“Stop it, BJ. You’re saying I morphed into Jesus Christ. Can’t you go with time travel or a parallel universe, something more plausible than becoming the Lord.”

“Mark, every time I close my eyes I see you in your Christ-form and hear the words. Your eyes, how you floated above us, and then the warning. You warned each of us about our sins.” She almost broke down again.

“Don’t you understand? I’m one of the chosen. Until this week I’ve been in a state of hate and loathing for twenty years. It’s all that mattered and it killed my career, my dreams-never good enough. But Monday you freed me; warned by God’s own angel. I got a long way to go but I know how to be saved. In Christ’s name I pray, Amen.”

And hearing her prayer, a part of Mark gave in, understood it was beyond him. He’d started it, tried to stop it, and now was going to be taken by it. Whatever happened Monday had run over his ass but it was the beginning, not the end. He had to find some control.

“… and I’m developing your faith journey for a CSN series. I’ve covered everything with my producers and they’d prefer film and eyewitness reports, but doesn’t matter. We believe your transformation started with Miss Daisy and *continues* to evolve. There’s no more talk about fraud or exploitation. Lord, I’m so sorry about that. We took the wrong path.

“All’s forgiven, BJ. Let’s just forget it.”

"Didn't you hear me? You are a phenomenon and we want the nation to know it. So we're going with a new version of Chamber's original storyline, *An Accident Of Faith*. We're still working on the production details but CSN is totally inspired and committed to it. It's going to air just as soon as we're ready," she said as if he had already signed on.

"Now you are hallucinating. I know you're sincere but it's not going to happen. You and the guys at the Christian Saturation Network will have to find another poster boy."

"We are serious about this, Mark. Monday was not just another day at the office. It's my calling and we are running with it. You *are* CSN. Your life, our lives, everything changed in the middle of Grant Avenue a couple of Sunday's back. And now all we want is a chance to tell your story, not crucify you."

Silence.

She had to back off before he brought the wrath of God back for an encore.

"Okay, that's my pitch and you deserve some time to noodle it. But now you're going to love how I make your day 100% better. No conditions, only a phone call. Can you write down a number?"

"Sure but---" She didn't let him finish the question.

"It's in Norfolk. Dial it in thirty minutes. You got that? I gotta go,"

"Yes but---" She interrupted him again.

"Just do it. You're needed again. You'll understand when you call. We'll talk later." She hung up leaving him staring at the phone.

For the next thirty minutes Mark analyzed everything about Bobbie Jean's delirium and what the Christian Sewer Network had planned for him. Her new 'calling' was a needed change but dangerous for him. He could only handle a one-front war so it had to stop. The network hack on this next call would be toast.

"Hey, Mark. You're right on schedule. Got someone here who wants to talk with you."

“This is a courtesy call BJ. Don’t get your hopes up. I won’t have a statement for you or anyone at CSN and I strongly disagree with your intentions.”

“Well deacon, I assure you my intentions are honorable. Lookit, I barely made it out of Central America and so how about some sympathy for an old war-horse.”

“John? John Chambers is that you? Hot damn, you’re back!” They found your ornery hide.”

“And I love you too. But I’m a little worse for ware. Broke my back and was nearly prime rib for the local felines. Can’t walk, don’t know if I ever will. They stabilized me in Guatemala City and now I’m here in Norfolk General.”

“But you are alive, man. Fantastic! I can’t believe it. We’d given up but I hate that you’re hurt so bad. What can I do to help?”

“Just tell your story to BJ. She’s my legs now. Oh, hang on a sec.”

He stopped to thank the nurse for the morphine pump and her smile.

“I’m counting my blessings just being alive. All night lying in a washed out creek bed paralyzed and terrified knowing I’d be fully conscious when they tore me apart. Never known fear like that. Life changing, deacon, life changing,” he said breathing harder as he recalled the ordeal.

“That was the worst of it-layin’ there waiting to be eaten alive and praying for a miracle. My prayers were answered the next day when my pilot returned with the posse. Right then and there I promised the Lord that I wouldn’t whine no matter how bad I was hurt. I was that close to being the main course in a jungle buffet.” he finished.

“John, I’m blown away. Think about it. Rescued from a rescue mission. That’s just the kind of story the network should promote.”

“Working on it as we speak-a tribute to the two who didn’t make it and those who came back for me, but let’s you and I cut through the chaff. This joy juice is kicking in so here's the deal," Chambers paused for dramatic effect and continued.

"Lookit. We are a mess, you and me, so let's face our problems together. From the git-go I knew your gift was divinely guided and it's going to get stronger as you accept it. That's the way God works. So, numero uno, you are now the human technology of faith. Believe it. Numero two, forget the usual self-analysis, your pea brain can't comprehend it and you'll just get in the way. Are you with me so far?"

"Not really. But, John, I know who the bad guys are now and I'm working on a plan."

"Who gives a rat's ass?" John blurted without thinking. "Oh God, I'm sorry Mark. It's the drugs, really, I'd never yank your plank like that. Oh, wow, there's another one. I'm talking like a hack on crack. Just say you'll forgive me, and we'll keep 'er goin'."

"Sure John. Calm down. I understand but I don't agree. Okay?"

"Hardly relevant. You're being snatched up, used and recycled for reasons known only by the Almighty. To some of us it's a wonderful thing, for others it's sacrilege, and to the fringe on both sides you are extremely dangerous. Worry about those last two groups because it's as clear as moonshine in a mason jar, they'll hurt you before they hear you."

Mark said nothing, amazed at how close John had come to the truth.

"And besides, my friend, it looks to me like you got exactly what you ordered from the Lord."

"Alright, now you are delirious, John. I never asked for this. I'm losing touch with reality and I'm not sure if I'm good or evil. A guy at work said I even *sounded* evil. I didn't ask for this torture."

"Sure you did, deacon. It's the wisdom from above. No doubt about it. Ain't that a hoot. For years you've prayed and primped and then demanded it. Well, now you got it. Get it?"

"No, well, yes. Hell, I don't know."

"Lookit, for the last time, it's not about you anymore. Just like me, there ain't no going back. The fat is cast. You've got to *feel* your way through it, from heart to soul. I swear. It's wisdom from above. Embrace it."

"Fine then. Fine as frog hair, John. But I can't just lay naked in the road mumbling a bible verse waiting to save somebody. I need a plan. What am I supposed to do next?"

"Hey, jeese, I'm not your personal coach. I'm just a reporter with insightful commentary and drug induced euphoria," he said as the phone slipped from his hand and fell on the bed. He was about to pass out.

"Mark, lookit, you gotta remember one thing. You, my friend, must turn and face the power. Yeah, that's it all right. Turn and face the power. Amen." He paused for effect. "How's that for a big finish?" But started talking to someone in the room before Mark could answer.

"They're telling me it's time for my a sponge bath with Nurse Myhinney or Myhoney. Matters not. They are all gorgeous. Gotta go. Call me tomorrow. I've extended office hours and cut my rates for you."

The line went dead.

Chapter 28

Feeling sad, alone and tired Mark hung up the phone and walked into the living room to rest on the sofa. Thank God John was alive but his sermon had been exhausting. It was time to resume naptime.

When he opened his eyes again the room was flooded with setting sunlight that intensified the wood grains in their antique furniture as well as the bright dyes in the oriental rugs.

"Perfect illumination," he observed and smiled, feeling refreshed.

The loud bell-buzz of the front doorbell spoiled the moment.

He didn't try the peephole, the sun would blind him, but when he opened the door the effect was nearly the same, strong western sunshine on a 100-degree late summer afternoon. He had to put his hand up to deflect it.

"Sorry to drop in like this Mark but I'm not able to take our meeting tomorrow morning so I hope you have a few minutes this afternoon. Should I have called first?" asked the familiar voice of Vick Springwell.

"Vick. I can't see a thing in this bright sun but I'd know those golden tones anywhere. Come on in and cool off. It's hot enough to melt the hide off a Gila monster."

"It's that and more but this won't take long. Is Charlotte in too?" Vick asked walking into living room. He took a seat in the early nineteenth century wing chair.

"Yeah, she's just come in and changing, I think. She'll probably be down to thank you for whatever it is you've done to get us back to normal. We assumed it was you that cancelled the speaking gigs I had lined up, right?" Mark asked trying to catch Vick off guard.

Vick sat back and raised a hand toward Mark. The wing chair framed him so that he appeared to be on a royal throne.

"That's right, deacon and I've come because once you showed me your true form I had to return to the scene of the blasphemy and settle this. I'm going to be blunt with you because I can't stomach what's happening in the name of my church. While I was gone and in direct contradiction to policy, you and that former assistant minister of mine had a field day with the media," Vick paused and sat forward to make the next point.

"Policy must rule or anarchy reigns." he said and sat back again in the tall chair to continue.

"Three days ago I came here to minister to you and how was I received? You and your heinous alter ego trashed my ministry, scared the piss out of me, and sent me running out of here in shame and humiliation. It's unacceptable to leave things that way." he said and leaned forward again to confront Mark.

"I believe that you were then and remain evil-possessed and must to be stopped. I'm here to test you and end this mockery of God's work. So go ahead; roll your eyes upside down, fly around the room and try to frighten me with more machinations straight from hell. Try to stop the exhumation of evil if you can. But I am here to teach you a lesson for the ages and will not fail." Vick said in quiet rage as he extended his arm and pointed a menacing finger in Mark's direction.

Then he contorted his face into a crazed mask, with wide wild eyes darting back and forth from Mark to the finger he pointed at Mark.

"Defixionum. Verispiro. Magniluminato." He uttered the three Latin words and then repeated them two times slowly.

After the third sequence, a spot of white light appeared on the tip of his pointed finger. Quickly the light radiated backward to include his fingernail and the end joint.

He smiled and said the three words again.

The light responded by becoming a slender white ray that began extending from his finger steadily across the room toward Mark.

"Vick, that's a nice light saber. Where do you keep the batteries for something like that?" Mark quipped as he moved down the couch trying to buy some time to form a counter strategy.

The beam moved with him and closed to within three feet.

"This is the light of Bethany and it is for your trial, deacon," Vick said as the light spike from his finger changed from white to fire engine red.

"Trial? What are you talking about? Bethany is where Christ appeared after the crucifixion. What do I possibly have to do with the last appearance of Christ?" Mark asked watching the red beam now ten feet long and waving within inches of him.

"God, Christ, and the Holy Spirit are separate forces joined in a governance of the universe. They are always good but not always together," Vick lectured as he maneuvered the beam toward Mark's head.

"This is Light of Truth that Christ left on earth when he ascended into heaven. It is the power Moses used to part the Red Sea. Christ used it to calm the stormy Sea of Galilee and to heal the infirmed and blind. He last used it to remain among the living after his resurrection and before his ascendance." Vick's crazed eyes followed the light to his target.

"He told us, 'I am the light of the world. He that followeth me shall not walk in darkness but have the light of life,'" Vick quoted the well-known bible verse and continued the ceremony.

"I am one of many chosen through the ages and taught by descendents of Christ's disciples to acquire the light and purge darkness from this world. The light you see will not hurt the innocent, the pure, or the uncorrupt. If you are virtuous, you have nothing to fear. If your power emanates from evil, the light will dissect you as it enters."

Vick grinned and stood up from the chair for a better attack angle. He planned to pierce Mark's throat and permanently mute the heretic.

Mark retreated to the end of the sofa and finally came to his senses.

"Alright, Vick, take your best shot and then we're going to see how it works when I turn it around and drill you with it," he said and sat up looking directly at the end of the beam.

It was about to touch his throat when Charlotte's footsteps hit the top of the stairs.

"Vick, is that you? I thought you'd never come back in this house but I'm glad---" She stopped the greeting as soon as she saw the bizarre situation in the living room.

"Charlotte, go back!" Mark yelled but she didn't move.

"Vick? What are you doing? What is that thing?" she asked startled by the red shaft of light threatening Mark.

Vick didn't turn to answer. Without taking his eyes from Mark, he pivoted his arm ninety degrees toward her voice. The beam grew five feet longer as it sliced through the air and painted her just below both knees.

The light looked harmless gliding across her legs but the red ray worked like a penetrating laser cutting cleanly through both bones without breaking the skin. There was no incision, no blood, and no way of knowing that her legs had been severed just below the knee.

"Mark! What happened? I can't keep my balance! Help me!"

She tried to bend and catch herself but her worthless legs couldn't lean toward the banister. Instead she fell backward with her lower legs and feet remaining on the step until her back slammed down on a higher stair. Legs flailing lifelessly and hands grasping air, she began tumbling down the steps.

Mark leaped from the sofa to run to the staircase. He could save her if he got there fast enough.

"Charlotte, Grab the railing! Grab it now!" he yelled as he ran across the room.

But she couldn't slow her momentum any more than he could reach out and catch her. Instead he heard a series of fracturing thumps, thuds, and quick gasping sounds as she flopped from stair to stair. He saw her hands reach out, desperate to stop, but failing to grab and hold anything down to the bottom.

An instant after she slid off the last step they met face to face on the small landing at the bottom of the stairs. Blood leaked from her mouth and ears and her head was cocked at a fatal angle against the closet door. Worst of all Mark was looking directly into her gorgeous green eyes. Eyes that didn't see anymore, that stared past him, past them and into the next life.

He tried to think of a prayer that would bring her back but no words came.

"She was not so pure as you thought, deacon. The Lord has dispatched her and shown you to be nothing more than Satan's right hand. Your punishment is to lose her, who you loved and corrupted. So sayeth the Lord, so shall it be," Vick preached as he looked down on Mark and Charlotte.

Mark ignored the minister's deranged judgment and picked up Charlotte's limp hand.

He looked into her eyes but they didn't look back. He knew she was gone, knew the best part of his life was dead and that he was alone. Hopeless.

He began to cry like he had wanted to cry earlier in the day when he talked with John Chambers. There was no reason to hold back now so he cried from his lungs, like he had as a three year old in mid-tantrum.

The tears gushed from his eyes and on to Charlotte's lifeless hand.

He tried to look into her face again but the flood of tears blinded his view. The world was a watery blur so he used his shirt to wipe his eyes over and over until… the antique furniture across the room came into focus.

Mark woke up sitting on the living room sofa wiping his face with his shirttail. Although instantly aware that it had all been a bad dream, he couldn't stop crying. He tried but coughed uncontrollably so he kept crying, crying because it felt so damn good.

As she came into the house through the side door Charlotte heard him sobbing but didn't know whether to run into the living room or tiptoe in quietly. She decided to peek in first hoping he was laughing not crying hysterically.

Mark saw her red hair and face and the relief intensified his crying. He couldn't stop bawling into his shirt and calling her name.

She couldn't believe her eyes.

"Oh no, Mark. How many flavors does this thing come in? Now you're having a breakdown too? Let's pull you together now," she said and sat next to him speaking softly, trying to get his attention.

"I'm here, honey, right here. We can get through this and if you want to cry, make it a river," she said, as her own tears couldn't be stopped either.

Mark tucked his head into her and kept crying, blubbering something unintelligible about a red light from Bath and Beauty that had cut her legs off.

"It's okay. I'm fine, never better, except my husband can't find the exit door from the Twilight Zone. Mark, honey, it's okay. If this is the way out for you let it go and cry your brains out. It works for some of us."

Gently rubbing his shoulders, they sobbed together, not afraid anymore, but together.

He gradually calmed down and ten minutes later was in the bathroom washing his face.

"Wow. You just bawled your eyes out because an imaginary death ray cut up your wife. That, you poor slob, was a 5-star catharsis," he said to his mirror image and continued. "It's like I turned myself inside out, hosed me down and flushed four decades of self pity out of the system," he said understanding why he felt better.

“Maybe a spiritual enema? Is that it?” The Debating Society asked.

“Don’t start, boys. Take a synaptic siesta or better yet, a cruise to oblongata. But give it a rest,” he replied into the mirror and leaned over the sink.

“Why don’t I look more like Tom Cruise? I really should. That would be so cool.”

He looked closer to discover if there was any trace of TC looking back when, out of thin air, without a sound, another face appeared next to his head. He gasped for air as a shot of screaming terror tore through his body and heart-pounding fear returned.

Vick was there, beside him, eyes closed, in repose, a stiff corpse in a thousand dollar suit. But as real as his own image.

“I’m awake. I know I’m awake so you can’t be there. For Christ’s sake, please leave me alone,” he whispered to them both.

The eyes of Vick’s image snapped open, locked on and jolted him again. They were black and soulless, meant to see him die.

“You cannot have me.”

“Too late.”

In self-defense Mark squeezed his eyes shut so tight the pain of the concussion buzzed back and he blacked out for a moment but held on to the sink as he crumbled to the floor.

Moments later he opened his eyes. Vick-in-death was gone.

“So, we’ll be shaving in the shower from now on?” Debating Society humor didn’t help when the lesson just learned was so devastating.

“I can’t trust what I’m seeing when I’m awake and my dreams are as real as everything else. Damn it all, I am losing myself.”

Chapter 29

Mark awoke the next morning with the bright sun of a bluebird day lighting the room. He had crawled into bed twelve hours ago and sleep did what it does best, a port in the storm. He felt nearly normal but the pit in his stomach reminded him of the meeting this morning with Vick.

"So here's the plan. We'll chat about my scaring the hell out of him on Monday and that, dear friends, will set the stage for a good deed to be done," he thought, admiring his new plan.

"The Right Reverend Jerry Tinsler will have his position back after Vick calls him and explains how it was all a mistake, a misunderstanding. I may have to convince him again but he believed me Monday (Did he really wet himself?) and now he's got to get religion about it," Mark felt the risk in his gut but ignored it.

"Count on it, genius. And we'd like you to meet the Chance Brothers, Tiny and Getouttatown. That's not a plan; it's a fantasy. Vick ain't rolling over for you or anyone else. Could even be another hit in your future," warned The Debating Society.

"You may be right, boys but I have to make a run at him. If he takes Jerry back I'll join the VickTV cast in my off hours. That's the deal. I'll be on the inside of the scam to keep Dominique in the loop so we can break it open at a time of our choosing. It's the old inside-outside strategy and a damn good plan," he thought as a cold sweat popped up just below his hairline.

He'd wait until after the meeting to cover it with Charlotte.

"Maybe I look more like TC today. That would be a hellofa boost." He smiled but didn't look in the mirror as he dressed for the confrontation.

* * * * *

The moment he arrived at church the aura of the place tugged on his confidence. The dead preachers lined up along the wall waited but he walked past without acknowledging their stares. He thought about praying in the sanctuary before heading to Vick's office upstairs but kept walking through the Narthex and up to Vick's outer office.

"If God's not already on point in this mission then I'll be out of here with my tail between my legs in less than fifteen minutes. But I know I'm right. Vick's a bully, maybe worse, and it's time to face him, he thought and remembered John Chambers' advice.

"'Turn and face the power.'" Very cool, John."

"Hello there, Mark," Virginia Bartell walked from around her desk and gave him a big hug. "It's good to see looking so fresh and rested but your young so we'd expect you to bounce right back. And just in time. There are some big changes brewing. He'll be right out," she teased.

Virginia's desk was gossip central at Commonwealth Church.

"So before I get the word, tell me what's really going on around here." Mark assumed she was talking about Vick's canning the assistant minister, Jerry Tinsler.

"It's so exciting. Channel 10 is talking with Vick about a Sunday morning news show and they're going with an ensemble cast. He's mentioned you as part of the on-camera talent. It's going to be taped and slotted as the lead in for the *Sunday Morning* network show," she whispered excitedly close to his ear.

"Wow, I'm impressed Mrs. Bartell. You've got the lingo down pretty good but I'm sure he didn't mean me. I'm looking to leave the Directorate in a few months and I want to talk with him about that this morning. In any case, I'm flattered to be considered if that's the case," Mark replied giving her another fresh piece of gossip.

"What? But Mark, that's not the plan. You were an anchor, you have the experience and we know you're just right for this project." She was surprised but recovered quickly.

"Oh, listen to me. I shouldn't gab so much and don't let on we chatted about this. He'll lay it out in his own way," she said and pressed the intercom button to announce him.

"I'll be right out," said the voice in the box.

"That voice, so smooth, so cool. He has got to go down," Mark thought as goose bumps covered his body.

Vick opened his office door and walked out, hand extended to greet his wayward deacon. Bright white teeth highlighted his insincere smile. He was a tall man, impeccably dressed with a Rush Limbaugh power tie atop a Brooks Brothers white shirt inside a Saks Fifth Avenue black wool suit. Alive and smiling he looked nothing like the death-image in the bathroom mirror.

He took Mark's right hand firmly and pressed his left across its back in an extra friendly hand-over-hand shake.

"Mark, you look great. Come on in and Virginia, will you bring us some coffee? We've got to be in and out in about twenty minutes but that's plenty of time for a cup of Joe, don't you think?" he asked knowing the answer.

"Yes sir. I'll be right in with a tray," she replied but didn't leave her seat.

"Come on in Mark we have quite a bit to cover," Vick said as they entered his office and closed the door.

Mark noticed the second line on Vick's phone light up.

"She's spreading the word. Now it's show time," he thought.

"Vick, I just wanted to go back over---"

"Mark, if you don't mind I'd rather not reexamine what happened Monday. I have no explanations. It was completely out of my realm of experience. It was spectacular and supernatural, maybe divine, maybe not. I don't know so unless you're here to tell me it's a continuing problem, I think we do what we said on the phone, move on."

"On to what?" He regretted giving up control as soon as he asked.

“Well it depends on how you want to be involved. It’s also why I was dropping by to see you Monday. We are calling it Phase One of the LIFE Campaign I discussed a few weeks ago with the Directorate. We are about launch it. I’ve been working with Seth Griggs at TV10 News. Our idea is to air a weekly program of Richmond area stories from a Christian perspective. We’ll team some of our leadership with reporters at TV10 to create a kind of grass roots talent mix. Are you interested in where you fit into that picture?”

“After what I did on Monday, why would you trust me with the heart of the project?”

“Because *that* was your message to me. You’ll be elected an Elder on the Directorate for a three-year term and your primary assignment will be to work with me on media and non-ecumenical communications. You’ll chair a new committee, External Communications, with a scope and mission covering TV, radio, the papers, you know, the media.” As Vick paused to let it sink in, a polite knock on his door broke the silence.

“Here’s some fresh java for you. It’s 9:20. Do you want me to ring you in ten minutes?”

“Yes, but we’ll be done by then. Thank you, Mrs. Bartell,” Vick said excusing her.

“That’s quite a post, Vick. You sure I’ll manage my power to your advantage?” Mark asked knowing that time to play his cards was running out.

“You love this church like I do and it adores you. So will our viewers. We need you to connect, to lead, to be the face they trust. You’ve done it all along, with a smile or a handshake, a lot of ways, but this week you became a star. Don’t you see it, Mark? Your past meets your future. You have experience and now celebrity. That’s why you are the perfect anchor for our flagship news show. Let’s turn your energy and talent toward LIFE, not to intimidate or threaten, but to educate and inform. That’s our mission,” Vick said and then leaned forward to speak quietly.

“I understand what you told me to do the other day in your house when you were about 6 feet above the floor. You told me to clean up my act. Well, that’s what I’m trying to do now. Can’t we agree on that?” He asked.

“You may fire when ready Mr. Justin. Time for the magic,” he thought.

“No, Vick I don’t think so. If you were cleaning up your act Jerry would be here discussing this with us right now. When are you going to take care of that?”

“With the package we gave him Jerry will prosper, be in a church of his own soon enough. I assure you that he and his family are being treated more than fairly.”

“Well I’m not so sure so here’s *my* deal. I’d like you to immediately reinstate him and, in exchange, I’ll not walk into the middle of Sunday service, levitate about fifteen feet above the congregation, and discuss the inadequacies of your ministry,” Mark said in a far more threatening way than he had intended.

Vick twitched a smile, expecting Mark’s gambit.

“Alright Mark, if you won’t play it my way you can walk out of here just like Jerry did, a rebel with a cause. But you’ll not intimidate me in this office with threats like that.” Vick leaned back, clasped his hands together and pointed steepled index fingers at Mark.

“Imagine the aftermath of that little scene. Think about your career, your family life, and the home you’ve so comfortably made. Personally I think it would be devastating,” he said and then leaned back to continue.

“We’d have a true demonic possession on our hands wouldn’t we? And you’d be attacking the spiritual leader of the church like some kind of fiendish antichrist. You *know* I would meet it head on. You *know* I’d be in the pulpit the next week with more media attention than we’ve ever seen. And you *know* that you’d be banned from the church, probably all churches except for the Satanic cults. That’s not the path you want to take, Mark. It will backfire, big time.” He said with the confidence of a ‘check mate’ declaration.

Mark believed it; saw the logic and consequence. Besides, he'd never been able to control himself to that degree.

"When am I going to learn that playing poker with Vick is like trying to swim up Niagara Falls," he thought but didn't respond.

Vick took the lack of response as surrender and continued.

"So, now that we have that out of the way, my offer still stands. You can help us spread the word on a weekly TV show or go your own self destructive way. It's your call." Vick tapped an index finger on the desk and looked at his watch.

Mark just stared at him for a moment. They both knew the meeting was over but instead of folding, Mark tried his bluff one more time.

"I understand the consequences for both of us, Vick. Do you really believe the membership would stay with you if something like that happened in the sanctuary? If a thousand members were told by an Archangel not to return to this church?"

"I won't quibble with your vision but let's just say I'm willing to take that chance. Are you?" Vick responded and then lightened up for his final appeal to Mark.

"Come on Mark. Join the team. You've proved so much in the past two weeks. The church needs your leadership and we have the right plan to take advantage of all your talents. Regardless of what happened in your house four days ago, your on-air experience makes you the man for this job. So please give it serious thought. I'm offering you a win-win proposition." He finished and stood up behind his desk.

"I'm sorry but I do have to go to my next meeting. I'll see you again Sunday for a few minutes after the service. I'll need your answer then. This is about to happen with or without you so please pray on it and let me know your decision this week," Vick said with the warmth of a father talking to his wayward son.

Mark stood up and extended a hand of friendship toward Vick. "You're right Vick. It is a good time to rethink old commitments and future moves.

Vick took his hand, shook it, and moved around the desk to see him to the door.

"I know you've been through a lot, we both have, but all of it for a reason. God's purpose for us right now is to join forces in LIFE Network. You won't ever regret it, Mark," Vick said with a fatherly pat on the shoulder.

"Oh, please tell Charlotte that I send my best and that we're looking forward to her leadership in Circle Ten this year. She and I really do need to get caught up soon. Maybe I'll drop by on the way home one day, if that's okay with you." Vick smiled and emphasized the last word by pointing a finger at Mark.

"Sure, our door is always open (*don't point that finger at me unless you mean to use it*). See you Sunday,"

But Vick didn't return the salutation. His office door was already closing and Mark was already off his radar.

"Mr. Justin, it's none of my business but I really hope you'll reconsider and work with Vick on the new committee and TV show. I just know it's right up your alley," Virginia encouraged him.

"Thanks for the coffee and confidence Mrs. Bartell," Mark said returning her smile as the phone rang.

"Oh, hello Mr. Griggs. Yes, he's right here and expecting your call. I'm connecting you now. And have a good day, sir," she replied and held a hand up as a signal for Mark to stop in his tracks. She quickly introduced the call to Vick and hung up.

"You may not know who that was but they've been talking a lot lately and I bet they're talking about you right now," she said with such schoolgirl impishness he wanted to slap her silly but encouraged her instead.

"Was that Seth Griggs from TV10?"

"Looks like you got the picture," she replied and smiled at her play on words.

"Yes ma'am, in Technicolor," he said and waved her off as he turned to leave.

He walked through the Hall of Dead Preachers feeling their eyes and sly smiles. They knew one of their own had just kicked his ass.

"With us." A whisper told him.

He turned to face them; looking, listening, threatened, goose bumps on every pore.

"Who? Who's with you," he whispered back.

"The pretender, Judas," the walls and air replied.

Mark wasn't sure if the voice was from the hall or in his head.

"Me? Vick?" He needed one more exchange.

"Soon," was the answer so soft it could have been a breeze from an open window.

"Talking to the dead preachers? You are beginning to worry us," the Debating Society broke his concentration.

"Yeah? Well who are you guys?"

Nothing heard, he turned and ran out of the building.

Driving home he tried to understand the dead preachers' cryptic message while also decoding Vick's conversation. "He knows your soft spot, ace. It's a real plum. Almost too good to be true." The Debating Society summed up.

"Hold it right there Deacon Dimwad. There are no new committees. And if a Channel 10 news show was in the works, don't you think Dominique would have mentioned it?" Mark realized his wasn't the only bluff.

"Vick, you are a piece of work and I fell for every word of it. There is no committee or anchor seat in the new network. In less than 30 days you'll take me aside for a heart-to-heart, apologize for the change of plans and explain that my real assignment is on the Stewardship Committee, begging the membership for LIFE Network pledges. By that time I'll be fully co-opted like the rest of your sheep," he reasoned out loud while idling in the driveway.

"That, dear friends, is elegant. And the disinformation to Mrs. Bartell-he knew she would bait me. Nice touch, but she *never* knows what's really going on." He smiled and cut off the engine.

"But he's been warned about this kind of crap. In Vick's world there are no threats only risks to be managed. The minister's gambit," he thought as he entered the house.

It was 9:45. The headache was back and throbbing. "How long does it take to get over a concussion?"

Chapter 30

At that same time, Seth Griggs had an even bigger headache. Like every other department manager at WVTV he was under pressure to cut his budget, again. He tried to move Springwell's thirty-minute Sunday morning show, *LIFE in Action*, out of News but Entertainment didn't want it and couldn't afford it. So, if Vick's project was going to air, News was going to pay for it and Seth was $250,000 short.

"I keep coming back to the same problem-a gold plated thirty minutes. Can't call it news, it's religion. Can't jack up advertising to make margins. And it's not the only PSA we have to air. My bottom line can't take it unless I cut some real news programming."

He squeezed the pencil hard enough to snap it in half.

"Damnation. I can't fit ten pounds of this kaka in my five-pound bag. He's got to scale it back. All I can handle is a few two-minute vignettes during the Sunday morning national pickups. Better yet, let's forget about it this year and we'll both pitch it in the spring."

He looked up to check the time. Budgets were due by 10:00 and the final drafts would be done by the end of the day. He had thirty minutes to figure it out.

"Okay let's compromise. I think I can squeeze in a half dozen of the Commonwealth spots and maybe that will keep him off my back. No matter what, I've got to make plan and this still gives him more face time than any preacher in town. We'll see what his holiness thinks about it tonight. He can do what he wants with the dirt he's got on me but he can't change the economics of the deal," he swore barely able to control his temper.

"He'd better not screw with me. This is a damn good alternative. In fact, he'd better show me some love for sticking my neck out this far." And with another click it was e-mailed the to Finance.

"What's done is done so get over it preacher," he thought as he picked up the phone to call Vick and confirm the meeting for tonight.

"This won't be a love fest so maybe we'd better meet somewhere off the beaten path like the station's little safe house outside of town. But I'm telling you Seth ole son, this cloak and dagger shit has got to stop. You're no 007. More like a 747." He thought as Mrs. Bartell answered the phone and forwarded his call on to Vick.

"Vick, Seth here. How's it going?"

"Very good as long as you're calling to say we're ready to send out the press release. I just met with Justin and he's a bit confused but he won't stay that way for long. He has the power to derail the whole project so we've got to get it in motion. Do you need any more encouragement?"

"No sir. That's why I'm calling. It's a done deal and I want to cover the details with you tonight? I've got a long day here but when it's over we can meet and draft the press release."

"I'm truly blessed to have you as a partner, my friend. We're set on corporate donations and God bless your fine station for coming through on production. I'll meet whenever and wherever you tell me. And don't worry about Justin. He's controllable and won't dare come after us once we are on the air."

"Sounds like you got it covered, preacher. By the way, let's not discuss this meeting with anyone just yet. The budget won't be set until late today and I'll have the final word tonight."

Uneasy but ready to do anything to launch LIFE, Vick agreed.

* * * * *

Driving out to the meeting so late Vick smelled the proverbial rat but the stench didn't matter now. His investors were pressing for a short-term 'pilot' strategy that would let them track ratings, demographics, run it by focus groups and fine-tune before syndication. If the numbers were decent the cable network launch would follow. They also warned that the funding window was about to close.

He couldn't afford to let Seth talk him into another delay.

"I hate to do it and hope it won't come to this but I have to get through to him. He knows I can ruin him with the New Orleans evidence but he doesn't believe I'll use it. Seth, my friend, this time I'm not bluffing. We launch or that stuff shows up in the worst places. Let us pray you don't force my hand."

"Lord, please let him believe me and please forgive me for the despicable act I'm considering. It is for Your glory. I know I am wrong but, Lord, the end will justify it. And, I know You are with me," he prayed out loud as he turned into the driveway.

The WVTV safe house was an out of the way two-bedroom saltbox that the station kept for interviews, witnesses, and sources the News Department didn't want to reveal. It was nearly midnight when he arrived.

He realized that Seth was actually *hiding* the meeting out here. For a second he wanted to turn around, drive home, and reschedule to a very public lunch at a window table in the Strawberry Street Café. But his TV show was right there, in that little house, and he was going in to get it.

"This is all too Mickey Spillane for me," he though as he parked behind Seth's car and looked around the yard, leaning over to see behind the bushes that lined the sidewalk. "No assassins or bogey men." He was on his own.

"Vick, it's good to see you. Let me pour you some sherry," Seth greeted him at the door. "Nothing heavy, just a little nip to celebrate," Seth said as he crossed the room to a Southern hunt board with several decanters and cut glass demitasse cups on a large silver platter. It was his third little nip.

"No thanks friend, but help yourself," Vick said. "This is a tidy little place for the station to keep. Nicely decorated too but why are we meeting here and why so late? Why not your office or mine?"

"Actually it was a gift to the station. Occasionally a reporter makes the big time and the guy that did this never forgot us, even after he went national. But he's not on camera any more, hell, he's not even above ground so let's us get down to brass tacks." Seth ignored Vick's questions and sat down on the overstuffed couch as he motioned Vick to sit in the matching wingchair.

"Like so many decisions we have to make, there's good news and bad. The bad is that we can't include the thirty-minute show in the Sunday morning line up. We made the final adjustments today and my budget was just too thin-warned you about that."

Vick was surprised at Seth's bottom line bluntness but didn't react and let him continue.

"Now, the good news is that I peeled off some PSA money and we can combine that with your funds to produce several sixty-second stories featuring your community projects. You can use the studio and up to six hours of production time with everything taped for rebroadcast. And I think there's syndication potential to boot. That'll make a nice package, don't you think?" he asked hoping for a quick agreement and exit.

"Well, Seth, that is not our direction, not even close and I'm very disappointed. It's the continuity of thirty minutes every week that we need and it's the only way we'll get our message across. This just won't do and you have to rethink it. This *is* God's work; it's for the children. Tell me, what could be more important than spreading the Word to the least among us?"

"I love the children too, pastor, and I would cleave them all to my bosom if I could. But there is just no way News has the kind of money to partner with you on a weekly show like this, no matter if Jesus Christ Almighty personally ordered it on Pay per View."

"Well, perhaps He did, Seth. We've already talked about that unbelievable sign and warning I got earlier this week," Vick said recalling Justin's transformation and threat.

Seth nodded, "Yes, but…"

"You weren't there. *You* didn't see what Justin became. I'm telling you I don't know if he's the devil, an angel or The

Creature from the Black Lagoon but this morning he walked into my office and threatened a repeat performance in the middle of my Sunday service. Imagine that scene-his body hovering above the congregation, damning them to hell-in-a-hand-basket. It would literally scare half of them to death. I can't let that happen. So, I lied to him to buy some time," Vick said and returned to his original point.

"Now listen to me. We've got to find a way to air the show *in its entirety*. It's for the church and the community. Eventually it's for national syndication. You know I'm under a lot of pressure here, we have investors to consider, and I'm sorry I can't compromise anymore. You don't have a choice. Understand?"

"Oh yeah, I get it alright. Justin's got you by the balls and you've got me on film with my dick hanging out in New Orleans. We all have our problems don't we?" Seth said standing up and walking toward the door. He was desperate.

"Come on Vick, let's go have some coffee at your house. It's not far and I think we need some air and a change of venue. You can drop me off back here when we're done." He said looking at the stunned preacher.

"My house? Now? Are you kidding?"

"No sir, dead serious. We've prayed in your chapel before."

"Well, yes but…"

"Like you said Vick, I didn't see Justin do his thing but I am convinced. You're scared, threatened by God knows what, and now you're threatening me with blackmail. Don't you see how out of control we are? We need help right now. We've got to pray together and ask for guidance and forgiveness. Your chapel is the only place I know where we can calmly think this through and make our peace," he said and opened the door. "You got a better idea?"

"Yeah. Let's do the show. That's why I'm here and my mind is made up about it." Vick stood up, walked across the room, poured two glasses of sherry and offer one to Seth.

“Come on partner. Don’t be so short sighted. We’ll make it nondenominational to be sure it’s syndicated. A thirty-minute show is the draw, not a bunch of PSAs. It’ll be a huge success for TV10 and the beginning of a bigger vision. Everybody’s a winner with it. All you have to do is bend the budget a bit. Besides, if you need more matching funds I’m sure I can make the arrangements. It’s just a matter of moving the dollars around. We are so close, let’s make it happen,” he said and flashed the smile that had closed a thousand sermons. “Let’s toast a new beginning shall we?”

“You know Vick, you could sell sand to the Arabs.” Seth took the glass and seemed to give in. “You’ll need to pony up another quarter mil and take the lead when we pitch it *and* you’ll have to show how it’s accretive to earnings. That’s a tall order, even for you. Assuming all that, I’m still not comfortable. It’s such a huge commitment for us this year. So I really want to pray about it in your chapel. Do you mind if we do that?”

Vick’s smile disappeared. “I guess not but I don’t understand your sudden need for prayer. It’s just a business deal not a life or death decision and *I’m* the one on the hook for 250 grand. So what’s you’re problem?”

“No problem, just looking for confirmation and guidance from above, that’s all. You won’t deny me that will you?”

“Well, before we go, let’s seal the deal with a toast, Mr. News Director.” Vick said as he raised his glass. “Here’s to a partnership for Christ, community and cable,” he said, proud of turning the phrase.

“Here’s mud in your eye.” Seth returned the toast and took both empty glasses back to the kitchen, rinsed them and returned them to their place on the silver tray.

“Shall we?” he asked walking toward the door.

“If you insist but let’s make it quick. We’ve got a long day tomorrow,” Vick said as they walked out the door and onto the front stoop.

“Wow. Check the fog. That came up quick.” Seth said looking into the fog through the veil of a far away street lamp.

"Doesn't matter one whit, my friend. I know the road like the Lord's Prayer. Hop in."

And they sped off into the clouds.

Chapter 31

3:30 a.m.-the phone rang loud and harsh in their bedroom.

Mark and Charlotte sat up simultaneously, both panicked, knowing it was the call every baby boomer fears. A parent in cardiac arrest or down with a broken hip or stroked-out; the dreaded hairpin turn from minding your own middle age to daily care and deathwatch. They had been discussing 'the call' quite a bit lately.

Mark shimmied out of bed and answered it.

"Dominique? What? No, what? Have I heard? Jesus! It's o'dark thirty. I'm not even awake. Why are you calling?" he asked and sat down on the blanket chest in front of the bed.

Charlotte pulled a pillow over her head, angry but secure in the knowledge that her mother was safely asleep in her own bed too.

"Look, I need to move to another phone. Can I call you back? Yeah, okay, if you have to but give me… Okay, I'll be on the front porch waiting." He hung up and grabbed a shirt and some shorts before walking out of the room.

On his way out the front door he yelled up the stairs to Charlotte.

"Hon, it's going to hit the fan again. You'd better unplug the phone. I'll explain later." He heard her footsteps hit the floor and he headed outside to wait for Dominique.

The summer night was stifling, like walking into a hot wet mattress. Not a leaf stirred in the muggy air and the cicadas' pulsating *wee-ahhs* signaled a temperature still over eighty degrees.

"Even at 4:00 a.m. the heat won't retreat. Shorter days bring warmer nights. How's that possible?" he was about to answer when she pulled into the driveway.

“Thanks for not bringing the van,” he said and waved to her as she stopped next to the walkway. She was in no mood for etiquette and didn’t return the greeting.

“Now that is a angry mug. Take us to Def Con Four boys and stand by for incoming,” he told his crew as he watched her tense expression.

“So what calamity brings you back to Sleepy Hollow? Forty eight hours ago you swore on my stained rug you’d never be back.”

“Vick Springwell was in an auto accident three hours ago and taken to MCV Hospital. He’s in a coma and listed in critical condition. He may not make it,” she said as if reading from a teleprompter.

Mark lost his breath and legs. His life energy gushed out through his belly button onto the stoop and he grabbed the banister to cushion his fall as he sat down heavily on the first step.

“I’ve been there since we heard about it just after 1:00 so I’m pretty far ahead of you. Just stay with me. I need to know if you’ve talked with Vick since he ran out of your living room Monday afternoon,” she asked pointing to the front door.

“I’m, I’m, damn it,” he stammered shaking his head, “He’s been in an accident? You don’t think I had a hand in it, do you? I mean his family, the church, his life. So many people depend on him. Was Marlene hurt?” He asked, shaking his head, still not looking at her.

“Answer my question first.”

“We talked eighteen hours ago. Now, tell me what is going on.”

Dominique sat on the brick stoop but didn’t want to comfort him.

“Looks like a routine single car accident on his way home from working late, appeared to be alone. There’s some dense fog out that way and he might have fallen asleep or swerved to avoid something in the road. You got any information on it?”

"Me?" Now he looked at her.

"You cannot be serious. I may be a lot of stuff but psycho-killer is not on the list yet. Believe me this is just another episode from the Justin corner of the Twilight Zone." He said and looked away.

"Is the family with him?"

"Marlene and their three sons were there but gone home for the night except Marlene. She's dazed and confused. Totaled his car. Hit a tree head on at high speed. From the pictures it looks like he's lucky to be above room temperature. So, are you gonna answer my question or do we have a problem?"

"Sure. I talked with him twice, but I won't say another word until you prove this conversation is not being recorded from your purse *and* you tell me why I'm getting the third degree at 4:00 Saturday morning."

"All right, I'll show you mine then you show me yours," she said without smiling and opened her purse.

"Nothing there, just me and you. Satisfied? Sorry to be so grim but you're in this pretty deep," she warned and then continued. "I probably ought to call the cops and tell them you're material to all of this. I know what I witnessed here-your messages were prophecy. There is no doubt in my heart or soul about that. You told Vick there would be no more warnings. In my book that's a threat," she said ready to make her final point and stood up.

"The way I see it, miracles happen and shit happens. And it's pretty easy to tell the difference. So give me some reassurance that neither you nor some other form of you had anything to do with Vick's car running off a road he's driven a thousand times."

"Alright, for the record, except for dinner up the street at Lee's, Charlotte and I have been home all night. There have been *zero* transcendent dreams, telekinetic tantrums, or any form of unnatural hanky panky during the time in question," he said holding up his right hand as if swearing on a stack of bibles.

“Got it and let’s pretend I believe you. So why did you go to see Vick,” she said.

“We met in his office yesterday morning for about thirty minutes. We talked about the future and hardly mentioned the Monday incident. Truthfully, he wasn’t concerned about it. Now, it’s my turn to ask a question. What do you know about a Christian news program being developed by TV10 and Commonwealth Church?”

“A what? Christian news? That’s an oxymoron. It’s not news. It may be some kind of PSA deal. What the hell are you talking about.

“Ask your boss, he knows a lot more than I do. Vick went into some detail about it. Suppose Seth decided to dump it and Vick didn’t appreciate his lack of faith? Maybe a disagreement of some kind?” He speculated. “I don’t know, it’s just a hunch,” he said returning her raised eyebrow.

She couldn’t believe he was turning the story on its head.

“So that’s it? I wake you at 4am, show up on your front step to play 20-questions and I wind up pointed back at my boss? Are you saying we have an attempted homicide?” She stopped to consider it.

“You mean it about that weekly church production?”

“Every word. Check it out with your boss.”

“Ain’t that a bee-och. And you tell no lies, I know that, deacon. So, I’ll look into it today. Based on some other stuff I dug up there may be something to it. Anything else?”

“Yeah. I do have another one for your reporter’s curiosity. What would you say if I told you that Vick hired a crew to kidnap me and Charlotte and that they tried it twenty-four hours ago right here where you are sitting?”

“I’d say it’s the best reason yet for the preacher to have an accident *and* that you’d better have some damn strong evidence. It would also mean, among other bizarre things, there’s a war inside the church over some PSA deal. Are you telling me that?”

"No ma'am. It's a lot bigger than this church but not a concern at the moment. I was just wondering if it's a scenario that would be of interest, you know, as a potential thread to follow-up on, if there was something to it."

"It's gotta be crazy-ass drama everywhere with you doesn't it? You know I can't deal with another unsubstantiated Class 1 felony tied to this whole affair but, it is noted. And you don't seem any worse for ware except for that badly overdone pierced ear lob? Any connection?"

"To what?"

"Cute but no more games. This time *I* am warning *you.* If the padre's accident comes back this way, there will be tracks and I can find them. But for now you're out of it but damn it, you make things so complicated when I know it's not that tough.

She stood up and rubbed her stomach.

"Man, I miss my old news bugs. They'd be tearing me a new one right now. I really counted on those little cooties."

"Sounds to me like you got an upgrade-from old gas to a new voice. Think of it as another rung up the precognitive ladder."

"Precognitive ladder my butt. I wish I had 'em back, that's all. When those little buggers were crawling up my insides there were no doubts. That's all I know," she said and stood up to leave.

"Kidnapping? Really?"

He nodded.

"What a shit-fried mess. Get some sleep." She turned and walked down the driveway, waving to him with the back of her hand.

Mark watched her taillights disappear around the corner before going in to wake Charlotte and tell her about Vick's accident.

But as he stepped onto the small landing at the foot of the stairs he remembered her lying there, right there, dead in his dream, staring into oblivion. He stopped. Instead of taking the next step up to the bedroom he dropped to his knees and started praying, praying for Charlotte and for Vick and for his family and for the church.

"Good grief, Lord. Where's the wisdom in any of this?" he asked knowing it was his own question to answer.

He decided not to wake her and walked back to the kitchen ready to make the first pot of coffee for a long day. Staring out the storm door window he profoundly wished that Woodstock and 1969 were out his back door.

The downstairs phone rang at 6:15.

Tommy Robertson was calling with an update on Vick's condition (*critical but stable*) and a request for Mark to call four other deacons about an emergency meeting at 10:00 for the elders, deacons, and church staff.

Vick hadn't regained consciousness, the tests were inconclusive and the prognosis was not optimistic. The Directorate was meeting in a few hours to appoint an interim senior pastor, plan the transition and work on damage control. But Mark knew they would schedule this meeting only after the deal was done. Someone had already taken Vick's place as Senior Minister of Commonwealth Church.

So he agreed to make the calls and didn't ask any questions. He knew the Elders would tell them the plan at the meeting and be looking for a rubber stamp approval.

One thing was sure; a tidal wave of panic was going to break over the church so they'd best move quickly to show control and authority. There were thousands of members and millions of dollars in play.

Each deacon Mark called had the same shocked reaction and no idea what to do. Tim Flowers was typical.

"It's not fair, Mark, but the leadership will figure something out don't you think? And with Vick lying in the hospital near death we'd better have some world-class praying going on. I mean, do you know how we're going to make it without our head coach?"

"We'll appoint a new senior minister, make some sort of plan, and then get through it. Like we always do. Together."

"Let's pray for him right now, Mark." Tim offered and Mark couldn't refuse.

Tim prayed for Vick, Vick's family, the church and then each elder and deacon before Mark had to interrupt. After so many sports analogies he was beginning to think Vince Lombardy was the man in a coma.

"Tim, no disrespect but we only have two hours until the meeting. Can we say a joint 'amen' and score one for the Gipper?"

"Yeah, sure, guess I got a little carried away but I'm really scared."

"No, my fault," Mark replied, "and please keep praying. (*Somebody has to.*) I just have to make a few more calls, that's all. I'll hang up and you keep going as long as the spirit moves you."

"10-4. It's one of the things I do best and, hey, I'll put one together for the meeting. I'll weave in some soccer stuff too."

"Great idea Tim. That'll round it out. I'll see you there."

"Mark, you're one funny guy. Nice catch. I'll...

Mark hung up hoping for the silent prayer option later.

"Damn it. I know Vick's laying the hospital because of what happened in this house on Monday."

"Don't flatter yourself." The Debating Society piped up. "Vick's accident wasn't some link in a divine chain reaction. There's no cause and effect from here to there, Slick. It's just the crap of life. Stinks don't it?"

Mark didn't reply. He was already too tired to duke it out with them.

"On the list of life's dark days, this one's in the top five and climbing. And that meeting this morning. Sure, they've decided the important stuff but even they can't control what they don't know. There's bound be a surprise or two," he thought and gulped another cup of coffee thinking about how events were closing in now.

"Yes indeed. There will be a few of those. But you got some tricks up your sleeve too. More than you know."

Chapter 32

Mark and his Thunderbird arrived at the church parking lot fifteen minutes early for the emergency meeting. He was fidgety and depressed but the Debating Society rambled on.

"You haven't contributed much of anything to the church this year, mostly did your best to avoid it. You are one sorry deacon, Mr. Justin."

But George Jones answered with a different notion, sung in a strong song and a determined set of major chords.

It's high time to put that behind
And leap into the breach.
And if you can't do that then kiss my ass
'cause they damn sure need you now.
That's right and you know it.
They damn sure need you now.

He let it play back a few times until he memorized it.

"Thanks, George, I needed that. Come back later and we'll finish it," he thought and sang it out loud as he walked through the parking lot. When he opened the front door all his self-pity was gone and he was ready to help make the plans that would steer the church through the crisis.

"Mark. Hey Mark, can I talk with you a minute before the meeting."

He almost tripped on the bottom stair as he stopped and pivoted. It was Jerry Tinsler. Without returning the greeting, Mark trotted up the hall to meet him.

"What are you doing here?" he whispered as Jerry pointed toward the empty chapel used for overflow on crowded Sunday's.

Jerry smiled and wrapped Mark in a big bear hug.

"Jerry, it's great to see you but I thought they got you at the Alamo. What the heck are you doing here?" Mark said prying himself away but very happy to see his friend.

“I was waiting for *you.* We only have a minute so listen up, friend. First, no matter what you heard, they never fired me. Vick, God save him, put me on administrative leave and recommended dismissal but the Elders deferred voting and decided to let things cool off for a couple of weeks *then* revisit the whole thing. They thought he overreacted and many of them stood up for me. They told me to keep my mouth shut, take a vacation, and they’d get back to me. I got the call from Robertson at 3am and here we are.” He was speaking so fast Mark hardly recognized his voice.

“So here’s the deal. They want me to take Vick’s place until he recovers or they hire another honcho. No strings attached, like he never canned me-a straight interim promotion. It’s a hellofa thing,” Jerry said shaking his head.

Mark couldn’t stop the shiver-shake in his shoulders but talked through it.

“It makes so much sense I’m surprised they made the call this fast. But it’s about the only choice that will get us through with any leadership at all. I guess I was one of the few people that knew Vick tried to can you. I, uh, came here yesterday to negotiate your return but he flicked me off, big time. Afraid I was no match for him.”

“Really? You did that for me? What in the world made you think he would ever change his mind?” Jerry was baffled and grateful.

“Well let’s just say I thought I was taking a gun to a knife fight and leave it at that.”

“You really walked in here and tried to get my job back. Incredible, I don’t know what to say,” Jerry eyes teared but not to the brim.

“Yeah, but don’t get all choked up about it. Besides, it’s the Elders that saved your hinny, not me. I’m still trying to understand why any of this has happened.”

“We’ll have time for reflection later. Right now events are running over us. But one of these days you have to tell me about you're little chat with Vick," Jerry said and put his hand on Mark's shoulder.

"It's time to focus on beginning the recovery. This church is in trouble and we need you. We need you're strength and inspiration, Mark, so I'm glad we had a minute here because I didn't want to surprise you in there," Jerry said pointing toward the meeting room and continued in his hurried whisper.

"Part of my arrangement with the Elders involves a special election this morning. You, Rocky Sims and Louis Shotley are being elected Elders and you, sir, will join me on the Finance Committee. I don't know what your plans are but that's what we're putting on the table in a few minutes. Mark, the last two weeks you've shown us how to get ready to react and take charge of unexpected situations. They respect you here. A lot. And you know I want you on point with me. It's finito, already approved. Can you do it?" he asked not looking at Mark but at the large mahogany cross hanging on the wall.

"*They damn sure need you now*," was Mark's only thought and the decision was made.

"Sure, Jerry, I'll reup for as long as you're in charge but after that I'm going agnostic. The Lord works in mysterious ways, too mysterious around here," Mark said and smiled at his preacher friend. "Besides, you knew I wouldn't refuse a hell bent Texan on a rescue mission, didn't you?"

"I was hoping you'd see it that way," Jerry answered and sighed, shaking his head. "I just pray we've got the cahonnes to get through it. This is a mighty big pickle."

"But the Finance Committee? What's with that? I know those guys and there won't be any bear hugs and kisses from that group."

"Well, you know, that's the fun of it. Finance is the only way to redirect funding and there are too many dang pet projects around here so I want your pickle in there. And don't worry; they'll fall in line. It's part of the deal. Believe me, no one is going to mess with us now. There's nothing left to say but the 'Amens'," Jerry assured him and looked at his watch.

“Holy frijoles, I gotta go. See you upstairs and thanks again for taking this on. You’ll probably regret it. And just follow my lead if anything unexpected happens up there,” he advised shaking Mark’s hand again and then hurriedly left for the meeting.

Looking at the big mahogany cross and the gold plated communion chalice on the table in front of it, Mark was alone with his thoughts.

“Did he wink at me? Damn it, here I go again. Too many questions, not enough answers, and another three years to waste. Three more years? I can’t believe what just happened. Jesus, do I have control of anything anymore?” He asked and realized that from where he was sitting it was a direct question.

“Hey communion breath, you could’ve just said ‘no’ to your Texas buddy; tossed it back in his face and made tracks. Besides, he bushwhacked you right here in front of the Big Three. That’s pressure. You caved. Game over.” The Debating Society finished with the usual deductive signature.

“Yeah, well, well, so’s your mother.” He hated when they were right and he looked back at the cross. “We damn sure need *you* guys now.”

The first emergency meeting of the Directorate of Commonwealth Church in twenty-seven years was solemn but well executed. Tom Robertson began with a brief report on Vick’s condition and then lit three candles, one for Vick, one for his family, and one for the church.

The business part of the meeting then proceeded with the Senior Minister Henry Hanratty from the James River Ministry office seated between Mark and Jerry at the head of the table. By regional and national governance his duty was to approve the transition and sign the temporary changes drafted for Commonwealth’s charter. But Hanratty had requested certain guarantees before signing anything.

“What about your plans for the Finance committee? Could those changes impact certain projects critical to community outreach already underway?” he asked Jerry.

"I guess it's possible. We'll review everything and see what we can do without Vick. Then *we* will make the call on all of *our* projects. I assure you our contribution to the JRM is not at issue," Jerry countered.

"No, we've received that already. Our concern is for the media projects where your commitment of funds and leadership is so important to a number of interested parties. As assistant minister you may not be aware of those partnerships but...," he stopped and looked around the table. None of them had a clue about the extent of Vick's reach.

"Let's just say that it will be required for the Ministry's office to approve any changes in funding commitments already in motion. We don't want to upset the apple cart now, do we?"

The light came on for Mark. "Vick has the whole Ministry up to their eyeballs in this thing and old Henry here needs some cover. I wonder how much they've funneled into Vick TV?"

Jerry answered by sliding the one-page project revision document in front of Hanratty and signaled Mark with a nod-up to help the Ministry make up his mind.

With a friendly smile and a firm grip, Mark placed his hand on the Hanratty's shoulder much like he had laid it on Miss Daisy's two weeks earlier.

"There are no apple carts in danger here, pastor. All of us in the Directorate assure you that the wisdom from above will guide us through these troubled waters. Further, the Finance Committee will keep you and the Ministry informed of everything we discover. Will that do?"

Hanratty felt a tingling sensation bolt down his arm all the way through his right hand, not paralyzing but warm and getting warmer. Then he realized that this was the 'praying deacon' offering him the only deal he was going to get.

"Right you are, Mr. Justin. That is specifically what the Ministry expects," he said and quickly signed the charter after shrugging Mark's hand off his shoulder. "Now if you'll excuse me, I need to communicate this tragedy to our other members. I'm sure they will want the latest status. God bless you all. We are praying for you and let's talk often. Maybe at our offices next week?" he said getting up from the table.

"We'll call you." Jerry replied but Hanratty was already out the door.

"So, is everyone good with the changes? Vote aye or nay," Jerry requested. There was unanimous consent and the meeting adjourned. As Mark picked up his paper work Jerry moved close enough to whisper.

"Walk with me out to the parking lot? There's one more item on the agenda that only you and I can discuss."

"You expectin' trouble, sheriff?"

"Naw, just another favor to ask my new deputy."

Exiting through one of the side doors Mark caught a glimpse of a small crowd of local print, radio and TV reporters surrounding Tom Robertson on the front portico.

"We've got to get him a chain link fence and some pepper spray for his daily press briefings," Jerry said with a smile.

"How about a podium and an American flag?"

"That's not bad, Mark. Really, we'll set it up before the evening service tonight and he can use it after that if they're here. I think old Tom would appreciate some space and a couple of props." Jerry pulled out a folded piece of paper, made a quick note, and kept talking.

"Okay, here's my thought. I'd like us to go see Vick this afternoon. If they'll let us in, I want to pray for his recovery right there in the room. He needs to know we are tending the church while he fights for his life. I want him to feel us pulling him back from the outside and I also want you pushing him up from the inside. You know what I mean don't you?" For effect Jerry tugged a little on Mark's arm.

The image of Vick, dead in the mirror, sent a panic-flash through his stomach and he leaned on the Thunderbird for support.

"Jerry, I can't do that and I'm not going to explain it. I just can't. We need another way."

"All I know is that if anyone can reach him, it's you. I want constant prayers from the church and I want extraordinary prayer in that hospital room." he said and stopped to face Mark.

"So many people need him and I sure don't want the church the way I just got it. This is Vick's church, his staff, his congregation and we have to get him back here, God willing."

"Okay, how many ways do I need to say this? I have no business trying to mess with Vick or any one else in a coma. For Christ's sake, I couldn't get to him when he sat behind a mahogany desk. I sure can't do it now. You got that?"

"Yeah, you're stuck in denial. Well, screw that. You need to do this."

"Sorry to disappoint you, padre, but I've gone about as far as I can go. Find yourself a real psychic if that's what you need," he said getting into the car and quickly pulled away feeling drained and angry.

"Hell, I'm afraid to look in the rearview mirror; scared to death he'll be staring black-eyed bullets through me from the back seat. Why would I probe his comatose subconscious? What would I find in there?"

Chapter 33

Charlotte was eating lunch in the breakfast room when he walked into the house and sat down to tell her the short hand version of the emergency meeting.

"For a guy that was hanging up his spurs, you had a serious change of heart. Let me guess, the greater good got you. It's one of my personal favorites," she said while chewing on a cheese and ham sandwich.

"Oh yeah, I just rolled over, said three amens and now I've got a star on my vest. Even worse, it's going to take away more of our time together. You all right with that?" he asked knowing she would be.

"Fine by me as long as you don't think you can poke me with your badge any time you feel like it," she smiled knowing they would manage. "And, by the way, while you were getting pinned I also got the call to serve. They must have a coordinated strike force over there because you're lunching with the co-leader of Operation 24 X 7, continuous prayer for Vick. So I'll be over there quite a bit too. And I'm curious, dear. Have you ever made love in church?"

"Ah, well it depends on what you mean by church." He smiled welcoming the diversion.

"Really. You'll have to tell me about those revivals you attended. But with our commitments now don't you think it is a perfectly defensible position? Wait, don't answer that. We'll look it up in the Governology section of the library some night," she said not knowing what they would do in the library but pretty sure they would soon find out.

"Very warped, dear, but with that southern charm of yours I can't resist. It's a date. Do you mind if I change the subject?"

"Please do." She was red behind her freckles.

"Jerry asked me to see Vick this afternoon. Get this. He's as serious as a plane crash about me telepathically reaching out to Vick right there in the hospital. He thinks I can break through and communicate on some level. Unreal, huh? But I'm going to pass. It's kind of ridiculous. Me, a coma conduit? Hardly in my job description, right?"

"Maybe but you are writing the rules. Scary to admit but I see you getting stronger, fighting *with* it, using it especially when you had to protect us. You've been so far out there, just flat gone to who-knows-where and now we're talking about telepathic coupling with our comatose minister. Sounds kind of tame compared to the other stuff that's happened," she said and reached across the table to put her hand on his and continued.

"You are not in the Twilight Zone. It's all very real and part of being you so believe it or not Ripley, I think it makes sense for you to try it. Kind of a destiny thing and besides, you can't get hurt just standing next to him," she said and let go of his hand before continuing.

"The wildcard is that you still don't control that new mojo very well so you absolutely *must* keep some sense of yourself. That's the key and it's probably how things got away from you on Monday. But let's also be logical. Nothing is going to happen. They're saying on the radio that he's a deep coma. That doesn't bode well for a psychic-rescue. So, as long as Jerry is watching over you, my vote is to go for it. After all he is close to dying."

"But I've already seen him, dead, standing beside me upstairs in the bathroom. Did I tell you that one?"

"Oh God, no. Are you sure you were awake?"

"Yeah, damn sure and I know he wants to kill me. For all we know he's already tried to once. How can I face that again?"

"Because it was a hollow image in the mirror, your image of him, not some kind of telepathic bond. You have to use your warnings, not be afraid of them."

"You, kind lady, are 100% right. How'd you get so smart about this stuff?"

“You got your gifts, kiddo, and I got mine. We’ve been a hellofa team since you conducted the air-ballet with my dental tools twenty years ago. You still haven’t beat one.”

She smiled and kissed him. “Unbeatable,” he thought.

“So stay grounded, in control and fearless.” she said and looked away, suddenly embarrassed by whole conversation.

“Listen to me. I don’t know any more about this than I do screwing in church. You’re experimenting, Mark. You always have. Anything from zero response to total possession by Vick is possible.” Now that thought made her feel the panic.

“Wait. That’s ridiculous-not a chance. Just go with Jerry, pray for Vick and come back home in one piece. How’s that?”

“I love you and it is outstanding advice,” he said picking up the other half of her sandwich.

* * * * *

While the Directorate of Commonwealth Church met that morning, Dominique called Seth. She wanted to meet him at the station to review what she had the Springwell accident, how it would be reported and what else was needed for the 6:00 weekend show.

As usual he was ahead of her. It had been the lead story on their AM affiliate, News960, since 7:00 a.m. and he had talked with Vick’s wife, Marlene, earlier in the morning. He wanted to see Dominique in his office at 2:00 but warned her against turning the accident into some kind of climactic event.

“We are going to stay with the facts and focus on the impact to the church and the community. This is not going to be a tabloid piece linking everything over there to some kind of divine mystery. We are going to do this with respect for the family and that congregation. You on board?”

“Never thought of anything else, chief. But we don’t have any film yet. You want a crew at the 4:00 prayer service?”

“Let’s talk about that at two. Anything else before you get some sleep?”

“Just one thing. The cops are checking out some leads about the accident. May have been more to it than they are letting on, but I’ve got no corroboration. Do you want me to check it out with the precinct?” she asked innocently trying not to be obvious about her lie.

“I want to know your source on that and we’ll talk about it later. You get some sleep and I’ll see you in few hours.” He hung up without saying goodbye.

“Freakin’ hell, he called me on it. You can bet your koochie he’s on the phone right now checking it out. It’s okay though. I’ll finesse it as a rumor and deny any hard source. Damn it, I should have called the Third for some comment but I have got to get some shuteye. This is one very long strange trip,” she thought and flopped onto her unmade bed, asleep before the second bounce.

Seth punched up the Third Precinct desk sergeant without setting the phone down.

“Jake, hey, it’s Seth Griggs, TV10 News. Just a quick question if you don’t mind. Got word from one of my reporters that you’re working a lead on some possible foul play in the Springwell accident. Any comment?”

Chapter 34

Befitting a CEO, Victor Springwell occupied a private suite just off the ICU. The windowsills in the spacious bedroom displayed a tasteful number of flower arrangements but dozens more had arrived. The family asked to send the rest to the ward for elderly patients. After it was filled, the children's ward was next. By 2:00 Saint Gertrude's resembled a colorful garden nursery thanks to Vick's accident.

Jerry sipped a cup of coffee in the lobby waiting for the 2 o'clock visiting hour. He had called ahead to be sure he and Mark could see Vick. Now he hoped Mark would show. Marlene Springwell cried with joy when he talked with her. She was beyond frustration with the doctor's evasions and needed his counsel.

Slumped in oversized chair, he thought back to that final meeting seven days ago when Vick fired him-a quick dressing down followed by an ingenuous request for rebuttal and then a simple execution.

"I won't argue any of it with, Jerry. It was simply poor judgment. So it is with profound regret that I have to place you on immediate administrative leave leading to the termination of your services. The Elders will confirm it tomorrow afternoon. And I'm sorry but we'll only be able to support you for a few months," he had scolded then humiliated Jerry.

"I won't fight this, Vick. It's your church and I only want peace and love for the people here, but I *will* be in the meeting tomorrow with the Elders and I will defend my actions. They'll have to look me in the eye when they pull the trigger on this," Jerry recalled saying as he stood up and walked out of Vick's office.

But, the usually spineless Elders didn't cave this time. They did not approve Vick's unauthorized action and, instead, called Jerry with a different message. Tom Robertson delivered it early Monday morning.

“Just a quick update for you, Jerry. First, there is no discussion about your situation outside the executive committee. You’re on vacation for a week or two. Second, we think the best outcome for everyone is to get some time-slash-space between you and Vick. This is a family feud and not really a terminating offense, period. We’ll call you next week when the dust settles around here and *then* we’ll meet to put it behind us. In the meantime, enjoy your vacation. Ah, pastor, does that work for you?”

Jerry heard the real message. “Vick screwed up. Give us a week to unscrew it.”

“Short week,” he murmured.

At the entrance to St. Gertrude’s Mark was happy to be walking and not being gurnied into the place. The smell of it triggered memories of several other visits besides his latest. Twenty-one years ago their daughter was born in the maternity ward on the fourth floor and he first experienced the emergency room when she broke her arm (no more Supergirl imitations) and again five years ago when one of her girl friends passed out (vodka shooters) in their front yard.

But this time stepping across the threshold through the revolving door, he *felt* Vick, a shadowy pulse up there somewhere. Waiting. Maybe.

“Hey, padre, you look like you’ve been rode hard and put up wet,” Mark said walking up to see Jerry comfortably lost in thought.

“Justin. I can’t believe it. Man, I apologize for being such a …”

“Overbearing pickle salesman. Yeah, well do me a favor and let’s rethink the wisdom of this little parley. Could we buy him a stuffed animal in the gift shop and drop it off with regards for a speedy recovery?” he asked offering his hand to reinforce their friendship.

“Look at it like this, Mark. Maybe reaching Vick will help us figure out what you’re made of and why he’s here. That’s a two-fer if we’re lucky.”

On the fifth floor they checked with the head nurse at the main desk. She smiled at the sight of a white collared clergyman and pointed them in the direction of room 501, the corner private suite.

Beyond the large sitting room, in the French provincial decorated bedroom, Marlene, sat in a wingchair next to the bed. She looked up to see them enter the room and more tears flowed from her puffy red eyes as she quickly walked into the sitting room to greet them in a loving three-way embrace.

Jerry took her aside and asked if she would like to join them in a bedside prayer service but she declined.

"The doctors don't know any more now than they did twelve hours ago after he came out of surgery," she said dabbing the tears. "They say the bleeding is stopped, got it before any more damage was done but they went in pretty deep. Please, Jerry, ask God to send him back," she said and looked into Vick's room where Mark had was already standing at the foot of the bed.

"Look at that. I'm so pleased you brought Mark. He's charismatic and I know if anyone can reach Vick, the two of you will do it." And she kissed him on the cheek. "Bless your heart Jerry Tinsler. You, Mark and Vick need to come together now. God will listen." She smiled for the first time.

Vick was pale, lifeless, tubed and wired; more dead that alive, with a large bandage on the left side of this head. Pajama clad, hair perfectly combed; he was unrelated to the terrifying image in the bathroom mirror yesterday.

"Okay, the tough part is over. What am I supposed to do now?" His stomach flipped over and he panicked realizing how unprepared he was to do anything but stare at Vick.

"Breathe dumbass, breathe," he reminded himself. "You'll think of something."

But the nightmare featuring Vick's unholy light laser flashed back. Then Charlotte's awful fall, her dead eyes, all of it whipped by in piclets as he looked at Vick's lifeless face.

"I'm as lost as you are Vick, only I know it," he whispered.

When he glanced up Jerry was standing by the bed.

"How's it going over there, Slick?" he asked seeing that Mark was paler than the patient.

"Clear to partly cloudy, Captain. We're past the rough air now," he lied.

"Good to hear it. Let's begin, Elder Justin. I'll start with prayer and then you add to it as the spirit moves you. We have about ten minutes," he said holding his right hand out for Mark to take and placing his left on top of Vick's right. Mark took Jerry's hand and slid his right under Vick's, completing the circle. He nodded to Jerry and then looked back to Vick's closed eyes.

There were no notes or prepared text to read. Jerry was not so much praying as he was talking to God and Vick. Asking to be heard, knowing that all things have purpose, telling Vick that he was needed and missed, and how his church family was praying for him continuously. All recited in the singsong cadence that good preachers automatically slip into.

Mark never closed his eyes but focused on Vick and gently squeezed his left hand. It was warm, pliable, and limp. No response, not a twitch, but there was a pulse, strong and steady.

"Amen." He heard Jerry say and he automatically echoed "Amen."

"That's your cue, Elder."

Still holding hands he looked at Jerry and received a head nod that said, "Whatever you got over there, it's show time."

It didn't help.

"Jerry?" He said and found it hard to swallow.

"I'm not ready for this. I feel like Father Damien in *The Exorcist.* I'm drawing a blank and I'm afraid to do anything. I don't know how to go after him," he said dropping his hands by his side.

"Well, partner, what can I say?" Jerry replied. "On the bright side, I don't think he's going to wake up and spew green goo all over us."

Mark didn't laugh.

"Alright, alright. Let's take a minute. Regroup. Calm and collected we are." Jerry inhaled deeply, then exhaled. Mark did the same.

"Maybe you're not up for giving him a little telepathic tickle or opening one of those divine channels you've been showing off lately. It's perfectly understandable if you bail out and don't do anything. Truth is, it's kind of hard explaining all that shit you do anyway," Jerry said and started laughing.

Mark tried but couldn't stop himself from laughing at the minister's bedside cussing and almost lost it before recovering and wiping the tears away.

"So, Mark, what's it going to be? You got anything in mind for our friend here.

"You know, I think I do. Thanks for the reminder," Mark said as he reached out for Jerry's hand and slid his other hand back under Vick's.

Leaning down, Mark spoke in a firm voice.

"Okay Vick, I don't know if you can hear me but maybe God can back me up. I'm going to close my eyes and project my thoughts toward yours. Maybe we connect, maybe not, but I'll be looking for you so try your best to connect with me. I'm coming in to look for you now," he said and leaned in closer.

With his hand still in Vick's, Mark closed his eyes and quickly drifted away.

The first image behind his eyelids was a swimming pool. He was standing on the back end of the three-meter diving board at a public pool, closed, no lifeguards, no swimmers, fill jets turned off, glassy smooth surface. The sky was cloudy and boiling as if a storm would break any moment but the breeze was fresh and warm. Shirtless and wearing his favorite pair of red flowered surfing jams from the endless summer of 1969, he knew why he was there.

"Vick? Can you hear me?" he asked knowing there wouldn't be an answer in the open air above the pool.

“Talk about your leap of faith,” he thought looking down the board into the water.

“But, I really have to take a leak too so let’s take the plunge.”

He walked down the board, raised his arms and leaped off the end performing a flawless flip-and-a-half (just like the summer of ‘69) that ended in a vertical dive into the water.

Opening his eyes underwater, the floor drain was clear and magnified. Always a goal in his childhood but never touched, he headed down to the bottom at twelve feet of water.

“Vick, are you anywhere near me? Am I in the right place?” he spoke in a loud voice as he touched the drain cover and then stood over it.

Nothing heard so he tried again.

“Vick, I’m twelve feet deep in some public pool looking for you so please speak up. This is your place, not mine, so now’s the time if you want to talk to me.”

It was also time to relieve himself. He was enjoying the warm flow into his jams and the sense of breathing underwater when the silence was broken.

“Mark, I am here.” A voice responded from below the drain and stunned him out of the time warp.

“Vick? I wasn’t sure I could find you. I need to see you. Where are you?” Mark asked talking down toward the drain.

“I want to see you too but I can’t move very much. I seem to be mostly paralyzed and floating around in the dark. Where are we, Mark? I hear voices far away but I can’t understand them,” said the voice below the drain.

“You’re in a coma lying in bed at Saint Gertrude’s hospital and have been for most of the day. Everyone is praying for you to come back and I’m here to help you make it. I don’t know how long I can stay but I think we’ll be fine if I can get you out of there and up to the surface,”

“I can’t see anything but I’ll try to reach out in the direction of your voice. If you see my hand maybe you can you pull me out? Please don’t leave me here,” the voice begged.

“I won’t, I promise. I’ll stay as long as I can. Go ahead, try it now,” Mark said looking at the drain.

Amazingly, a hand reached through, all five fingers intact, blindly stretching for a grip. It might have been ‘Thing’ from the Adams Family as he looked at it.

“Mark, that’s the best I can do. Can you take my hand and pull me out of here? I want to go home.”

“You bet. Hang on. I want to get a better stance,” Mark said and was reassured by the ring on the hand’s second finger he recognized as Vick’s UVA class ring.

“All right, Vick, I think we’re set. Get ready to kick and swim and fight to get to me. We’ll be out of here in no time,” And he firmly grasped the extended hand.

The force that jerked back was overwhelming.

It squeezed his hand and then yanked him into a squat that bounced his butt off the cement floor. In a flash of panic and pain Mark instinctively grabbed his own arm and pulled it up as hard as he could.

“Come on down, Elder Justin,” Vick’s voice calmly insisted.

“You’ll adore the serenity of nothingness in here. and I’d love some company in my new world. It will be our own little corner of Purgatory. Remember, Justin, you *told* me this was going to happen. Now, by all that is Holy and just, you will eternally drown with me!” Vick was screaming as another jerk pulled Mark’s arm down into the drain.

“This just in,” Vick continued now imitating a TV news anchor while pulling Mark deeper into the drain.

“Newly elected elder joins pastor in hospital-twin comas stun community. Tragic auto accident continues to baffle police. Local news director covers his tracks.” Vick’s tone was maniacal. “How’s *that* for a lead in?” He screamed, yanking Mark down, slamming his chest on the drain.

“Vick. I can’t breathe. You’re killing me,” Mark was losing consciousness just as a giant flash bolted through the pool, pierced by lightning.

“Feel it. Fe-el all of it. But you’re not going to die. You’re going to---” The rest of the sentence was obliterated by crashing thunder that exploded through Mark and smashed him against the wall.

Jerry had to use so much force to pry Mark’s hand from Vick’s grasp that the momentum sent both men falling backward with most of Jerry’s two-hundred-fifty lbs. landing on the smaller elder.

“Sweet mother of Mary, Harry, and Skip Carey. What a grip! You with me, Mark?” Jerry said rolling off of his smaller friend. “That was some arm wrestling match you and Vick had going. Looked like you were getting the worst of it so I untangled you the hard way. Sorry about the rough landing,” he said still not facing Mark and not yet hearing a reply.

“So how about saying something, Ace?”

“He’s in there,” Mark whispered, “and he’s really pissed.”

Jerry got to his feet and was lifting Mark the way a guilty lineman picks up a sacked quarterback, when the ICU staff and Marlene rushed into room.

They first looked to the patient. Vick was lying in bed eyes closed, arms at his side, monitors chirping and beating normal, seemingly undisturbed by the commotion made by his two visitors.

“I’m so sorry,” Mark said to break the silence.

“I was deep in prayer and I turned to fast on my gimpy ankle. It just gave way on me, does that occasionally. Jerry tried to grab me but I couldn’t catch myself before tumbling in a heap. I apologize for the racket. It was entirely my fault,” he said turning red and embarrassed.

“Mr. Justin, that was a nasty little fall. Maybe you’d like to step into an examination room and we’ll take a look at your ankle. Sounds like it's unstable," Nurse Kendall said, knowing a loaf when it was dropped.

"No ma'am. I think you've seen enough of me. I'm finished here," Mark said and looked to Jerry for support.

"Uh, yes, that's right, we are done but we'd like to talk with Marlene before leaving," he said looking at the minister's wife.

"I'd like that very much Jerry. This has been so difficult for all of us," she said wiping new tears from her eyes. "I'll talk with the minister and the elder in the sitting room, nurse," she said and turned to walk out of the sick room.

"That's fine dear but just for a few minutes. There is entirely too much raucousness in here to suit me. And this isn't your first time either, young man. I got my eye on you. Do I make myself clear?" She knew about Mark's visit to Dan Campbell's room (everyone did) and he acknowledged her warning with a nod.

Marlene could hardly wait until the staff left them alone in the sitting room. "Mark, something happened with Vick didn't it?"

"Yes ma'am, it sure did. As I prayed I sensed him, very strongly, no question about it. I'm sure he's fighting to be with us," he said as she burst into more tears.

"Oh God, I knew it. I just knew it. I felt him trying to reach out to me too. What can I do to help him?"

"Let him know you're here, Marlene. He can hear voices but it's not easy. He seems close but I don't know if he'll break through. I'm so sorry I couldn't bring him back with me."

"Maybe not this time, Mark, but you give me hope; you give us all hope. Bless you for this wonderful thing and don't pay any mind to the battle-axe out there. She's just the mother hen up here but I can get you in anytime you feel up to it," she said and then cupped his face with both of her hands to make sure he was listening.

"I want you to know something, Mark Justin. Vick admires you. He talked about this past week and his plans with so much passion these last few days. He is determined to make you his shining star." And the tears flowed again as she gave him a quick kiss on the cheek.

"Yes ma'am. He's really pulling for me. I'm sure of it." Mark smiled.

"And Jerry, you be sure everyone keeps praying for us," she said more composed again. "We're going to get him back. There is no doubt about it now. But I have to tell you both something. I don't believe what they are telling me about the accident. I mean, I can't make any sense of it," she said but knew they didn't understand yet.

"I don't know if they told you but Vick wasn't in his seat belt when the car crashed. I can't help but think he'd be fine if he'd had it on. And it's not like him to be so careless, especially at night in bad weather. I guess it doesn't much matter now but, for the life of me, I can't understand why he wasn't wearing it."

They walked out of the room and said their goodbyes in the hall. Marlene made Mark promise to return and contact Vick again if he wasn't better soon.

Mark and Jerry stopped in the hospital parking lot to finish their conversation and plan next steps.

"Seth Griggs is a problem. I don't know what he did to Vick but he's involved, big time. I mean, *that* is one enraged preacher, very afraid too. There's no telling what he'll do when he wakes up but it will be righteous," he said rubbing his still tingling arm.

"Mark? Do you know what's going on with you?" Jerry asked looking at him. "Just reflect for a second and tell me what you think you're doing and how you're doing it?"

"Sorry padre but I don't know or care. I'm playing it by ear. Hell's bells, the way Shotsy talks it's nothing more than a quarter-volt of power I can super charge and direct some how. For now, I'm going with that over the even more problematic divine intervention theory."

"Right. And Edgar Cayce was just another guy with a headache. Come on Mark, we can't minimize what just happened. You found your way into another man's soul. It's the most powerful thing I've ever seen. Admit it or not, you are a phenomenon," he said smiling and shaking his head. "But I hear you. Like I said this morning, now's not the time for reflection. I'll just refer to you by your super hero name, Electro. We'll work on the uniform later."

"Right and don't forget the comic book rights. I gotta go," Mark said.

"But when are you going to reach out to Vick again. It could work next time, right?"

"Don't think so. He's calling the shots in there like you wouldn't believe. No matter what I promised Marlene, it's a bad idea to wander around in Vick's head again. Besides, Dominique is in more trouble. She's at the station about to confront Seth with our suspicions and that guy is about as stable as Mount St. Helens. I'm headed down there-got a bad feeling about it," Mark said and realized how hyper he sounded.

"I know Seth pretty well. He's got a bark but not much bite. Nobody's going to be hurt, Mark."

"You may be right but flash back fifteen minutes ago when you yanked me out of another man's nightmare and five days ago when I was cold cocked by the lunatic fringe and our head pastor is laying there paying somebody's dues. No sir. You watch your back. I don't think we know all the players yet," he said shaking hands with Jerry and then slid behind the wheel of his Thunderbird

With no idea what he was going to do when he got there, Mark headed downtown toward the TV10 tower and the studio underneath it.

Chapter 35

With a Slim Fast milkshake at home and a Starbuck's triple espresso on the way in, Dominique was finally waking up and feeling alert enough to meet Seth at 2:00.

Her desk was a mass of 'while you were out screwing around' pink slips and white news copy from the week's stories. On top of it all was the storyboard for reporting the Springwell accident.

"Wow, this is a tight and tidy little package," she said aloud and looked around to see the office was cleared out again like last weekend.

"Where is everybody?" She asked and listened to the echo.

The phone rang. It's small green screen showed Seth's name.

"Hey boss. This town is either on vacation or on fire and everyone is covering it. What's the word?"

"Another slow Saturday so we're going to run the Springwell piece up front at 6:00. Come on in."

She walked into his office with two copies of the story outline and tossed one on his desk.

"We've talked about most of this except what you got from the cops," he said after glancing at her storyboard for thirty seconds, and continued. "You know there's nothing in the accident report about foul play or an on going investigation. Sounds like 'case closed' to me so tell me who you talked to at the precinct."

"Just some temp working a desk said he heard a rumor about some foot prints at the scene. Pretty weak but worth a phone call or two. Funny thing. The report said that Vick wasn't wearing a seat belt and that his car didn't break and swerve prior the running off the road. It was more of a 90-degree turn into a tree. Not likely he went to sleep and made a sharp turn like that so they're running down a few leads."

“That’s a reach. With all evidence to the contrary you can’t just toss attempted homicide into the mix. This ain’t no cable station. Like I say, ‘factoids not tabloids.’ This one has legs without adding sensational rumors,” he replied and leaned forward in his chair.

“I think the network will pick it up if we play our cards right. Not much prime time material here in River City so let’s take a look at your pitch,” he said picking up the storyboard copy.

“Jesus, Seth. Your friend and minister is lying comatose in the hospital. He may die for all we know and you’re talking about a network spot. It’s not like you to be so coldhearted.”

“That’s because you don’t get it. This story is our tribute and I want the widest possible audience. That’s why we are rushing. It’s a terrible situation but *this* is what we do and you’ve only got a couple of hours to get it into editing so, let’s drop the platitudes and focus on the story. *That’s* how we are going to pay our respects. Any questions?”

Thirty minutes later she finished her pitch and again understood why Seth was the director of the news. He was a great storyteller-how to make it feel, reveal facts, manipulate the sequence and finish with maximum impact.

“So I’m still trying to connect a few dots. Can we take a minute and go over what we know about the accident?” she asked as he looked at her with a perfect poker face.

“Alright Dominique let’s do that. I’ll go first,” he replied and sat back in his chair.

“It’s late, heavy fog, car going too fast, swerves to avoid a deer and heads into the woods or maybe he goes to sleep and cuts the wheel dozing off. No skid marks, no faulty breaks, no latent prints in the car, no nothing. The cops have told us that much. Do you prefer a different scenario?”

“Well, for openers the unworn seat belt, lack of skid marks and possible footprints *are* issues. They tell us that maybe we have two people in that car. Suppose the passenger grabbed the wheel, cut it into the woods and did something to Vick’s seat belt? Vick would almost certainly be injured, even killed, and the passenger could slip away unhurt."

"Wait. I've got a better one. An evil force was taking control of his body and he wrecked the car to save the planet. Or maybe a civil war ghost regiment marched out of the swamp and scared the crap out of him. Happens all the time in these parts. Anything else?"

"Just one more question." she said and swallowed hard.

"How far along were you and Vick in discussing a weekly production?"

"Sounds like you want to do more than connect some damn dots so let's get it straight. That project is the preacher's pipedream and he never gets tired of pitching it. A new TV empire or some silly shit. How-eh-ver, it always dies a quick death when it gets to this desk." He stood up and walked around to confront her.

"I know what you're driving at and I've had more than enough of it. Either you take that crew and do your job or get the hell out of my station. Is that clear?" he said with barely controlled anger.

"I'm going, boss," she said standing, daring to face him down. "But we're not done with this. I'm sorry if that threatens you but I was told to expose the source of the violence I despise and I won't hold back on that."

"Well here's my warning to you, Dominique. If you try to pull that reporter's curiosity crap in this office again I'll have you working PSAs and commercial cut-ins until you're singing the jingles in your sleep," he said moving closer, face to face with her.

"What's done is done and I won't stand for you're little insinuations. My relationship with Vick is not the issue, not now or ever. I should---" He was interrupted by a knock on the office door and it quickly opened.

Mark popped his head in to see Seth Griggs' large frame towering over Dominique.

“Hi there, folks. Gee, Dominique, did you forget our interview?” he innocently asked.

“Justin. What the hell are you doing here? How’d you get past security?” Seth yelled at him but Dominique answered.

“He’s here to interview for our Citizen of the Week award. I told the guys at the desk he might show up. You know, they watch the news too.” she replied sliding out from between Seth and the chair.

“Just get me that story and do it fast. You don’t have time for what this guy is selling. Citizen of the Week? We’ll see about that. And for the record Justin, after this tribute to Springwell we’re coming back around to look at you. Be back here in two hours, young lady,” he demanded as she closed the door.

“Wow, Citizen of the Week, I’m honored, but looks like Seth was about to make you Dead Reporter of the Week. You’re putting it together aren’t you?” he asked as they walked to her desk.

“Yeah, maybe.” she replied and spun around so fast to face him he almost ran into her.

“Damn it, Mark. He said there were no latent prints but the cops never dusted the car. That’s not in any report. Why would he say that unless he knows more than he’s telling,” she said the last sentence slowly like sliding the last few pieces of a jigsaw puzzle into place.

“I gotta go over to Commonwealth with a crew. I’ll see you there,” she said grabbing her purse and walking toward the back door.

“Hey, don’t you want to know why I got here in the nick of time?” he half yelled to her.

“To save my ass. Thanks,” she said and disappeared through the door.

Mark turned around and walked back toward Seth’s office ready to confront him, *mano y mano,* but three feet from the door he turned left and took the stairs down to the lobby. A crystal clear picture of Seth's meaty right fist crushing the side of his head about ten seconds after walking in there changed his mind.

"Come to think of it, that's the quickest way to join Vick in Comaville," he thought crossing the lobby and tossing the visitor's badge on the security desk. "Sign me out, fellas. Many thanks," he said with a quick wave and exit.

As Justin was taking the stairs outside his office, Seth Griggs stood on the other side of the closed door weighing his options. Amazed and seething mad at how fast his reporter had fingered him, he sat on the edge of his desk thinking out loud and trying to simmer down.

"Well chump, let's go through the possibilities. With less than nothing, she's nailed it and me but does not believe it. Yet. Thank God she's a better reporter than that." He began pacing and wondered if he'd have to trade his office for a jail cell soon.

"And now for the good news. As far as the cops are concerned, they're closing the books on the righteous reverend's accident. That means I just have to gut it out and play some mind games with Dominique until the end of the news cycle. Now that's damn doable."

He felt better but then had to consider the unexpected.

"This ain't the crime of the century and somewhere in the spectrum of possibilities my ass is caught and prosecuted. If Vick wakes up, it's all over except doing the time. If he doesn't, he just rots there and life as we know it keeps on keepin' on," he mumbled to himself and then remembered the last thing they talked about in Vick's car.

"He just had to have that weekly show and it had to be a top drawer production. He wouldn't back down like last year," he thought and then recalled exactly what Vick said that made him snap.

"It's a community project, Seth. You've got to make it happen now for all of us, especially the children," he remembered Vick saying through an insincere smile.

“It was that wicked grin of his, so condescending, so damn white. I couldn’t stop myself,” he thought and recalled the accident.

“How many times have I imagined that wreck? At night, on a remote interstate, wife in the driver’s seat. Never thought it would work but damn, like a charm. In one motion. Reach over, click the belt, and yank the wheel. Clobberuski!”

He winced at the collision flash back.

“I thought he was dead, bleeding and out like a gigged toad. It didn’t even crease my slacks. A thirty-second wipe-down and it was over. Maybe I was stupid to run away without knowing he was dead but I was too scared to finish him off. And now I can’t just mosey over to the hospital and put old Vick out of his misery. Very slim odds I’d make another clean getaway and besides, asphyxiation shows up in an autopsy.”

He’d decided.

“Nope, Seth ole son, you and Vick are here and there. But the food’s a lot better here,” he thought and plucked his coat off the rack.

“Maybe I’ll do some praying at his church service. Pray to be forgiven and pray that son of a bitch doesn’t come to and remember who put him there.” He rubbed his chin knowing that could happen any minute.

“After I ask forgiveness I’ll come back and run the hell out of this story. Consider it my memorial to the man who pulled my chain once too often,” he said to the empty office and turned off the lights on his way out the door.

“Shitty world, shitty choice.”

That thought produced a flood of old regrets he couldn’t stop and The New Orleans incident was always at the top. But he had to smile at the memory of being such a heathen at a church conference.

“At least I had some fun for one glorious night. Drunk on hurricanes and humping my bones off in a three-way with the two loveliest working girls in the Big Easy. Hellofa night. But I never get away with anything," he thought and realized what that could mean now.

"Pictures. It's so trite but Vick got 'em. Never believed that bogus story about a concerned Christian turning them over to him, a man of God, so that I could confess my sins and be forgiven." He tripped but grabbed the rail to right himself and kept descending the stairs.

"Don't kill yourself now, Seth ole son, he ain't worth it. Setting me up like that. I should have killed him right then and there. Finally, the deed is done so let's keep moving."

He opened the door to the entry foyer and headed across the marble floor.

"Good night Mr. Griggs," the security guard interrupted his thoughts as Seth walked in front of the guard desk. "You going to pay your respects to Reverend Springwell?"

"That I am, Tony. And while I'm thinking about it, would you make an entry in the security log to stop Mark Justin from heading upstairs alone. If we have to entertain him again he'll need an escort."

"No problemo, Mr. Griggs. He just left so I'll key it in right now." The guard was anxious to serve and protect.

"Thanks, Tony. See you after the service."

Glad to see the bright sunshiny day, Seth was ready to fake his respects and enjoy a newfound freedom. And he cleared his thinking of the bilge from New Orleans for the last time.

Chapter 36

Charlotte knew the Justin phone drill and had unplugged all 4 in the house as the theme music for *The News at 6 on 10* began. During the last week she set up external voice mail through their carrier so unplugging the phone redirected the outside world but didn't cut it off.

"People who want to always get through one way or another," she thought knowing Mark could be the target of another zealot or assassin from God knows where. "This isn't going away, not now, maybe not ever. Note to self: Give Madame Surgio the Golden Turban Award and then set it on fire while he's wearing it."

She settled on the couch to watch the broadcast and snuggled against Mark thankful they had made it though the week.

* * * * *

"Hello. You've reached the Justin telecommunications bunker. All of our operators are helping other callers come to their senses. Leave a message and we'll take your case," Mark announced through their new answering service.

6:30 PM: "Hey Mark, BJ from CSN here. We just saw that local six o'clock piece and looks like you're getting some regular airtime up there in Richmond. Third one this week, but who's counting huh? Shame about Vick. I guess he ignored your warning, God forgive him. Well, any who, I'm calling because we've got something important for you to consider. In two weeks we'd like to feature you on the New Leaders segment of CSN's People Making a Difference show. I need to get a crew up there and shoot some promo cuts. You know, Mark, CSN is where your story belongs. We'll respect your privacy and won't interfere with your career. It's information to inspire the nation. Catchy hook don't you think? Anyway, God bless you, Mark. I know we can do this the right way. Call me."

7:45 PM: "Hello Mr. Justin. Dan Rather, CBS News. Maybe you're surprised to hear my voice on your answering gizmo. Well don't be. We at CBS News often call washed up newscasters after they make their comeback as evangelicals. Happens more than you think and we want you to know there's a place where the news and heaven meet on earth. No, not CBS, it's CSN. Now, we understand that courageous reporter John Chambers is trying to reach you. He's busted up like a Texas oil monopoly but can still tell your story along with the other young bucks at CSN. They're the best in the biz and old John is on the mend so give him a call. Appreciate it," said John Chambers doing a ridiculously bad Rather impersonation.

9:00 PM: "Hey Mark, Dominique. Wanted you to know this thing is off the charts. The combination of Springwell's coma, his church in turmoil and your escapades has torqued this town into some kind of religious fervor. Scary but incredibly good for ratings. Seth is running it again at 11:00 and again tomorrow on Good Morning Richmond. Everybody wants to tape it and we're announcing the schedule. Unbelievable. Speaking of the unbelieved, I'm not getting anywhere on solving that phony Springwell accident. I know what I know but I don't know how I know it. You owe me for obliterating my bugs. Later."

10:00 PM: "Mark, Dominique again with breaking news. The network is picking up the story. We used the East Coast uplink and New York went crazy. So, bottom line is that we can't run it tonight or any other time and they want to talk on Monday about setting up something midweek with you, Miss Daisy, Tinsler and the whole cast from *Elder Justin's Road to Glory*. I'll call you Monday to talk about the schedule but wanted you know we're going national. Have a damn fine weekend while you can and call me if you want to talk before Monday."

Mark listened to the messages without taking a note or a phone number and couldn't hold back the smile. But the Debating Society wouldn't let him enjoy it.

"Your ego over flows, boss. This is a flying leap in to the network cesspool. They eat their young don't they?"

"Lovely image, boys. Club any baby seals in there today?"

“Just warning you, hero. Expectations have left the building and you’re chasing them down a dark alley. On the bright side, it beats grinding through the network affiliates looking for a break at the anchor desk. How’d that work out? You think *that* was a crash landing? This one’s going to be fast and bloody. So bask in the glory or hide and be crucified. Anything else?”

“No thanks, gentleman. I’m totally underwhelmed. Go find an Embolism Suites and get a room.” He smiled at the thought and decided to call for backup.

It was midnight but he dialed his best friend’s portable phone. Louis was a night owl too.

“Hey Shotsy. You still up?”

“Yeah, suture face. I’m at the hospital finishing a late case. I was about to call you anyway. You want to tell me about your little visit with Vick today?”

“Not really, I mean I can’t talk about it. It was a confidential…”

“So why’d you call me?”

“Just to talk. I found out the network will be here next week…”

“Really? Gosh that’s swell and I’d love to chat about who you’ll be wearing on the red carpet but we have some unfinished business. I’m looking at the results of Vick’s confidential EEG and I need to know what you did over here. That’s what’s important right now, cuz. So why don’t you confidential your butt over here and I’ll find us a sound proof room to talk about it.”

“Hold it Lou, you’re babbling. I warned you about humping the anesthesia tanks.”

“Okay wise guy, I’ll spell it out. I’ve got more charts for you to peruse. Remember Dan Campbell and your little midnight prayer service a few days ago? I chalked up his recovery to a rare case of perfect therapy meeting a responsive patient. Delusional, I know, but in Vick’s case I can’t do that. He’s still unconscious and I need to talk to you about it right now.”

"But not necessarily at the hospital, right?"

"Wrong, little buddy. It has to be here. I can't take case records out of building and besides, after we talk you may even want to peek in on him.

"Highly unlikely, Dr. Spazinoff, and I sure don't need to see no stinkin' charts. So I'm going to hang up now and we'll see where he is in the morning."

"Hold it Mark, I'm not kidding. I need you to look at this stuff. We may be at a turning point that only you can understand. I'm just asking for a few minutes to work with me."

The silence beat a dial tone. Louis knew he was in.

"Shit and double shit on your best suit, Lou. I'm dead on my feet tired."

"And I don't need that cleaning bill but it's all connected and you're in the middle so drag your butt on over here. I'll reheat some rancid coffee and you can tour the morgue if it'll make you feel better."

Dial tone.

Without waking Charlotte, Mark locked up the house and drove to the hospital playing his favorite tunes at the pain threshold to preempt any thoughts about what might happen when he got there. It was his fourth visit of the week.

Louis was waiting by the elevator and they took it to the second floor without exchanging the usual insults. The coffee was 6 hours old and as bad as advertised.

"You've got to see the EEG charts. The differences in brain activity between now and twelve hours ago are beyond the pale. So, we've officially termed whatever it is you do, the Justin Effect. We'll let you know when it shows up in the prayer section of our text books."

"But I didn't exactly pray for Vick," Mark clarified. "I was just trying kind of poking around a little to see if he was in there."

“Well my wayward psychic friend, you must have poked him in eye with your johnson because this is radical.”

Louis spread out both of the Springwell ‘before’ and ‘after’ EEG charts on a desk and waved his pen at them before stabbing the ‘after’ chart near a series of spikes in the reading.

“This is not a comatose patient. Bear with me a second and learn something. First thing, there’s no Beta activity, nada. That’s the same as it was when he came in and symptomatic of cortical injury so we know he’s hurt pretty bad. His initial CT scan showed a left hemisphere subdural hematoma and we drained that bad boy as soon as the neurosurgeon got here. But even after that he still didn’t present us with much to work with. Not a big surprise.”

Louis drew large circles on the ‘before’ chart. “See, he came in with just some lazy Theta activity and some short Alpha waves but mostly it was lights out, comatose.”

Mark didn’t understand the brain wave lingo but he did hear a faint and familiar background buzz crank up. He decided to ignore it and nodded for Louis to continue.

“Ok now we are here, *after* your visit, and even you can see what’s going on. Beta is still flat, pulse slow, respiration deep and he outwardly remains comatose, but the other activity waves are leaping around like sugar plum fairies on steroids. Fact is we’ve *all* been poking him with something but only you got a response.

“Now,” he said looking directly at Mark, “we don’t see any more internal bleeding and that’s a good thing but he’s still remarkably unresponsive so I want you to focus on these charts and tell me what you see.”

“How would a temper tantrum look on them?”

“I don’t know. Is he having one?”

“Maybe but this stuff just looks like a bad year in the market to me. What am I supposed to see?”

“I’m not sure. Come on Marko. Focus. Tell me what’s there.”

He tried to think through the irritating buzz saw and concentrate. Suddenly there was a prickly stinging vibe in his hands and arms. It throbbed down both shoulders and seemed to emanate from the base of his skull.

The more he squinted and concentrated the more his hands stung but he kept his eyes focused on the wavy lines in the 'after' chart. Given he was near exhaustion, Mark wasn't much surprised when the lines moved vertically, projecting above the paper in full 3-D graphical fashion.

"Very creative hallucination," he thought.

He expected the graphics to slide off the chart and slither across the floor but instead, spewing out in all directions from his finger tips, stubby sparks, lots of them, pulsed across the chart like a thousand tiny bolts of static electricity. And the charts responded.

"Far out," he whispered.

"Whoa! Look at that! Mark, you're doing it man. You are doing it with a capital I-T!" Louis screamed as he backed away from the desk.

Both EEG charts rolled up into tight scrolls and then, even quicker, rolled back out flat on the desktop making a sharp snapping noise at the end. It was over in less than five seconds.

The little finger tip sparks disappeared but Mark still felt the prickly vibe as he stood up and flicked his hands back and forth trying to wake them up. Louis leaned in to put his arm around Mark's shoulders to help settle him down but Mark pulled away.

"Lay off and listen to me. Did you see what I saw?"

"Well, I don't rightly know, son. What did we see?"

"The little sparks coming out of my fingers?"

"Oh wow, you're not kidding. There were sparks too? That would have been so cool to see. But I don't care about attendant hallucinations. We both know you and your extremely long Head Line just moved those freakin' charts. I mean it's not like the air conditioner kicking on could do it. No sir-ree, Mr. Justin.

You got the touch. And you got it good. I knew it, knew it for sure when you blew up Mr. Slurpee the other day."

He smiled from ear to ear and leaned over to give Mark a squeeze before looking closely again at the charts lying flat and fully extended. "I wish we had a couple of cigars and some cognac to celebrate, even if it is a federal crime to smoke in here."

"Maybe it really was the air conditioner, Lou. It's pretty chilly."

"It's always a meat locker in here but check this out." Louis was pointing at the rolled out charts. "Hey, did you see this? The lines on the 'after' chart are gone. Man, look at that. It's lily white, like they were never there."

His mood changed when he looked back at Mark. "You found me out didn't you? How could you possibly know?"

"I really hate to ask this but, 'Know what?'"

"It was a fake. The 'after' one was a fake. I made it an hour ago using a demo program. Just entered the symptoms and printed the chart. The other one is real but the one you erased came straight from my laptop."

"Why would you do that?" Was all Mark could say before the buzz in his head, amplified by the hurt of a betrayed friendship, sawed his thoughts in half.

"Don't look at me like that, Marko. You ought to be thanking me. Really, I saw the 6:00 news piece and figured with everything you've done this week maybe one more nudge would get you across the finish line. That's all. Just trying to free your mind. And it worked, didn't it? Hells bells, you not only moved it you actually changed it. That's beyond any explanation."

Louis paused, awed by what he had just witnessed.

"It's beyond anything, man." He was near tears as he tried to express what he'd seen. "I believe in you, Mark. I have since I read your palm. That's why I did it. Don't be mad. It's all good. Right?"

Mark was too angry to look at him and the buzz in his brain shut down any analysis. “I don’t know what it is Lou. I only know you tricked me and I am mad as hell about it. I ought to sue you for impersonating a doctor and a friend. Screw you and your experiment. *You* had no right to do it.”

And in one quick move he rolled up the charts and threw them at his friend. For a moment they appeared to be wrapping around him from head to toe but then fell unrolled to the floor at his feet.

The buzz was louder, much louder, like a chainsaw gnawing through his brain. He instinctively covered both ears hoping to block the painful sounds and sat down expecting his head to explode in his hands.

But instead, it all stopped. Suddenly silent. Not a buzz, a voice, or thought. Quiet. Relief. In a few seconds he was back in control and about to confront Lou when a familiar voice spoke up.

“He is your friend but I am your victim. No rescue now. It’s time to pay for your sins, demon. So nice of you to return. So nisssssssss...”

Chapter 37

A cold shiver ran up Mark's spine and across his shoulders as the voice drew out the last word to sound like a hissing snake.

"Lou, damn it. Did you hear that?"

"Hear what, Marko. You know you're not looking too good over there. How about let's take you to the ICU downstairs? This time of night I can find you an apple flavor IV and a big-eyed nurse."

"Listen to me. It's Vick. He found me. We've got to go back to his room right now. This time take that EEG machine and get a reading. A real one. No trickeration. I'm at the end of my rope and it's time to know if it's him or me thinking it's him."

"You hear Vick?" Lou asked but then realized that now anything was possible with Mark. "Yeah, you do. I know you do. You're becoming supernatural and I guess there's no predicting it, huh? You still mad at me?" he asked holding up his stethoscope for protection.

"Bite me Doctor Quackenstein. We have to see Vick right now. I'll burn your bridge later."

Nothing had changed in the room. Vick looked just as he did twelve hours earlier. The heart monitor was chirping sixty two times per minute, the EEG quietly recorded brain activity, and the food tube was grotesquely taped into his nose.

Louis stepped beside the bed to start the printer while Mark stayed at the foot staring at Vick, remembering the pain of the earlier pool dream.

"Feel it? The fear? Fee-ell me?"

Louis was still busy with the monitoring equipment and hadn't said a word but neither had Vick. Mark decided to close his eyes but kept his hands near the bed just above the lumps he knew were Vick's feet.

“Vick, you don’t belong here. I’m sure you know that and we want you back. Come with me now. Right now.” And he opened his eyes.

Or did he?

Vick was staring back with vibrant green eyes and a sly grin so frightening that Mark could only mouth the scream that formed in his throat.

“You *do* feel it. Pulling you under. Filling your lungs. Drowning in sin. But it doesn’t have to be that way. I can protect you.” Vick said out loud this time.

Mark was so afraid he couldn’t breath or move-terrified by the suffocating panic of his own imminent death.

“Please Vick, I’m trying to help.”

Vick spoke again, reassuring, beckoning. “So many prayers, so much strength and pain. Sometimes they reach me but I can’t go back to them now. Take my hands, Mark. You and I need to be together. Free together. Take them.”

“I don’t think so.”

The EEG printer snapped on and immediately presented Louis with highly amplified patterns across all of the signature waves.

“Mark. This is unbelievable. It’s identical to the chart I created in the demo and it…

He looked back over his shoulder just in time to see a bolt of lightning leap from Mark’s hands and strike Vick squarely in the chest. It vanished into his pajama shirt, making a soft crackling sound, but sending a violent whole body quake through Vick’s torso, legs and feet that yanked against the tight sheets.

“No! Stop it! Are you trying to kill him?”

Quick answer-Vick’s body functions shut down. The EEG flat lined, the EKG chirps became one long monotone and he stopped breathing. Just like that he was gone.

Louis jumped to the side of the bed and applied the first chest compression on Vick, then the second, third, forth, and fifth in rapid succession.

"Come on Vick, I know for a fact that wasn't enough juice to kill you," he scolded his patient.

On cue, the EKG chirped once, then again. Louis grabbed his stethoscope to begin checking vitals when Vick suddenly took a deep breath, turned toward him and opened his eyes. Louis was inches away when they looked at each other and Vick's eyes widened as if he recognized the doctor before they closed and he relaxed on the exhale. Within seconds the irregular chirps resumed their one-per-second rhythm.

"Vick? Can you hear me?" Louis needed to catch him before he slipped back.

No response. Again, with a clap of his hands close to Vicks ear. Nothing.

He had no way of knowing if Vick was better or worse but at least his vitals returned to normal. It occurred to Louis that this whole show might have been a bad idea. "Mental, physical and spiritual crap I can't comprehend cutting through him dark knives. I could lose my patient and my license."

He looked back at Mark who hadn't moved and was still at the foot of bed, staring at Vick. "Hey, Sparky. What the hell are you doing to my patient?"

"Self defense, Lou. He's coming after me but I am not going down there with him." Mark said and continued flicking his hands back and forth to wake them up.

"Just get the hell out of here and don't come back. This hospital is off limits. You got that?" Louis barely contained his anger while examining Vick's eyes with a pin light.

"No problem, Lou. I'm done here, anyway. He's stable isn't he?"

"He was stable before you zapped him with your, your… What the hell was that, Mark? No, wait, don't answer," He said shining the light into Mark's eyes to emphasize the point. "He hadn't moved a muscle, you freak. Just leave before I call the cops. I mean it."

"Calm down and check your new chart over there. You'll see I didn't hurt him. But what you won't see is that he's closer to us now than he was five minutes ago. So run your little diagnostics and I'll wait outside for someone to cuff me and Miranda my ass."

And Mark left the room for the last time. He was exhausted. Collapsing on the couch in the waiting room he wondered where to find enough strength to even crawl out to the parking lot.

"Wisdom from above? Turn and face the power? Dynamo hum? The hits just keep coming," he thought and blanked out until Louis walked in with the EEG printout in hand.

"Hey you bum. No loitering in here. Now wake up and smell the righteousness," Louis said while gently nudging Mark's feet off of the couch and sitting down.

"I won't admit it outside this room but it looks like you called it a while ago. He's stable, not agitated any longer. Resting like you gave him a full body massage."

Louis had spent the last twenty minutes thoroughly examining Vick and was relieved enough by the results to reconsider Mark's intervention. He'd reviewed the continuous EEG printout and brought the last few minutes of it into the waiting room hoping Mark would telekinetically roll and unroll this one like he had done earlier.

"Most of it looks pretty normal, kind of a deep sleep, I think. In any case we'll continue the concussion cocktail and I've ordered a bed check every thirty minutes just to be sure he doesn't put on his dancin' shoes. You interested in looking at this?"

He tilted the printout toward Mark but then realized that Mark looked worse than Vick. "Guess you're not up for more reading between the lines, huh?"

Mark glared at him and at the same time Louis felt his eyeglasses slide backward atop his nose and press hard against his eyebrows.

"Whoa there, Mark. What the hell was that?" He asked standing up, yanking off his glasses, and stuffing them in his lab coat pocket.

"What was what, Dr. Boner?"

"Forget it. Let's just get out of here. Can you drive?"

"Don't think so. In fact, can you get me a wheelchair? Feels like I'm the loser in a cage match with a grizzly bear."

"A truly confused metaphor you are, little buddy. But after your mind-bending performance tonight we're going home in style. Bound to be an available ambulance downstairs headed your way."

"Good idea but you still suck and after this you always will."

"Yes, I do and I'd do it again as long as I could be at your coming out party. Now hop in, buckle up, and stop whining. You'll be home in ten minutes." Louis said as he grabbed a wheelchair from the corner of the room.

Mark's legs shook; barely strong enough to walk from driveway-to-stoop after Louis drove him home. It seemed closer to dawn than midnight when he collapsed on the couch but it was just past one, only an hour since he'd called Louis.

"Vick in my mirror, in my dreams and me in his coma-that guy wanted to kill me fifteen ways to Sunday. But my new shock therapy put the quietus on that one. He'll be a changed man when he wakes up. Right?" He asked himself.

"Yessssssss."

The little bit of energy he had left gushed from his stomach on the floor and a million goose bumps pricked him from head to toe.

"The snake wasn't Vick."

"Very funny boys. Give it a rest."

It was all he could do to find and click the remote. He turned the weather blather loud enough to generate a snake-proof sound barrier and crashed.

Sunday service was less than ten hours away.

Chapter 38

Another hot and sunny Sunday morning at the front door of Commonwealth Church. The duty sheet showed Mark meeting, greeting, and glad-handing at the back door but Jerry moved him to the front where he would handle more traffic. There were now so many celebrities at Commonwealth that he was able to return the “Oh, I saw you on TV” greeting as they filled in.

Miss Daisy gave him a big hug and said she’d never felt better. Everyone wanted to know about more about Vick and he assured them that Vick was strong and fighting to be back with them. Mostly they wanted to sign up to pray and he pointed them toward Charlotte and her friends at the sign up table.

Jerry was going to announce the ‘interim’ leadership changes and even Tom Robertson looked more comfortable talking to reporters from behind a podium set in one of the small memorial gardens around the church. Mark was surprised by how quickly they had come together after Vick’s demise; like they were ready for it or maybe just glad to get out from under his thumb.

“Truth is Vick’s so close that a knee to the groin might do him more good than anything else. How’s that for tough love?” Mark smiled as the picture of rupture therapy for Vick popped into his mind’s eye.

“Telling yourself a joke Mr. Justin? Do you know something the rest of us don’t?” Seth Griggs asked walking toward Mark from the other side of the portico.

“I should be asking *you* that question, Seth. Looks like your mood’s improved. Anything you want to confess?” he replied.

“Cute. You may not know it yet, Justin, but I’m your best friend this morning,” Seth replied but Mark knew about the network plans for the story.

In a flash of anger Mark put his hand on Seth’s shoulder and leaned in close to make sure his comment would not be overheard.

"Friends don't let friends drive unbelted. Hope you enjoy the service," he said in a harsh whisper and then added a friendly slap on Seth's back before turning around to shake hands with the next sinner.

"Catch me if you can, elder asshole," Seth thought as he walked into the church and up to his usual seat in the balcony.

Mark glimpsed Dan Campbell across the narthex entering the sanctuary from the other side and waved to him. Dan looked up, spotted him, but kept walking, avoiding eye contact.

"Come on Dan. You made it out of that deathbed for a reason. You should've figured that out by now and besides, walking in here beats the alternative doesn't it?" He wanted to yell that question across the crowded entry but Dan was gone. "You're still upset about missing an early exit. How strange is that?"

"How strange is what?" asked another familiar voice.

Mark looked around to see Dominique dressed in a black skirt with a coordinated short sleeve top and made up to accentuate her eyes and high cheekbones. There was no hiding his surprise-had she read his mind?"

"Welcome back. Is this visit for business or forgiveness? He asked looking around for the TV10 van.

"Both. Need to talk with you after the service. Big doings in River City," she said and took a bulletin out of his hand as she passed by.

"Read this thought lady. 'Your career path doesn't run through this yard.'" He was relieved when she disappeared into the sanctuary without giving him a backhanded wave.

In fifteen minutes all the sinners were coralled and seated. Duty done, he took his customary seat on the second step of the stairs leading up to the balcony. It was the part of the service he usually cranked up The Debating Society sermonette but this week he wanted silence. Peace.

But slicing the quiet, a voice sang out. Not from the sanctuary, it was clear and precise, like an angelic diva floating above him near the ceiling.

Faith Hill's voice was pure and peaceful in a two-chord song line he'd never heard before.

The wisdom from above is luh-uve.

He looked around but no one was there.

The wisdom from above is luh-uh-uve.

Faith curled the last note as if in the middle of the song's chorus.

It comes to you on the wings of a dove,
The wisdom from above is luh-uh-uve
You know the wisdom from above is love.

Four beats later with the elation of 75 voices, 150 hands clapping and overpowering gospel harmony, the Hallelujah Chorus launched the first stanza of the new song.

You don't need a diamond ri-ing,
No, you don't need to own a thing.
Just lose yourself in His peace and luh-uve
The wisdom from above is luh-uh-uve
The wisdom from above is love.

Then the vision of the whole production leaped into his mind's eye. It *was* in the church sanctuary, right through the doors in front of him, complete with a twenty piece orchestra, a huge bank of Marshall amplifiers, a back center stage drum set, and a front stage stand up microphone.

With the Hallelujah Chorus swaying, clapping, and singing on either side, Joe Cocker staggered up to the mike and picked up the second verse.

You-oo-oo don't need a cause to dee-fend
You don't need a little help from your friends.
Just rock and roll when it's your time to shi-ine
The wisdom from above is luh-uh-uve.
You knooooow the wisdom from above is love.

Then the back stage spotlight silhouetted Eric Clapton as he broke into a guitar solo and the orchestra joined in along with drummer Ginger Baker and bassist Jack Bruce playing the refrain on stage with Clapton.

The Halleluiah's and the stars joined together to play the chorus and build it to a crescendo. Loud and overwhelming, all the voices and instruments performed with the precision of a national touring group.

The wisdom from above is luh-uh-uve
It comes to you on the wings ---"

The muffled thunder of 1381 fannies hitting the pew cushions jolted Mark away from his all-star gospel concert and back into the narthex. But instead of sitting on the balcony stairs he was standing in front of the memorial slab of marble with James 3:17 inscribed.

"That's so cool. It's the No Fear Tour. It's We Are The World meets The Cream and the Philadelphia Philharmonic. It's the Wisdom From Above Extravagalooza! Smooth tune, outstanding arrangement and the Faith Hill intro is so strong."

"It's nothing but a fantasy tour and you're still the leader of The Wannabes." The Debating Society interrupted. "You're way over your head Marko, so we decided to book the reality tour. Check it out. You're suppressing the most bizarre two weeks of your life and you've got no clue what's up with the next two weeks or with this church, or with Vick, that comatose rascal, or Miss TV10 reporter right there in the other room or those bible beaters at CSN. You don't even know if you can control your thoughts, your fits, and those new voices. Divine or satanic? Important questions. We won't let you just make up another loser song and blow off your so-called life. Time to face the real music."

Before he could answer, the Hallelujah Chorus was back clapping in rhythm but this time Paul McCartney, seated stage right behind a baby grand, was in the spotlight and picked up the next verse singing loud enough to overwhelm any internal debate.

You don't need to be afra-aid

No, you don't have to feel ashamed,
Just open your heart and let it be-ee
The wisdom from above will set you free-e
The wisdom from above is luh-uh-uve.
The wisdom from above is love.

The tune and Paul's piano gracefully faded out but there was no response from The Debating Society. He looked up again to the words on the marble memorial to a long dead minister.

There they were. They were always there.

Reading them again, feeling the music in his head, instead of the buzz and the pain, he closed his eyes to enjoy the rare moment and replay his new tune.

"Finally, the end of it," he thought. "The reason and the lesson. The wisdom and the truth. Now that I know it, I'm going to live it. But first, let's play that tune again.

But the music didn't return. Instead, as soon as he settled back on the steps and closed his eyes, a bright light flared up behind his eyelids. It changed so quickly he thought he was falling backwards. The music, the wisdom, and the joy were gone. All replaced by a new vision in his mind's eye.

Chapter 39

Mark was standing in the doorway of a large modern kitchen. The red tile floor was a Southwestern design and led to an oval shaped cooking island with drop-in stove and small bar sink in black granite countertop. With wrought iron racks holding all manner of cookery and large jars of various pastas lining the back countertops, he recognized it as a well-stocked gourmet kitchen.

"This is not funny. Am I here to cook my own goose? Where the heck is here?"

Perfect as it was, something was gut-wrong, too sterile, unnatural and isolated. He realized this handsome kitchen was like a prop, never used but appearing fully functional and inviting. The only thing missing was a fresh pot of coffee.

"What kind of home has an unused kitchen equipped to the 9s like it's waiting for Julia Child to drop by?"

Then other senses kicked in. From somewhere in the scene a piercing high frequency smoke alarm was steadily growing louder.

"At least it's not the buzz of another chainsaw headache but it is going to burst my eardrums in about two minutes. Otherwise this will be a great hallucination when I can find the eggs and bacon."

He moved into the scene toward the cooking island. Moving was walking without sound or footfall, feeling-floating with feet and legs in motion. As cool as that felt, there was no time to analyze it. He stopped to peek behind the mahogany paneled center island. The irritating smoke alarm was louder and he was getting near its source as he looked up toward the ceiling.

"Now I see you. But there's no smoke or fire in here so you can shut up now and let me hallucinate in peace."

But it continued and reached the pain threshold.

"Hey, boss, hallucinate this. Very bad things are happening in here and you've got no control over any of it so we think you'd better skip the garden tour and get the hell out. Right now."

The Debating Society had come along for the ride, a bit panicky, so he ignored them and continued looking around the cooking island to see the area in front of the oven. But the blinking red numbers of an alarm clock sitting on the oven's surface caught his eye first.

"That's wrong. It's out of place. You should be on opposite counter top not on the oven."

But he instantly dropped that thought and stopped in his tracks as he looked down to see the figure of a woman, dressed only in a bra and panty, lying belly-down on the open oven door, her head fully inside the oven, hands tied behind her back, knees on the floor.

Her skin was smooth but not young. She was middle aged, slim, and petite with jet-black shoulder length hair, perfectly cut, and immaculately dyed.

"What is she doing here being tortured like that? Wait a second, Marko. You know she's not real. None of this is so play along and ask her the obvious question. Believe me, there won't be an answer."

He tried to speak but it was more like telepathy-he thought toward her. "Are you real? Are you alive? How'd you get here?" he blurted and stepped closer to see a little further into the oven. "Hey lady, can you hear me?"

But then she moved *and* she saw him.

Actually she turned and backed out her head a little by leaning over on one knee so that her eyes could peek under the lip of the oven. Her mouth was duct-taped but her eyes were open, huge and brown.

If she tried to talk, he couldn't hear her over the screeching smoke alarm. But she flicked her eyes and ticked her head upward to get him to look in that direction, above the oven.

"The clock? I don't care about the clock, lady. We have to get you out of here."

But as he looked again at its blinking numbers, he realized the clock wasn't a clock, the red digital numbers were declining.

Worse, the smoke alarm wasn't a smoke alarm. It was a carbon monoxide detector.

3…2…1

The detonator charged the igniter and a fireball engulfed the stove, the woman, and the kitchen in an instant of heat and light without sound.

He was dead for sure; executed along with the oven lady. Dead and drifting, blinked away by a bomb and the gas that blew away a home in Nowheresville.

Sailing. Back into black. No dialog, no music. Silent night.

But a creaking-snapping noise directly in front of him broke through the dark after-blast. He jerked open his eyes to confront yet another hallucination. The dead preacher's Wisdom From Above marble memorial was crooked and becoming more so, slowly rotating and pulling itself out of the wall, sink-bolts breaking from an invisible twisting force.

"No, no, stop it." But the heavy slab was already 90 degrees turned, horizontal to the floor. "This is not going to happen. Stop right now."

And it obeyed for a moment, suspended sideways, pulled away from the wall; briefly the world's only floating marble memorial. But then the force let it go.

The 300 lb. slab fell so hard and so fast it looked to Mark as if he'd plucked it off the wall and thrown it down to the floor a la Charlton 'Moses' Heston heaving the Ten Commandments at the infidels below Mount Sinai.

The crashing noise was hellecious.

Like a car wreck in the hallway, it thundered through the walls and echoed into every corner of the church. Mark stood three feet from the wall looking down in stunned silence, shoes covered with holy shards.

There they were. They had always been there. But not much more than dust on the floor, now they were gone. Oddly, instead of panic, he felt a distinct and comforting sense of relief.

"How irrational is that? You just destroyed your only real connection with God and you feel good about it? Better check your oil, son. That ain't right," The Debating Society has also made it back from the blast.

He looked back at the big doors to the sanctuary knowing that the deacons on duty would be through them in one second.

"Come on guys, let's get it over with."

And the doors flew open on cue.

Tim Flowers was the first through; running down the center red carpet of the sanctuary, he shoved the heavy sanctuary doors open with enough force to bang them against the wall, sending another thundering echo through the building.

From the pulpit Jerry could see into the narthex through the open doors and all appeared to be well. He knew Mark's habit of sitting out the sermon and frowned at the thought of what he'd done out there. So, he loudly cleared his throat and raised his hands to refocus his congregation.

"Friends, yes, friends let me get your attention back up front here again. Yes, Tom Showalter, that means you. And Francine, don't pay any mind to that little fracas. Let's all be seated now. Yes, thank you friends," he said holding up his hands as if to baptize the lot of them.

"It's nothing the deacons can't handle. Probably just that old furnace cutting on for the first time this season or maybe freeway exit construction." No one laughed but he had their attention again.

"Anyway, the deacons will sort it out I'm sure. So, friends, sit back down, face this way and we'll continue the lesson without added sound effects I assure you." He dropped his hands, cleared this throat again, and resumed the sermon.

In the narthex Tim skidded to a stop beside Mark, mouth agape, looking at the pile of marble chunks and shards and the small crater made in the floor.

"I don't know, Tim." Mark said shaking his head, still looking down.

“Christ Almighty. Lord Jesus save us all! It’s a sacrilege and blasphemy. You got an explanation for this mess, Justin?” he said in a harsh whisper.

“Nothing to explain, Tim. It fell down. You know how gravity works don’t you?” Mark answered with a question as he turned and walked toward the wide-open sanctuary doors.

“It’s not funny, Justin. The Lord doesn’t yank our sacred memorials off the wall and smash them to the floor.”

“He did today.” Mark shot back and kept walking.

“Then you march in there and tell them all about it, Mr. High And Mighty. Tell them any clever lie you want but there’s going to be an investigation, I can promise you that.” Tim yelled the last sentence to be heard in the sanctuary.

Without fingerprints Tim’s threat was baseless but Mark was going to face the congregation in about five seconds. Walking the few feet to the open doors he tried to think of something clever. But above all he dare not go supernatural on them. Vick had been right about what that would do.

He stopped at the sanctuary’s entrance and quickly read the room. Instead of everyone staring back waiting for an explanation, most of the congregation was facing forward, listening to Jerry’s increasingly animated sermon. And Jerry was working hard up there in the pulpit.

But a few were still stirring in their pews, looking back toward the narthex, and waiting for an ‘all clear’ signal. To them he coolly nodded, adding a reassuring smile to back it up.

“Oh yeah, the power of a reassuring head nod from the new Elder. That’s one I didn’t count on,” he thought as he looked each one in the eyes and repeated his confident nod.

And the moment would have been resolved except that Dan Campbell decided that a nod and a wink from the devil wouldn’t do. He stood to confront Mark.

“What have you done, Mr. Justin? What other disaster are you visiting on us? Your prayers are a curse. You are a curse on the church! Please leave us and take it with you!" He yelled from his pew in the front of the sanctuary.

"Sit down this instant, Dan! No one is cursed in this church. There is no evil here. So sit down. Do you hear me?" Jerry said from the pulpit.

Dan pointed his finger at Justin, before taking his seat.

"We'll find out all about it in a few minutes," Jerry assured him. "But there's nothing to be concerned about so everyone, please, let us finish the sermon."

"I'll clear it up right now." Tim Flowers spoke up from the back of the sanctuary, loud enough even for Dora Elkins to hear.

"He's destroyed one of our most sacred memorials. It's pulverized all over the floor. He's desecrated this church. That's all I'm saying but it's the Lord's truth. Right, Mr. Justin?"

At that moment in that gigantic room, 1381 sinners sat in stunned silence, heads pivoted toward the sudden debate and all eyes cut to Mark.

In the past ten minutes he'd experienced a life changing epiphany and two supernatural fits. What he needed was a timeout in a sunny room filled with his favorite antiques but instead he was cornered with no cute come back. Without a defense there was only one way he could respond.

The old buzz snapped back so fast it almost took his head off and he felt his guts fall to the floor. His eyes began to roll backward but on their way up he caught a glimpse of Jerry and a uniformed policeman at center stage.

And, at that moment a hand clamped down on his upper shoulder, near the neckline. It pinched the nerve hard enough to make him blink back.

Pain trumps fear and all doctors know it.

"Don't pull that crap here, armadillo breath. All these believers will never join your fan club if you do." Louis warned him loud enough to have been heard by most of the congregation if they had been paying any attention to Mark.

The cops, the one with Jerry and the four in the back of the sanctuary, had stolen the show.

"Just smile for the folks and keep your hands down. We're in some pretty deep do-do right now. So you're going to mosey back toward the doorway and listen to Jerry. Are you with me?" Louis asked and started moving them in tandem.

"You bet, but easy on the death grip, Dr. Spock. I'd sue if I weren't so glad to see you." Mark replied and began backing toward the door with Louis.

Jerry raised his arms to quiet the congregation and the uniform moved away leaving him alone on center stage.

"Everyone please sit down and listen to me. I have some very sad news about Vick that you have to hear. Everyone please listen to me. Today, at 10:30 a.m., Mathew Victor Springwell passed away in his sleep at St. Gertrude's Hospital."

Above the gasps and muffled cries of most everyone there, Jerry continued.

"This is the saddest day in our long history. We've lost our leader and our friend but we not alone. Vick is with our Lord and Savior and will hear us as we pray. 'Our Father who art in heaven. Hallowed be thy name…'" And in a unified reflexive response, they all joined in. It was all Jerry could do to finish The Lord's Prayer.

But the cops weren't there to pray or pay their last respects. This was a business call to arrest their leading suspect. Springwell's accident was now a murder case and they planned to close it in time for the 6 o'clock news.

Detective Joshua Pedding had asked Jerry to string out a eulogy, to keep everyone seated for a few minutes while his five officers positioned themselves to move in and make the arrest. But after the Lord's Prayer was finished the detective signaled they needed more time. Still with his arms raised and a congregation in audible shock, Jerry continued.

"Friends, please stay seated as we comfort each other. Now, in our grief of, uh, terrible grief, and with heavy hearts and the sure knowledge that we are all sinners and saved only by the certainty of Your, uh, certainness, let us recite Psalm 103, no make that Psalm 23. Yes, that's right. Psalm 23 for Vick, a fallen bother, son, and father to many of us. Well, I mean he's been a father figure to so many in the community. Lord, we, uh, beseech thee to listen to us repeat the words You taught us to say. Now, everyone, all together with feeling. 'The Lord is my Shepard…."

Although two cops moved to a position just behind Mark and Louis, they didn't stop to collar Mark. Instead, after scanning the sanctuary they quickly huddled in the back of the narthex. Their suspect was in the balcony. In pairs, and with hands at the gun-ready position, they quick stepped up the marble stairs on both sides of the narthex.

"They're looking for Seth," Mark realized and he pivoted around Louis to run up the stairs behind the cops. Charlotte was up there.

The balcony spread across the width of the church with fifteen rows of short-long-short pews. It was an attached perch for up to 400 sinners and Seth was sitting front row center pew for the perfect view of the bizarre scene on the sanctuary floor.

In the last five minutes his emotional swings had been so extreme he was now bent forward, almost on his knees, crying uncontrollably, unable to contain the joy of total victory. Years of extortion and threats were over; the extorter dead and he was free.

Those seated around him, including Charlotte, knew how close he and Vick had been and tried to comfort him with hugs and the kind of empathizing back rubs meant to console someone in overwhelming grief. The irony wasn't lost on Seth and it made the catharsis even sweeter.

For a few moments.

"Mr. Griggs, sir, we'd like to talk with you." Detective Pedding said in a quiet but firm voice from the aisle at the end of the pew. "It won't take long and you can get right back to your bereavement." He couldn't help his cynicism.

Except for Jerry and the cops, no one else in the church knew that thirty minutes ago, ahead of a massive cranial hemorrhage, Vick had been fully conscious and talking about the automobile accident that nearly killed him.

Pedding appreciated how rare it was to get an eyewitness description of a murder from the victim. Although Vick had died in mid sentence (suddenly looking up and asking, "Lord?") he had detailed the meeting with Seth and the accident down to the instant of the crash.

But Seth had heard the nuance in the detective's request and understood everything. His tears instantly stopped (and his heart too) as another extreme emotional swing shook his body and obliterated any sense of himself.

He simultaneously convulsed and panicked, grabbing Charlotte by the back of the suit collar and squashed her under his arm in a paralyzing headlock that could easily break her neck. She was chocking and his grip was too strong to even hope to turn and bite the arm that was crushing her.

"She's going with me so back off copper!" Seth yelled a line from a Jimmy Cagney movie. He looked down at the sanctuary floor and realized his only chance was to leap off the balcony, break his fall with the innocent lady he was strangling, and run through the back of the church to his waiting car.

Pedding and the other 4 officers in the balcony all drew their guns to take down the about-to-turn psycho killer. But no one had a clear shot.

"Get down everyone! Get down right now! I've got a gun on him! Let your friend go and no one will get hurt. Okay?" Pedding warned.

On that command the attending 1381 fannies dropped to the floor. At the same moment, still chocking Charlotte and shaking her like a rag doll, Seth jumped onto the ledge and leaped off the balcony, air borne in the first part of his escape plan.

Mark had watched it all. Now he looked into Charlotte's eyes as she tried desperately to grab on to the ledge to keep from dying with Seth in the twenty-foot fall to the sanctuary floor.

They were the same green eyes he looked into when they died at the bottom of the stairs in their home; killed by Vick in a nightmare he'd never forget.

Now and again he was too far away to rescue her. He knew that unless he changed the course of events in the next two seconds she would be crushed by Griggs' huge frame when they hit the floor below.

Dead for real this time.

"You're not taking her!" he yelled and jumped onto the ledge of the balcony. Never breaking eye contact with her he reached out across the air between them and projected a long silent spark of white light that first struck Seth's death gripping arm, making it reflex away from Charlotte and then, wrapping around her as she separated from the falling Seth, it yanked her back toward the balcony and into Mark's arms in a fleshy collision that propelled them backward to the safety of the balcony floor.

At that same instant, Seth's poorly calculated flight was ending. No matter how he'd planned to stick the landing, Charlotte's rescue left him horizontal, flying out of control. Wide eyed and arms flailing he came down with a sickening thud-crunch across the tops of three pews, crushing his windpipe, splintering his pelvis and breaking both legs above the ankles before flipping over to crash land head first, unconscious, bleeding, and dying on the white marble floor.

Pandemonium and panic, screaming and crying, fainting and shock, Griggs twitching and oozing, cops calling for all available ambulances, doctors and ministers tending the most needy including Mark Justin, lying on his back on the balcony floor, semi conscious, flicking his hands back and forth.

After their landing Charlotte immediately rolled off of him but the damage was done. She propped herself up, hugging and loving him for loving her.

Louis was beside them within moments and could see Charlotte was unhurt, but Mark was another story. Again.

He gently moved Charlotte to one side comforting her as best he could while trying to get a better look at Mark.

“Okay hero. You really can’t afford all these house calls. But just for grins, tell me where it hurts.”

“Everywhere but especially my back and ribs. Lou, this may be my last breath. I have to ask you something. Come closer, I can’t see much anything,” Mark pleaded.

Louis bent down, his face nearly on Mark’s chest.

“Is it true you were a buttface baby before the surgery? I have to know, Lou.” Mark asked without a smile, like it was a deathbed request, but Louis smiled and knew his best friend was going to live to insult him for years to come.

Chapter 40 - 4 Weeks Later

Many Commonwealth Church members wouldn't return. Ever. In the next few weeks they transferred their memberships by the dozens.

But there were new members too. The media coverage was extensive and in every interview Jerry invited viewers to join and witness the healing of the church.

And they came; the curious, the devout, and the spiritually adventurous. The church had an entirely new feel. No pretense, no snobbery, and no ulterior motives. In the month following Vick's funeral Jerry announced more changes in leadership, creating a new working core with the goal of an open and joyous experience each week.

But that core didn't include Mark and Charlotte Justin.

They hadn't officially resigned or moved their membership but after so much publicity they couldn't be a part of the solution. Although Mark was physically recovering from exhaustion and four cracked ribs, life wasn't ever going to be the same.

What he'd done in church that day was so fast inside of so much confusion and panic, that only a few actually saw his supernatural handiwork. Most of them, including the cops, told the story that Mark had reached out and grabbed Charlotte from the arms of a madman, using an inexplicable strength to pull her back to safety.

It was a desperate lunge in the nick of time, near miraculous, but didn't defy basic physics. The power of love, some called it. Not far from the truth.

And Dominique missed it all. She had been running up the balcony stairs trying to catch up with the cops and the story when her boss had gone berserk.

But one eyewitness did confront Mark with the truth, choosing to believe exactly what he saw and then act on it. Charley Tobberman, CEO of Whyecliff Pharmaceuticals and a Vietnam War veteran who found Jesus in the rice paddies three decades earlier, hadn't ducked or hid when the detective screamed for everyone in the church to take cover. He had a perfect view of those few seconds when his employee, Mark Justin, did something so uncomprehendable he believed it could be a threat to his company.

Toberman's assistant left a voice mail for Mark to arrange a meeting as soon as he was up to coming in. A professional meet to cover product campaigns or any Whyecliff business would gone through channels so this had to be about the Sunday disaster. Good news or bad he wanted it over and made the appointment for Thursday morning, the first day he could walk through the rib pain.

It was going to be a short meeting and after coolly but politely seeing him in, Charlie started at the end.

"Justin, there's a lot about this job that keeps me up at night and I'm not about to add you to the short list. Bottom line is that no one so unpredictable, that can do what I saw with my own two eyes, should be in a position of responsibility on my leadership team or anywhere in my company."

And then he summed it up.

"We have a deal for you-two year's full salary with benefits plus half salary with benefits for three years after that." Charlie pointed to the paper on the desk and continued explaining the deal.

"And we won't deny your twenty years of exemplary service. Candidly, I wouldn't dare use your inexplicable behavior as the cause for dismissal. You and I both know the press would have a field day if I tried that. So, you're not fired but I can't have you around here either. You know this tune, don't you?"

"Sure, Charley. It's a RIF. I've been on the other side of the desk when we had to layoff staff. It's no fun."

"Exactly and you know we're officially consolidating your position with another." Tobberman broke eye contact for the first time, looking down at the paper on this desk, and continued.

"Now, after this five year package expires you also get the early retirement option with its benefits in tact. In return you'll leave your position immediately. There are only two conditions for this offer. First, you will not bring suit against Whyecliff for wrongful dismissal and, second, you will not discuss or make any public statement about this agreement. It is a difficult choice made by the Whyecliff in these difficult financial times. You good with that?"

Charlie slid the agreement letter across the desk. "And I don't want any lawyers to monkey with this. I just want you out of here."

The letter stated that his position was being eliminated and that the terms were included in his RIF package. It also noted that Whyecliff appreciated his twenty years of dedicated service.

"Yes, sir. I understand and agree."

"Well, sign on the dotted line and we'll be done."

"How close were you?" Mark asked about Sunday's violence at church.

"Griggs missed by daughter by one row and I was directly below the balcony. You saved Charlotte but you could have saved them both. That's a problem for this old Marine."

Mark signed both sets of originals and then reached out to shake on the deal.

Charlie refused his hand.

"I don't know what you did in our church. I don't know if it was good or evil but I do know it came from that very hand you're offering me. With all due respect, I'll pass."

"I did what I had to. That's all."

"Sure. And so am I. No matter though, I'm thankful Charlotte is well. Please tell her that we're just trying to do the right thing for everyone. Goodbye Mark."

Charley, his wife, and their two children never returned to Commonwealth Church. Their pledge was missed for years.

And TV10 did its share of house cleaning too. The homicide investigation broke open a scandal that widened to include the underbelly of LIFE TV, its hidden contributors in the James River Ministry and the TV10 connection.

The interim news director that replaced Seth made her best decision by assigning Dominique to run with the TV10 internal investigation. And they didn't let the departed Seth off the hook. She detailed Vick's blackmail scheme, even found the New Orleans call-girl who remembered Vick buying the infamous pictures. They were never recovered.

But there were bigger fish to fry.

Vick had recruited two board members from the TV10 parent company, Broad Rock Communications, to sit on his new company's board of directors. The separation of religion and main-stream media had been breeched at the highest levels of Broad Rock and more resignations followed.

TV10 News ratings skyrocketed. Two weeks later the national network aired a five-minute Nightly News segment produced by Dominique. From the prayer for Miss Daisy through that terrible bloody Sunday and the scandal that followed, she narrated and stared in their feature story.

It was also the break she needed to be recognized by a larger market. The next week she was on the air in Houston, a weekend anchor and weekday reporter for the NBC affiliate in the fifth largest market in the country. A quick move she was ready to make.

* * * * *

Much of this ran through Jerry Tinsler's mind as he marveled at the pace of change during the past month. Although Mark wasn't directly involved with the church any more, he had agreed to meet this morning to just 'catch up'. Until they were one-on-one here in the office, Jerry didn't dare tell him the real agenda

The last time they talked, Mark called to tell him that he and Charlotte were leaving town for a few weeks. After being politely but summarily fired by Tobberman they could take some time off. He wasn't management material any more.

"You'll be fine, Mark. Something will come to you, don't worry. The Lord will make you ready for your next calling. Now get some rest and when we talk again things will have changed for us both."

True enough. But he had no business, no right to ask Mark and Charlotte to head down another dangerous and radical path. But the situation was dire and his prayers had been answered with Mark's name. There was no other choice.

He'd been up all night fretting about this meeting, conflicted to the bone, and was relived when the light knock meant Mark was finally there.

He had a friendly hug for Mark followed by a warm hand-over-hand handshake. He was genuinely glad to see him looking fully recovered.

"Have a seat there on the sofa and tell me how you've been."

Mark had almost returned to normal. No sparking, telekinesis, or transformations and he heard very little from the Debating Society. Getting away had done the trick even though he and Charlotte were still ducking the CSN reporters. They hated getting shut out on the big story and were still angling for what was left of it. John Chambers remained in Norfolk General and Mark had visited him in rehab so that kept the relationship alive.

But he did not tell Jerry (or Charlotte) about the dreams. He had slept in front of the TV most every night, ear buds now required to achieve shut out volume. But most mornings just before sun up they got through anyway.

These were nothing like the vision of the kitchen explosion he had experienced four weeks ago in the narthex. These were impressions, feelings. More death, more horror, and extreme suffering on an overwhelming scale, as though he was a blindfolded witness to a mass execution. The death machine, whatever it was, constantly changed and always delivered. His nights were definitely getting worse.

"My days are fine and Charlotte's happily back to a semi-normal life and fall in Virginia is beautiful. But what's this about, Jerry? Sweaty palms aren't your usual calling card. Problem?"

"You have no idea so I'll just blurt it out. You know my father is a minister in Houston, right?"

"Steven F. Austin Tinsler as I recall. Yeah, you've mentioned him and his big Baptist church. You two aren't theologically simpatico as I recall."

"Yeah, he's from the fire and brimstone school. Not my approach. Anyway, we've been talking again since all this happened at Commonwealth. He's been more help than I could have expected and now I know why. The most awful things are happening down there too. Bottom line is that he's had some tragic loses in his congregation."

"Well, preacher, that doesn't much sound like the bottom line. Don't tell me they're worshiping idols and rebelling in Texas."

"No, not rebelling---dying." After a painful silence Jerry added, "Murdered to be exact."

Instantly, Mark knew the agenda. His stomach and heart and the Debating Society ("No way, Jose!") also knew what was coming next.

Jerry saw and felt his reaction.

"Please don't jump to any conclusions. I'm not asking you to go down there *(yet)*. He needs help and lots of it. The cops even created a special squad. Truth is he's lost three of his members in the worst kind of murderous ways. And there are no leads. His flock is scared, Mark, and leaving faster than a fire drill. The cops are totally frustrated and Dad is desperate. He's thinks he's a suspect but believes he's going to be one of the next victims." Jerry was near tears.

"That is beyond bizarre, Jerry. What in the world would point the cops in his direction?

"Substantial parts of the three estates were left to his church. But there is no way in Christ he's involved."

"So, what do you want me to do?"

"Take a look at this. Just glance over it and tell me if you get anything."

"Get anything? You mean like the killer's name, phone number, and shoe size? That's not fair Jerry. I can't tell jack about…."

He was looking at the front page of the Houston Chronicle, Metro Section, from four weeks earlier. The headline: 'New Home Explodes; Realtor Missing'

No need to read it. He had been there-teleported. It was the lady in the oven in the grommet kitchen. The explosion had blown them both away.

The buzz snapped on in his head and he recoiled back against the sofa pillows. Mark was gone again.

"Oh God. What did I do? Just relax." Jerry said leaping from his chair and almost falling on top of Mark. "Stay with me, friend. Let me see you blink."

He poured a glass of water not sure if he would throw or offer it.

Mark's vision cleared. He wasn't in Jerry's office but it was an office with a man (*his brother?*) seated at a desk directly in front of him. The man was leaning over, using a magnifying glass to inspect a document and speaking in another language as he moved the glass from left to right reading the text. He kept looking up at Mark, so excited. "Do you know what this is?" He asked. Mark didn't have time to respond.

The cold water Jerry threw in his face slapped him back into the present. Mark leapt off the couch and was standing over Jerry in an attack reaction that was so fast it startled them both.

"For your information I was baptized 47 years ago, preacher," Mark said wiping off his face and turning toward the door. "I'm outta here."

"Mark. Don't go just yet." Jerry stood and grabbed his arm. "When did you pick up German? You saw something, didn't you?"

“Enough to know I’m not going to Houston and I don’t speak Germish. My brother is fluent but that doesn’t get us anywhere does it?”

Jerry’s grip meant business. He needed Mark in Houston.

“I just saved your butt for the second time. Remember Vick’s grip at the hospital? You’re damn lucky to have me around when you blast off. So will you hear me out?”

“No sir. I’ve heard enough. We’re done. I can’t help your father and I can’t help you. So, padre, if you’re going to claim my arm you’d better say so or I’m taking it with me?”

Jerry released him without another word and Mark walked out of Commonwealth Church swearing he would never return.

“To hell with it all. I can’t control it, I can’t work with it, I can’t hide from it and, God, I don’t want it.” He was sobbing, tears flowing in a steady stream when he reached the Thunderbird only a few feet from the back door.

“Damn it. I can’t see enough to drive.”

“Let’s walk a minute, get some air. Find yourself.” Good advice from the Debating Society.

At the southeast corner of the main building, in a small plot off the parking lot, Commonwealth kept a pet cemetery where, since 1840, anyone was allowed to bury any critter that was loved for any length of time. It was rarely used any more and Mark never had reason to explore it but now it looked like sanctuary.

He opened the rusty iron gate and sat on the weathered bench facing the miniature graveyard. It was filled with odd shaped little burial stones, all flat in the ground, most carved with only a pet name like Fritzy, Little Bit, or JoJo. His depression deepened, tears still flowing, as he remembered the pets he had buried through the years.

“I guess it all comes down to the one big truth,” he thought.

Ashes to ashes, dust to dust,
Life is a rental and return it we must.
Burma Shave

"Hey rainbow. You're still beaconing like a psychedelic search light out here. I love that about you." He recognized the voice of the mystery brunette in black from his living room a month ago and his van twenty years earlier. She was intruding again but this time he welcomed the distraction.

"You know, lady, I spent a small fortune on window locks, deadbolts and one of the finest alarm systems known to man. Didn't do us a damn bit lot of good. They came in anyway, but you know that don't you.

"Yeah, and the bad guys changed their plans because of that security system and then you got 'em good, rainbow. Mighty proud of you. Just the beginning."

"Just leave me alone, will you. I've got a great sulk going on here and a lot of crap to consider," he said.

"Sorry love. You don't think all this happened so you could retire and feed the dead goldfish around here. We both know you're going to Houston and take on the bloody horror down there," she said walking, almost swaying, toward him.

"And give up all this?" he said still looking at the pet markers. "Are you even real?"

"As real as you, silly. I told you I'd be around. I know when you need help and when you're moving on. I also read the papers and understand the terrible danger in Texas. It's real simple. You kick its ass before it kicks yours."

"Before it sees the old beaconing rainbow and comes after me like a certain other hit team?" He asked and finally looked at her. She was striking, almost angelic in the sun. Bobbed black hair, sly smile and killer blue eyes seeing right through him. He looked back down at JoJo.

"There's more, rainbow," she said and sat down close to him. "The thing you'll be hunting is both good *and* evil. It's wicked and kind, hateful and loving, murderous and benevolent. It is an absolute rouge and it knows you are here. But for now it doesn't where here is. That's not a secret you can keep for long."

Mark smiled understanding that he too was a rouge.

“So my target is the clairvoyant incarnation of Charles Manson and Mother Theresa. That would be Mother Manson. You know I don’t need some fractured fairly tale right now. I got no grasp on reality as it is.”

“You’ve looked in the mirror and down the abyss. You know what this is and those dead people in Houston are no fairy tale,” she said and leaned closer to him.

“It’s still insecure, conflicted, so better now than later when it’s done in Houston and focused on you. Time to put on your traveling shoes.”

Staring out his window, trying to cool off after their meeting, Jerry looked down on an even more disturbing conversation.

“I know he’s upset but why is Mark sitting in the cemetery arguing with himself?” he asked, shaking his head. “Lord? Are you there? In case you haven’t noticed, we’re falling apart down here.” He dropped the blinds and continued praying quietly in his office.

“I get it,” Mark admitted to her. “You’re my guardian angel and I’m a freak of the universe that you’d like to stalk a kindhearted psychopath. So do us all a favor and tell the cops about this maniac, let them make a newsworthy arrest and we all live happily ever after?” He was past enamored and becoming angry.

“That’s the problem, rainbow. I don’t know who it is. I only know *what* it is and the cops will never figure it out. No evidence, no trail, no real suspects. But you will draw it out into the open. You will make it make a mistake. That’s how it goes down.” And, message delivered, she stood up to leave.

He watched her walk away, confused but convinced she was right. The thing in Texas was real and it would get him and those he loved if he didn’t join the battle in Houston.

“Shit.”

“You are so cool, rainbow, and you will kick its ass. No matter how desperate and surreal your situation is, don’t ever forget that fact,” she said and winked at him before disappearing around the corner of the church leaving him alone with the dead pets.

"Medic! That was insane advice from the former Miss Ameralarm. And did you see those boots? She's really a demon from Neiman's. Do not listen to her," advised The Debating Society.

"Well, boys, you have to admit that was industrial strength mojo in Jerry's office-Technicolor, stereo, and crystal clear. It nearly took my head off. It's been all Houston for a while, no doubt about that. You know I don't want any of this but everything points to Houston. Anyway, it's been too long since I've been back in the oil patch. Back home."

"Right, coffin breath. Home to homicide. What part of the term serial killer don't you understand? And where do you think Dominique Johnson is plying her trade these days? CSN is there too. You go hunting a church killer and there will be hell to pay," the Debating Society warned.

"Besides, you'll never make it anyway. Charlotte will kill you first."

He had to grin knowing how right they were but he was already walking toward the Thunderbird, dry-eyed and ready to drive.

Leaving the cemetery Mark never looked up; never saw Jerry peering out his office window, praying for divine intervention. And he never saw the other watcher, above Jerry's office window, glaring from the bell tower. It loathed him, seethed in silence.

But Mark *had* seen it in the bathroom mirror and had collapsed in fear of the black-eyed harrowing apparition of Matthew Victor Springwell. Newly dedicated in the Hall of Dead Preachers, Vick's 30" X 40" portrait joined the other twelve. He would always be there, kind smile and black eyes staring into the heart of the church. But trapped by hate, revenge and a dark spirit, he was also plotting the demise of the beaconing rainbow walking below.

And so the murderous rouge in Houston didn't know yet but it had a new partner in the bell tower as well as a common enemy who was on the road to confrontation.

www.ingramcontent.com/pod-product-compliance
Lightning Source LLC
LaVergne TN
LVHW091031080826
845145LV00002B/453

9780578004297